CRAVE

part one

e.k. blair

I0640442

Crave, Part One
Copyright © 2017 E.K. Blair

Cover Design: E.K. Blair
Editor: Ashley Williams, Adept Edits
Interior Design: Stacey Blake, Champagne Formats

ISBN: 978-0-9989997-3-9

All rights reserved. No part of this publication may be reproduced or transmitted in any form, or by any means, electronic, mechanical, including photocopying, recording, or by any information storage and retrieval system,) without the prior written permission in writing.

This is a work of fiction. Names, characters, places, brands, media, and incidents are either the products of the author's imagination or are used fictitiously, and any resemblance to any actual persons, living or dead, events, or locales is entirely coincidental.

The author acknowledges the trademarked status and trademark owners of various products referenced in this work of fiction, which have been used without permission. The publication/use of these trademarks is not authorized, associated with, or sponsored by the trademark owners.

All rights reserved.

dedication

To Ashley
who believes in this crazy dream of mine.

CHAPTER
one

Kason

I often find myself wondering if I have always been like this, if I ever existed without being afflicted with this craving. When I think back, I reach static before finding a time where I was free. Maybe I've never been free. Maybe I was born with some sort of displacement. A wiring gone wrong.

I was six years old when I saw my first set of tits.

I woke up in the middle of the night, thirsty for a drink of water, when I walked into the living room and saw my babysitter naked from the waist up while kissing her boyfriend. I didn't understand at the time exactly what I was seeing, but I knew I liked it. Not in a sexual way, but the visual intrigued me.

Her name was Shannon.

I don't remember much about her. She was one of a number of babysitters that would stay overnight while my mother worked her second job. I often found myself staying up late, hoping Shannon's boyfriend would show up. To this very day, I can still remember the excitement I felt when I saw her on the couch with him, when I heard the sounds they made. I would crouch on my hands and knees and watch them as I hid behind a fake ficus tree that sat in the far corner of the living room.

The excitement of watching her dry hump her boyfriend didn't make my dick grow like it does now as I clench my hand firmly around myself. Memories play behind my eyelids, and I cum quickly, shooting my load into a wad of toilet paper before flushing it.

I wash my hands and then run damp fingers through my hair as I look at my reflection in the mirror. I stare into green eyes, eyes that bear no resemblance to my mother's, and tell myself under my breath, "Seven hours," but I already know I won't be able to last that long. I only set these trivial goals to give myself the illusion that I'm being proactive about controlling whatever this is.

The idea that maybe I'm uncontrollable has been weighing heavily on me lately, but I shrug it off as I walk out of the bathroom.

"Bye, Mom," I shout and then grab my backpack and the keys to the shitty old Camaro I recently bought. I was finally able to save enough money from the part-time job I've been working after school to buy the damn thing. It's old and rundown, but it gets me from point A to point B.

The car fits in with the apartment complex, but I tell myself that I don't. The thought of this being my life has never sat well with me. I've grown up threadbare with an absentee mother who works herself to the bone for every penny she makes, only to fall short every month. She's drowning in debt, and I refuse to go down that same path.

I toss my backpack into the passenger seat and pump the gas a few times before cranking the ignition and bringing the car to a grumbling start.

Most would look at a kid like me and make the stereotypical judgment call. But I'm smarter than the other dopeheads that live on this side of the tracks. The only way I have a chance of getting out of here is by going to college and making something of myself. All I have going for me is academics, so I've made them my priority, and in return, I've maintained a solid four-point-oh GPA semester after semester.

Pulling into the parking lot of South Shore High, I park in my usual spot next to Micah's pristine truck where he and our buddy Trent are already waiting on me.

Micah claps his hand obnoxiously against the old metaled hood of my car and gives me a shit-eating grin. "Kason, what the hell happened to you last night?"

"Got tied up with stuff."

"Speaking of stuff," he hints as we head into the school building.

If it weren't for my association with Micah, I'd be just another roughneck outcast. But with his money and popularity and my ability to score him weed on a consistent basis, we've forged a friendship that benefits my social standing in this school. I guess that's one of the perks of living where I do—pot is an easy score for the rich kids. I've never touched the stuff myself, but I'll happily buy it off my neighbor, inflate the price for the naïve Micah, and pocket the profit.

"I gotta work this afternoon, but I can meet you when I'm done."

He turns to face me as he walks backward down the crowded hall, telling me, "Indian Rocks. The guys and I will be skimming there."

"Dude."

He smiles, ignoring my irritation, and then turns the corner and rushes to his class.

"That's way outta my way, man!" I holler before colliding into another student. "Fu—"

"I'm so sorry." Her voice comes before I'm able to gather my bearings enough to see who I bumped into. When I do look, she's already kneeling and grabbing the books she dropped.

"I'll get those." I squat next to her, and when I hand over her books, I finally get a look as we stand.

Long blonde hair frames her face, which is soft in color compared to most of the overly tanned girls in this town. But when you live in Tampa and the beaches are the main hangouts, what else can you expect? Her cheeks flush with embarrassment, and when she looks me in the eyes, she apologizes again, saying, "I'm sorry. That was my fault."

"I wasn't paying attention either, so no need to apologize." She shifts nervously on her feet and hoists her backpack higher on her shoulder. "What's your name?"

"Adaline," she responds and then shakes her head as she corrects herself. "I mean Ady. People just call me Ady."

"You new?"

"Is it that obvious?"

"Not in a bad way, but yeah. You have that lost look in your eyes."

"And here I thought I was blending in," she says and then smirks. "That is, until you ran into me and sent my books flying across the floor, causing a scene in front of everyone."

"I thought you said it was *your* fault? You even apologized for it."

"I was being polite. You know, new girl and all. Wouldn't want to make any enemies on my first day, but you should really watch where you're going."

Her humor cracks a smile on my face. "All right then. I'll take the blame if it'll make you feel better."

"It will. And thank you," she responds with modest perk.

"I guess I'll see you around then."

I start to head to class but only make it a few steps when she shouts, "Wait." I turn back, and she adds, "You never told me your name."

"Kason. People just call me Kason."

"Very funny."

"See you around, Adaline."

"It's Ady," she corrects as I head down the hall to first period, and I chuckle before making a detour that causes me to show up tardy.

I knew I'd never make it the full seven hours.

The day moves along in the same pattern as every day before, but it isn't until sixth period that I see her again. I sit in my usual seat at the back of the classroom and watch her eyes skitter around the room to find an unoccupied desk. She tucks a lock of hair behind her ear while kids file in behind her.

I typically mind my own business with girls, avoiding interactions that could possibly lead to an interest on their part. It's safer that way. But for some reason, I decide to put the poor thing out of her misery.

"Adaline."

She raises her chin and smiles when she spots me.

"I told you, it's Ady," she says when she approaches, but I ignore her reminder.

"No one has ever claimed the desk in front of me."

"Seriously? It's March."

"Your point?"

She hangs her bag on the back of the chair and shifts to the side to look at me when she takes her seat. "No point. Just wondering why you've sat back here for nearly the whole year by yourself."

"Maybe I'm a loser."

She laughs. "That's a stretch."

"How so?"

"I saw you at lunch. I can tell you're not a loser."

"Spying on me?"

She unzips her bag and takes her notebook out. "Don't flatter yourself. I'm the new girl, remember? It's kinda my job to be observant."

I catch Micah from the corner of my eye as he walks down the aisle, and Adaline looks up, following my line of focus.

"You again," he says to her before taking the seat to my right.

"You've already met?"

"Third period English," he tells me and then turns to her, saying, "And for the sole purpose of you being new, I won't hold it against you that you're sitting in my desk."

She shoots me an annoyed glare, to which I smile.

"In my defense, he told me no one sat here."

"Figures. This dick would throw anyone under the bus for a good-looking blonde."

"You think I'm good-looking?" Her tone is playful and full of mockery.

"His words, not mine."

"That isn't a denial."

She then turns in her chair, closing off the conversation, and I'm already somehow intrigued with the new girl and her air of confidence. Looking to my side, Micah mouths *she's hot*. I shake my head at him and then open my notebook, trying to redirect my focus when I feel the fangs of urgency bite.

I shift in my seat, hyperaware of my surroundings, but as I take a quick scan of my classmates, I find them all lost in their own conversations.

The teacher calls everyone's attention and begins her instruction while I struggle to pay attention to the lecture. I take notes and listen, all the while counting down the minutes until the final bell. When the last tick hits, I grab my bag, scrape the legs of my chair against the floor, and rush to get my fix.

"Dude," Micah calls. "Don't forget. Indian Rocks tonight."

"Got it," I throw over my shoulder, not wanting to look back and risk the chance of catching another glance of her. Sitting behind her and smelling the sweet scent of her shampoo was torture enough. So, I hightail it to my car and speed home to quell what's starting to feel like a curse.

CHAPTER
two

Adaline

He runs out of class so fast that I don't even get a chance to say goodbye. Maybe it's a good thing. I don't know how much longer I can put on this charade of the easy breezy self-assured new kid.

"What's Indian Rocks?" I ask Micah as we're packing our books.

"Pretty much the only decent place around here to skim."

"Your words are totally lost on me."

He drags his hand through his over-grown blond hair and walks with me out of the classroom. "Skimboarding. We're trying to get our fill before spring break hits and the beaches are filled with kooks for the next few weeks. You should come."

I have no clue what a kook is, but I nod, feigning understanding because I don't want to look like a complete moron. "I still have a lot of unpacking to do."

"Suit yourself, Guppy. But if you change your mind, we'll be there pretty late."

"Guppy?"

He laughs. "I could toss you in my pocket and you'd still have room to grow," he teases of my petite stature. "Gotta run, though. See you later?"

"Maybe. Like I said, still unpacking and all."

"Micah, come on," a guy hollers from down the hall, and Micah shoots me a quick, "Later," before catching up with his friend.

I make my way through the congested halls and watch as everyone clumps off into their groups of friends and heads out to the student parking lot while I walk solo. The humidity hangs heavily in the air, and when I hop into my car, I blast the air conditioner and release a somber huff. Since I'm still learning my way around this town, I plug my address into my car's navigation, and when the pin drops, I shift into drive.

Palm trees line the streets that take me to my new home, but I feel so far from paradise with the density caged within my chest. When I pull into the circular drive in front of the house my mom and I just moved into, I park and rest my head back against the seat and look through the sunroof.

Deep green palm fronds hang overhead against the bright blue sky. The moment I found out I would be leaving Plano, Texas, for Tampa, Florida, I was excited. I mean, who wouldn't want to trade landlocked pavement for water and sand? I psyched myself up for the move, but I didn't consider how lonely I'd be without my friends and family. I'm a million miles away from comfort and familiarity.

Inside the airy, two-story, stucco home, the echo of my shoes against the tile of the foyer is the only sound that greets me. I make my way up the stairs and into my bedroom, which overlooks the pool out back. Tossing my bag onto my bed, I pull my phone out from my pocket to check the time.

3:27PM

I'm an hour ahead of my friends back home, so I drag myself into my bathroom and unpack a couple of boxes to pass the time until they get out of class. Once my belongings are put in place and organized, I toss the empty boxes over the railing that overlooks the foyer, too lazy to walk them down the stairs.

When I go back to my room, I hear a splashing from outside. Looking out my window, I find the pool guy cleaning out the filter. It's only after he stands that I recognize him. A voyeur, hidden behind the white plantation shutters that are closed over my windows, I spy on Kason as he walks over to grab the leaf skimmer. I slant the shutters to face upward so he can't see me as he takes the hem of his white work polo and uses it to wipe the sweat from his forehead.

His long athletic cuts are evident in his arms and also his legs that show beneath his khaki shorts. I wonder if he plays any sports or hits the gym, because he's more defined and filled out than most of the boys my age. I debate whether to go say hi, but talk myself out of it when I remember how fast he bolted out of class when the final bell rang.

The buzzing of my cell phone pulls me away from the window, and when I see Molly's name lit up across the screen, I smile and take the call.

"Finally. I've been waiting to talk to you."

"How did it go?" is the first thing she says, and the sound of her voice has a wave of homesickness washing over me.

I flop onto the bed and groan. "Ugh. Okay, I guess. Being the new kid blows, especially since it's nearly the end of the year. Everyone is already secured in their cliques, and then there's me . . . the Texan with a hick accent."

"We're not hick," she defends. "We're . . . *Southern*."

"Well, whatever you want to call it, it isn't what these kids are. My blonde hair fits in, but these girls are walking around in shorts that barely cover their tiny butts."

"Seriously? At school?"

"Apparently, the dress codes aren't enforced, if there's a dress code at all," I remark. "And I need to go on a diet of X-Lax and water."

Molly bursts out in laughter. "You are certifiably crazy. You don't need to lose a pound!"

"Not according to Texan standards, but I doubt these people feast on fried pickles and ranch."

"More like kale salads and soybean smoothies?"

"Totally!" We both giggle, but mine is weighted in sadness. I wish Molly were here with me. No one gets me like she does.

"Hey, can I call you later? We're all going to Finn's house before the basketball game tonight."

"Tell everyone I said hi, okay?"

"Of course," she says before adding, "I miss you, Ady."

"I miss you, too."

I sit on the edge of the bed and sulk my shoulders as I look around my half-unpacked room. These items may have come from my old room back home, but nothing feels the same. My mom and I only moved here a few days ago, but it's enough time for me to feel the loneliness setting in. With her starting her new job, I know she'll be working longer hours than what she used to back in Dallas, which make me just that much more lonely.

When I hear the wrought iron gate *clank,* I move toward the window to find that Kason has left. I look at the pool and think about how, back in Texas, we'd have to wait until the end of May for the pools to open and then only be able to swim for a few months before they closed back up. Here it's hot enough to take a dip right now, and then I think about what Micah said about Indian Rocks.

In need of a little weight to be lifted off me, I decide a drive-by might help me clear my head. But it won't be enough. I've always been a person who finds security within friends, and unless I put myself out there, I'm going to be miserable. As much as I hate having to be overly extroverted, I know I'm going to have to fake it until I make it.

I kick off my shoes and dig through a few boxes in search of a pair of flip-flops, which will be more suitable for the sand. After I drag the boxes from the entryway and out back to the trash cans, I get into my car and plug my destination into the GPS. When I hit the Gandy Bridge and have water all around me, I open the sunroof, roll down my windows, and breathe in paradise.

At least that's what it feels like for this girl.

I try not to think about my friends back home as the breeze whips through my long hair, but the mind is a difficult thing to control, so I blast my stereo to try to drown out my thoughts. Before I know it, I'm pulling into the first parking spot I can find at the beach. When I kill the engine, I pep talk myself, similar to the way I did this morning before school.

I step out of the car and shove my cell into the back pocket of my shorts before making my way over the wooden walkway that leads to the sand. Using my hand as a shield against the blazing sun, I look down the beach in both directions, not having a clue as to where Micah might be. Only a few people are scattered about, so I decide to kick off my flip-flops and opt to head left over right.

Water rushes over my feet, carrying away my footprints with every ebb and flow as I wander aimlessly down the shore. I watch the boats in the distance as pelicans dive beak-first into the water. The sound of the gentle waves soothes beyond what I imagine, and I relish in the reprieve as my head clears. Collecting a few random shells, I tuck them into my pocket and then look over my shoulder to see how far I've walked. When I turn back, I see a cluster of guys down a ways.

Micah's sun-bleached hair stands out from the group. With his board tucked under his arm, he watches one of his friends. The guy runs parallel to the water before dropping his board, jumping on, and skimming onto a small wave. He then flips the board beneath his feet and dives into the water.

I'm hesitant to approach but do my best to bury all social apprehensions as I begin to walk over to them. Thank God he spots me.

"Look who decided to come out and play," he teases with a big smile as he jogs lazily toward me. A few of the other guys look my way.

"I needed to get out of my house for a while."

"So you came to see me out of boredom?"

"Something like that."

He punctures the sand with his board, digging it down so that it stands on end before he drops to the ground. I follow suit and sit next to him, squinting against the sun as it starts to hang a little lower in the sky.

"You come out here a lot?"

"Every chance I can."

"It's nice," I murmur softly.

"First time?"

I nod. "I moved here just a few days ago."

"Where from?"

"Texas. I lived in a suburb of Dallas. But my mom got a job offer that moved us, so here I am."

"That must suck," he remarks, and I turn my head to the side to look at him when he adds, "having to move in the middle of the school year."

"You have no idea."

"In a way, it could be nice, though. Getting to explore someplace new; meeting different people. I've always lived here. I love it, but I'd like to experience other places, ya know?"

I shrug my shoulders. "I guess, but I miss my friends."

He runs his hand through his hair, slicking it back. "You'll make new ones, Guppy."

I shake my head and smile at my new nickname.

"Micah!"

I look over my shoulder and find Kason standing on a wooden bridge that leads out to one of the many small parking lots that weave between beach rentals.

"Be right back." Micah jumps to his feet and jogs over to him.

Kason wears the same white work polo and khakis as he did when he was at my house a few hours ago, and I can't deny that I find him extremely attractive. His eyes catch mine, but when I raise my hand in subtle acknowledgement, he turns and walks out of my view with Micah following behind. His shift in demeanor from this morning when we bumped into each other has me conflicted, and I think back through what little interaction we had today, wondering if I said anything that offended him. Nothing comes to mind, but I can't shake the feeling that I've done something wrong.

"Sorry about that," Micah says when he returns a few minutes later.

"What was that about?"

"He was dropping something off."

I pause for a moment and then decide to mention my unease. "I think I might have irritated him."

"What do you mean?"

"I don't really know," I tell him as I push my toes into the sand. "He was really friendly when I met him this morning, but—"

"Just ignore him. He sometimes gets into these . . . *funks*. Don't get me wrong, he's a solid guy and all, he just . . ."

"What?"

Micah hesitates to go on, and as curious as I am about Kason, I feel a twinge of guilt for trying to be intrusive. "I'm sorry. I shouldn't pry."

"People make a lot of assumptions about him. As popular as the kid is, he's pretty closed off. He keeps his circle of friends small."

"Have you two known each other long?"

"Since freshman year when he transferred in from his neighborhood."

"He doesn't live in our area?"

"Dude, you coming or what?" a guy shouts from the water.

"They go to our school?" I ask, eyeing the guys who are now looking our way.

He points over to the tall lean one. "Trent does. And those two," he says pointing to the one who just caught a wave and another who's standing on the shore, "they graduated last year from Shorecrest Prep And that guy over there, Brandon, he's a senior at a school in St. Pete."

"I'm sure I won't remember any of that." I laugh under my breath before standing and wiping the sand off my shorts.

"Who's the bunny?" one of them questions as he walks over to us.

"Ady, this asshole here is Brogan," Micah says and then turns to his buddy. "And she's no bunny. She's new in town."

Brogan ticks his head up and reaches out to me. "What's up, Ady?"

We shake hands as beads of water drip down his dark tan chest, which is inked with a few tattoos.

"I was about to leave."

"So soon? We just met." He exaggerates his flirtation with a charming smile, and it causes my lips to lift as well.

"Ignore him. He has a hard-on for anything that's breathing."

Before Brogan can say anything, I turn to Micah. "Thanks for hanging out."

"Any time," he responds. "You have your cell on you?"

I pull my phone from my pocket and he takes it from my hand, adding his number to my contacts.

"Shoot me a text later, and I'll add your number to my phone, too."

I linger for a beat as he grabs his board and heads into the water before making my way back down the shore to my car, but it isn't Micah that creeps into my thoughts while I walk— it's Kason.

CHAPTER
three

Adaline

"**A**dy. There you are."

"Hey, Micah."

"Where're you off to?"

"The quad with all the other derelict youths," I exhaust with a dramatic eye roll.

"Funny." He smirks because this school is filled with elitist offspring of the rich and richer. "We're heading out for lunch today. Wanna come?"

"You sneaking out?"

He laughs. "It's an open campus, Guppy. Come on, let's get out of here."

I follow him to his truck and hop in. "Where are we going?"

"The Cheesery is at the bay today."

"The Cheesery?"

"Best food truck in the city. It's normally over in Palm Harbor, but every now and then it comes to South Tampa," he tells me before turning up the music and laying a heavy foot on the gas pedal.

Micah is the epitome of what I would imagine any surfer to look like, but it's his easygoing attitude that draws me to him. It's only my second day at school, and he's gone out of his way to ease my awkwardness. Not that I show it. I do my best to feign indifference to the dread of trying to fit in.

When we arrive, Micah introduces me to a handful of other kids from our school that are already there. The girls give me a fleeting hello, and I stick to Micah's side, not wanting to be the odd man out.

Once we have our food, we carry our Styrofoam containers to the park that edges along the water. All of us scatter about in small groups and sit on the manicured grass as business men and women stroll about, enjoying their mid-day break.

"Got any plans this weekend?"

Micah catches me with a mouthful of melted cheese and caramelized apples.

"Shit's good, huh?"

I nod with an awkward laugh from my belly as I swallow the massively unattractive bite. I wipe the back of my hand across my mouth, and then Micah leans over and takes a bite out of my sandwich.

"Hey! Eat your own."

"Dude, that's good," he says around the food in his mouth.

"Next time, you should order it instead of stealing bites out of mine."

"A woman territorial over her food. I like it."

I playfully nudge his shoulder and catch a few glances from the group of girls huddled across the lawn from us, sipping their Diet Cokes. "Is this the typical welcoming, or should I be bothered by the disaffection?" I give a slight nod in the girls' direction.

"Ignore them. They're starved-for-attention bunnies." With a questioning glance, I wait for him to explain. "Bunnies are chicks who flock to the beaches and hope to get noticed. They pretend to be down, but most of them are too uptight to get a little salt in their hair."

I dip a fry in some ketchup and toss it into my mouth.

"But you . . . you're of a different breed than that of around here."

"Is that a bad thing?"

He shakes his head and stands. "I'm gonna go grab another drink. Need anything?"

"I'm good."

I drop the other half of my gourmet grilled cheese into the container, too full to go on in my gluttony, and wipe my greasy hands on a napkin. With the sun beating down on me, I lower my sunglasses over my eyes and enjoy the warmth of this much-too-hot spring. As I look around, I give a friendly smile to the girls when they glance my way, but I don't stay on them for more than a beat before moving on. When I spot Kason, who I hadn't realized was here, he's alone on the edge of the wall that drops down to the water.

I stare curiously from behind my dark lenses, wondering why he's isolating himself from everyone. Not wanting to stew in my thoughts, I decide to make my way over to him. A tinge of insecurity flares with each step I take, but I figure I have nothing to lose by going over to say hi. I notice he has earbuds in, and he doesn't sense my presence until I climb onto the stone wall and sit next to him.

"What are you doing here?" he asks after pulling the buds out of his ears.

"I rode with Micah."

He looks out over the water, and the silence that strings between us does nothing for the awkwardness, so I force myself to speak.

"How come you're sitting over here all by yourself?"

"You say that as if solitude is a bad thing."

"Just as long as you avoid hermit status," I respond lightly, and I relax a little when he breaks a slight smile.

"You seem to be easing in quickly."

I shrug.

"You don't think so?"

"There's nothing easy about moving halfway across the country from all my friends and family only to be the new kid."

I shoot him a quick glance from the corner of my eye to see him looking at me.

"I'm impressed."

"By?" I question.

"Your fakery," he responds with a smirk. "And here I assumed your confidence only to find out it's all an act."

"Well . . . not all of it."

"So, tell me, where's home?"

"Texas."

He gives an exaggerated nod. "That explains it."

"Explains what?"

"The accent," he says before adding with jest, "and the way

you were inhaling that grilled cheese."

I push my hand against his arm as he laughs. "So, you were spying on me?"

"That's a stretch. You're sitting out here in the open."

His smile is infectious, and the uncertainty I was feeling is no longer present as I laugh right along with him.

"In my defense, and to appear slightly more on the delicate side, I only ate half of it." His amusement drags on, and I change the focus off me when I ask, "What are you listening to anyway?" I grab one of his earbuds and am surprised when I hear a narrator. "What's this?"

"*The Metamorphosis.*" He closes the app, pops the bud out of my ear, and sets his phone down.

"Why are you listening to an audio book?"

"Because I work and I don't want to fall behind in this class."

I refrain from mentioning that one of the houses he works at is mine.

"What class has you reading *The Metamorphosis*?"

"It's an AP course."

"Book nerd?"

"Far from it." He chuckles. "Just thinking ahead."

Going back to what Micah told me about Kason not living in a neighborhood that floods into the school we go to, and also the fact that I doubt many of the kids at the school hold down a job, my curiosity about Kason piques. I want to ask more, but I don't. The last thing I need to do is butt in where I'm not wanted.

"I haven't given much thought to college." I instantly regret my words after hearing how flippant they sound when spoken aloud when he's clearly given purposeful attention to what I haven't. "That sounded trite. It isn't that I don't value—"

"You don't sound trite."

"Ady," Micah calls as he and Trent walk over. "Do you mind riding back with Kason?"

"Where are you going?"

"Beach."

"You're ditching?"

"Brogan just called. He has the jet skis out at Clearwater," Trent says. "Wanna come?"

Kason stands and shoves his phone into his pocket. "It's her second day. She isn't ditching with you two drones."

"You good, Ady?"

I give Micah a nod and then take his hand when he reaches down to help me up. "Yeah. I'll be fine. And Kason's right. I can't skip out on class."

"Text me later if you wanna meet up after school."

The two of them run off, leaving me behind with Kason, and my chest flutters at the thought of spending more alone time with him.

"We need to get going," he says, and I follow alongside as he leads me to his car.

He walks over to an old muscle car, unlocks the passenger side door, and opens it for me. I shoot him a smile and slip in. His scent blends with the aged leather, and I can't help myself when I take in a lungful.

When he's behind the wheel, I buckle my seat belt. He works the pedal a few times before turning the key that brings the car to life.

"Is this a sixty-eight?" I ask, and his eyes dart over to mine in questioning surprise, to which I respond, "My dad used to take me to a lot of car shows when I was younger. It was kind of our thing."

"Sixty-nine, actually."

"Close enough."

The engine rumbles, and I find myself sneaking glances his way, wishing for traffic to slow us down because I'm not quite ready to return to school yet. The way the muscles in his forearm constrict with every gear he shifts is mesmerizing. The littlest movement causes the biggest chemical reaction within me.

"You two still go?"

"Ever since my parents divorced, he's sort of been doing his own thing."

"How long ago did they divorce?"

"When I was thirteen. So, it's been around four years," I tell him without going into any detail of how my dad managed to almost entirely exclude me from the new life he's created so effortlessly. "What about your parents? They still together?"

He turns into the student lot, completely dodging my question when he parks the car, saying, "We need to hurry before we're late."

I curse the tension that returns, but it doesn't do anything to curb the curiosity I have about him. Why the heck is this guy so evasive when I attempt to dig the same way he does with me?

"Thanks for giving me a ride."

The both of us step out of the car, and he gives me a half-hearted "See ya later," before we head in different directions once inside the school.

I make it through my next two classes before sixth period comes around, all the while trying not to dissect Kason when I know nothing about him. He's already sitting at his desk with his notebook open when I walk in.

"Hey." My voice comes out meek when I take my seat in front of him, and he responds with an equally meek, "Hey," of his own.

I don't attempt to say anything else, and it isn't even a solid minute later when our teacher takes to the front of the class, offering me only a shred of distraction from the guy who sits behind me. Then, like yesterday, when the bell rings, he rushes out of the class and leaves me behind to pack up my bag and wonder what his deal is.

When I arrive home from school, my mother's car is already parked in the circular drive.

"Mom," I call out as I walk through the front door.

"In the kitchen, dear."

"What are you doing home so early?"

When I walk in, she turns away from whatever she's cooking and gives me a tight hug. "I had to go get new tags for the cars and decided to come home instead of going back to the office."

I take a seat at the bar as she stirs whatever jarred sauce she's heating up. *If there's one thing my mom is not, it's a cook.*

"I'm sorry I didn't come home last night until after you were already asleep."

"It's okay."

"Tell me how your first day went."

I watch my mother, who shares the same bright blonde hair as I do, tend to her cooking in her high heels and pencil skirt, and smile. "I'm happy you're home."

Looking at me from over her shoulder, she shoots me a wink. "Dish, girl. I want to hear all about it."

"You act like my life is soap opera worthy."

"Honey, you're seventeen. Everything should be soap opera worthy."

I shake my head and proceed to tell her about the past two days. I talk about Micah and yesterday's afternoon trip to the beach and today's lunch out at the bay. I then go on and mention Kason and my limited interactions with him. My mother and I have always had a close relationship, despite the fact that her job demands she spend more time in the office than at home with me.

"I get the feeling that he finds me annoying and only talks to me out of politeness. I mean, Micah practically gave him no choice but to drive me back to school after lunch."

"My two cents?"

"Please."

"Guys don't behave out of politeness, especially teenage boys."

"He's just hot and cold," I tell her and then retract my word choice. "Not hot. More like warm."

She fills two plates with store-bought tortellini, spoons vodka sauce over the top, and places them on the bar top before taking her seat next to me.

"So, I take it this Kason is good-looking."

"Extremely," I gush, stabbing a tortellini before taking a bite.

"It's day two, Ady. Give him a chance to warm up to you."

"Oh, that's another thing. He only calls me Adaline when he knows I prefer to be called Ady. It should annoy me, but . . ."

"But he's hot, so you like it?"

"You're crazy," I accuse jokingly.

"And you're not denying it," she shoots back.

I shake my head at her.

"I wanted to talk to you about work. The firm has wasted no time handing me over my first case. It's a pretty intense one that's going to require a lot of long hours in prep for trial," she explains. "I know we just moved here, but—"

"Don't worry, Mom. I understand." And I do. My mother is a criminal defense attorney and has an impressive record of wins under her belt. That doesn't come to those who don't put in the hard work and time. At this point, I'm used to taking care of myself.

She sets her fork down, and with an endearing expression, she tucks a lock of my hair behind my ear. "Have I told you how much I love you?"

"All the time," I respond. "Seriously, though, I'll be fine."

"You're my favorite." She takes a bite of pasta. "I was thinking that since we're having an early dinner we could go to the beach and do some exploring. What do you think?"

Most seventeen-year-olds probably wouldn't be caught dead hanging out with their mother, but not me. And when she offers her time, I take it, knowing how precious it is to the both of us.

"I'd love that. Just ditch the heels."

CHAPTER
four

Adaline

There should be laws against creepers like me, but I can't help myself. Although, at this point, I should really make it be known to Kason that the pool he's been cleaning for the past two weeks is mine.

I've continued to grow closer in my friendship with Micah while Kason still keeps me guessing where I stand with him. I don't even know if I have any standing at all, or if he's nothing more than the teenage daydream living in my head.

Crushes suck.

It's the constant wondering about what could be, only to be tormented by what might never be. For now, I push those thoughts aside as I head down the stairs to say hi before he figures out on his own that this is my house and questions why I never said anything.

I slide open the large glass doors and step out onto the veranda. The movement catches his attention from across the yard, which makes him look up.

"Hey, stranger."

He lifts his sunglasses, only to squint against the bright sun as he looks over at me. "Adaline?"

"I was upstairs, and when I looked out my window and saw you, I thought I'd come say hi." *Even though I've been secretly watching you all the other times you've been here.*

He tosses the skimmer back into the water with a loud splash. "I didn't know this was your house."

With an uncomfortable smile, I nod as he starts to round-up his supplies. "You already done?"

"Yeah."

This interaction is so awkward that it edges on painful.

Why is he so hard to talk to?

"You thirsty?"

"I have water in the truck." He grabs his belongings and then looks over to me with a fleeting, "Have a good weekend," before opening the gate.

I give up. I swear I've never had to struggle so much with simple conversation than what I do with him. At this point, I'm sure he sees me as nothing more than annoying. I mean, if he cared to talk to me, he's had more than enough opportunities to do so.

My phone buzzes from my back pocket.

Micah: Got any plans for the day?

Me: None. I'm turning into a loser over here.

Micah: Come be a loser at my house.

Me: Let me throw myself together and I'll be over.

Micah: Throw yourself together? It's after 3:00.

Me: Again . . . loser status. I'll head your way in a bit.

He texts me his address before I go back upstairs, take a quick shower, and get dressed. While pulling my hair back into a ponytail, my phone rings with an incoming call from my mother.

"Hey, Mom."

"Hi, dear. I wanted to let you know that I purchased your plane ticket for spring break. I emailed the confirmation to you and your father, but I haven't been able to get ahold of him."

That isn't surprising.

"Look, I'm slammed and don't really have the time to track him down, so would you mind trying yourself?"

"Do I really have to go?" I sigh.

"Yes. You really have to go. If anything, look at it as a chance to hang out with all your old friends."

"This borders on child abuse, you know?"

"There are worse things in life."

"Are there?" A muffled laugh comes through on her end. "I heard that," I accuse.

"Your dramatics are amusing."

"I'm so glad I can be your source of entertainment."

"Just call your father, will you?"

With a reluctant groan, I agree. "Fine. I'll call him."

When I end the conversation with her, I scroll through my contacts and call my dad, who I haven't spoken to since the move two weeks ago. But it isn't like he's blowing my phone up to talk me, so I don't feel bad. His voice mail picks up, and I breathe out in relief before leaving him a message to call me back. And with that taken care of, I dab on a touch of lip gloss and grab my keys.

Micah lives on Harbour Island, so it's a quick ten-minute drive from my house in Hyde Park.

"Where are your parents?" I ask when he opens the front door.

"Anniversary trip to Connecticut," Micah responds as I walk through the foyer and back to the living room, where I flop down next to Trent on the couch.

"What's up, Ady?"

"Not much. What've you guys been doing all day?"

Micah grabs his T-shirt off the back of one of the chairs and shrugs it on. "You're looking at it. Just been hanging out."

"We should go do something then," I suggest, but Trent can barely drag his eyes away from some movie that's playing on the television. Micah, who's now lying on a loveseat with his legs dangling over the arm, is equally distracted by whatever he's reading on his phone. "Okay then," I mutter to myself as I lean back into the plush cushions. "This works, too."

"There's pizza in the kitchen if you're hungry," Micah offers before his cell vibrates with a buzz.

"Dude, this movie blows. I'm gonna go out back for a smoke. Wanna come?"

Micah lifts his eyes toward Trent. "Nah, man. I'm good."

"Ady?"

"No thanks."

He heads to the pool out back, and I take the remote and flip through the channels when Micah's phone buzzes yet again.

"Who are you texting?"

He doesn't even acknowledge me as his thumbs tap against the screen at record pace.

"Micah," I call loud enough to get a mild, "Huh?" in return.

Abandoning the remote, I walk across the room to where he's lounging, lift his ankles and squeeze myself onto the loveseat before dropping his legs on my lap. "Tell me who's got your attention."

He lowers his phone. "Not a chance."

"You're acting suspect."

"And you're acting nosey." His phone buzzes again.

"I'm a girl. Nosiness is engrained in all female DNA."

"Is that so?"

With curiosity heavy in the air, I reach my hand to the underside of his thigh and jab my fingers into the muscle. I crack up laughing when he lurches off the loveseat with a high-pitched squeal, surrendering with, "Okay, okay. Damn." He tosses the phone into my lap before dropping back next to me.

"Who's Jen?"

"Some chick I met at a party last weekend."

I toss the phone back without reading any of their texts. I might be nosey, but I'm not entirely intrusive.

"Just some chick, huh?"

"Are we seriously doing this?" He shifts and gives me a nervous smile. "I don't have any other female friends that I spend as much time with as I do you. And as chill as you are, I'm not down with painting each other's toe nails while gabbing about who I'm texting or whatever shit you girls like to do."

"This Jen has you wound up," I tease. "And to be honest, I don't expect you to *gab* to me about anything. And while we're on the topic of gabbing"—I look out the panoramic windows to the billowing smoke floating above Trent's head—"is he smoking weed?"

Micah chuckles under his breath. "Yeah, why?"

I lean forward and look back at him from over my shoulder, stressing, "Oh my God. Are you serious?"

"Dude, relax."

Turning away from Micah, I stare out at Trent as he takes another pull.

"Are you *that* sheltered?"

"Apparently," I murmur. Back home in Texas, I hadn't known anyone who smoked pot, let alone had the chance to watch someone smoke it. "Do you do it, too?"

When I look at him, he holds an expression of amused disbelief, as if my asking is completely asinine.

"I'll take that as a yes," I answer for him. "Where do you even get it?"

"From your little buddy, Kason."

"Kason? Seriously?"

At this, he laughs at me. "Dude, you look like you've seen a ghost. Take a breath. Whatever afterschool specials you've been watching have really warped your head. It isn't a big deal."

I sit back and look to my new friend who is clearly amused by my reaction, and I play it off when I tell him, "I met McGruff once, you know?"

"Who the hell is McGruff?"

"The crime dog," I exclaim. "He came to my school when I was in the fourth grade."

His smile grows, and he slings his arm around my shoulders. "I bet you also have a framed photo of George Bush somewhere in your house, too."

I thicken my accent for his benefit when I joke, "Right next to my framed NRA membership certificate."

A moment passes, and when our laugher dies down, he

surprises me when he says, "Don't ever do it."

I tilt my head to the side and look at him. "Do what?"

"Pot."

"I thought you said it wasn't a big deal."

"Not for us, but it is to you, and I like that whatever conservative town you were raised in has kept you green."

I smile, feeling lucky to have him as a friend. When he picks up his phone to continue texting Jen, I feign indifference when I respond to his previous statement, muttering, "And Kason isn't my buddy. He hardly knows I exist."

Trent bursts into the room, takes one look at the television, and groans, "Not the fucking Food Network," to which I crack up.

Hours waste away while we hang out and watch television. I listen as the two of them talk music and skateboarding. They make plans to hit up a new skate park over in St. Pete next week, and I text Molly off and on. It's a comforting feeling to simply hang out with these two and do nothing together.

The room soon begins to darken as the day fades, and I step out back where the pool overlooks the bay to watch the sun before it kisses the water. My bare feet step into the thick blades of grass, which are cool beneath my toes, and walk out to the dock where an impressive boat sits. Water gently laps against the fiberglass.

"Ady," Micah hollers from the house. "We're going to get takeout. You coming?"

"I'm going to stay and watch the sunset. Just get me whatever; I'm not picky."

I sit on the edge of the dock, my toes barely skimming over the top of the water. The sky is painted flawlessly in burnt oranges and almost fluorescent pinks. Colors that burn so brilliantly above, I can feel their heat on my bare shoulders.

I snap a photo and text it to Molly.

Molly: I'm so jealous.

I smile, but it doesn't feel good on my face, so I let it go.

Me: I miss you. Wish you were here.

Molly: You'll be back here soon enough. Spring break!!!

I brace my hands behind me and lean back, tilting my head to soak in the last few rays of light before the sun submerges itself beneath the water.

Tranquility is interrupted by my ringing cell, and my stomach sinks a little lower in my belly when I see it's my dad calling.

"Hi, Dad."

"Your mother sent me your flight information, and I needed to touch base with you," he says. "I won't be able to pick you up from the airport because Parker has his soccer game at that time, so can you see if one of your friends can give you a ride?"

"Where's Gwen going to be?"

"She'll be at the game, too."

Irritation pricks from within. "Can't you miss one game? He's her son, not yours."

"He's my stepson, Ady."

And I'm your daughter. Flesh and blood. Shared DNA.

"Look, it's a busy time right now—not that I expected your mother to retain that when I told her—but Parker is out for spring break at the same time you'll be here. So, you'll be spending most of the week with him and Gwen."

"You're not taking off work?" I question a bit too harshly as the heaviness in my chest grows.

"You know how it is. I can't just take off days at a time."

"Why am I even coming then?"

"Because I miss you." He's quick to answer, as if he's become so well rehearsed in his response that it's second nature. I know better, but it still hurts. Deep within the walls of anger and annoyance I've built up lies the pain of rejection—of being so easily replaced.

"You haven't even called me since Mom and I moved. I started a new school, and you haven't even texted me to ask how it's going," I tell him as I hear chatter in the background on his end of the call.

"Is that Ady?" I hear Parker's small voice call out, and I want to hate the kid for having the dad that used to be all mine, but he's only seven. It isn't his fault.

"Can I call you back later?"

"Are you going to make time for us to hang out . . . just the two of us?"

"Parker and Gwen just got home," he says, completely distracted. "We have dinner plans that we need to get ready for."

"Whatever," I grumble under my breath and disconnect the call without another word spoken. My nose burns as tears form in the corner of my eyes, and I hate that my dad is able to puncture the softest parts of me. I wish I was more detached than what I am, but he's my dad, and I love him. I just hate feeling as if I'm disposable, especially when I used to be his entire world when our family was still intact.

CHAPTER
five

Kason

Breathless and sated, I roll off my indulgence and stare at the water stains on the ceiling to avoid her eyes. Her heavy panting slows as I lose focus in the fan above. The blades stir the thick air that smells like our sex, and I close my eyes to draw out the lasting remnants of my high as it radiates through my limbs.

The moment she speaks is the moment I sit up and rip off the condom.

"I'm glad you stopped by," she says as I pull my shorts on. "This week has been crazy at work. They fired a few people, and I've been picking up the extra shifts to try to stash some money away."

"For what?"

"I don't know. Been thinking about taking a couple of cosmetology classes or something. Working in a salon could be fun," she says, and a part of me wants to tell her that she could do so much more with her life than scrubbing calluses off strangers' feet, but I don't. "It's not like I want to be a grocery store cashier for the rest of my life, you know?"

I grab my shirt off the floor and turn to look at her as she stares up at me. She lies on the bed, completely naked, with no sheets covering her body. Her eyes are needy. They always have been. Not for me, though. They're needy for self-worth and hope for a better life. Krista uses me, just as I use her, but where I use her to satisfy my physical needs, she uses me for something far more unfortunate—a false perception of importance.

Having the attention of the boy next door fulfills her in a way that allows me to keep coming back for more, and I do. For years, I've been knocking on her door and fucking her on her bed.

"You should look into classes if that's what you really want to do."

Krista rolls onto her side and props her head up with her hand. "Yeah, maybe."

I shove my feet into my flip-flops and pick up my keys from the nightstand before asking, "You okay?"

"You don't have to ask me that every time you leave. I'm a big girl."

And I know she is at the age of twenty-two. That's why this arrangement works so well. Neither one of us has to worry about emotions getting involved, since neither of us is interested in anything more than sex.

"See you later."

I step out of her ground-floor unit, walk over to the adjacent building, and climb the stairs to my apartment. Walking in, I find my mother in the kitchen, boiling a pot of water.

"What are you doing home?"

"It's nice to see you, too, Son."

"I didn't mean it like that," I say as I walk over to the stove. When I see the box of dried pasta and a tub of margarine, I take the fork out of her hand. "Why don't you sit, Mom."

She purses her lips before taking a seat at the rickety linoleum table that's pushed against the wall.

"Why aren't you at work?"

"I had an appointment with my doctor."

I turn to my mom, who looks years beyond her age, with deep-set wrinkles and brittle hair. She's had a tough life raising me as a single mother, and although she's been absent for the majority of my childhood, there isn't a single day that I don't appreciate her efforts to keep us afloat. "Is everything okay?"

"Everything's fine. It was only a checkup. Nothing to concern yourself with."

I hate when she brushes my warranted concerns off and claims there's nothing to worry about.

"How was work today?"

When the water comes to a boil, I toss in the pasta. "Same as every other day," I tell her, leaving out the fact that the girl I can't seem to get out of my head lives in one of the houses that's on my route.

"Any plans for tonight?"

"I'm supposed to hang out at Micah's."

"That sounds fun."

I continue to watch the pot, stirring occasionally until it's done.

"You want parmesan?" I ask as I drain the noodles and toss some margarine into them.

"We're all out."

Sprinkling a dash of salt over the noodles, I set the bowl in front of her, kiss her cheek, and wish I weren't so self-sufficient. For once, it would be nice if someone would tend to me, to ask me if I was all right. Not that I'm *not* okay, but it's the knowing that I'm being looked after that's been my missing piece in life. Again, I don't hold it against my mom, but the feelings of abandonment are ever-lingering.

"I'm going to jump in the shower and then head out. You need anything else?"

She shakes her head and thanks me for cooking before taking a bite.

After working out in the heat all day and then stopping by Krista's, I opt for a cold shower, which soothes my sunbaked skin. Not knowing how late I'm going to be out tonight, I give in once more and jerk another one out before finishing my shower.

Running my hand through my wet hair that's long overdue for a trim, I walk over to my dresser and pull out a pair of shorts and a T-shirt to toss on. With the money I earn, I've been able to accrue a decent collection of clothing to replace the thrift store hand-me-downs of my younger years. Thankfully, most of the kids I go to school with couldn't care less about labels—at least for the guys. It seems those who don't come from wealth desire the "look" of luxury more than those who are privy to it. Take it or leave it, they're fine with shorts, T-shirts, and flip-flops, so my fitting into the visual standards of those down in South Tampa has never been an issue.

But where I live, just west of the University of South Florida, is the armpit of Tampa. Rusty mobile homes and run-down apartments like this one line the streets. The city does its best to hide our dilapidated presence behind restaurants, sports bars, and retail sites that dominate the scene near USF.

I'm one of the lucky ones, though. With some help, I was able to leave my neighborhood school and transfer to South Shore High in South Tampa, where the city's most valuable properties line the impeccably manicured streets.

"Dude, you coming over?" Micah says when I answer his call.

"Leaving now."

"Trent and I are about to head out and grab some takeout. The house is open, so let yourself in."

"Sounds good."

Getting into my car, I crank the windows down since the air conditioning finally gave up the good fight the other day, and start driving south to Harbour Island. Thirty minutes later, I cross the small bridge over to the gated community. When I pull up to Micah's house, I see Trent's car, along with a sporty, white Mercedes hatchback, the same one that's parked at Adaline's house every time I've been there.

My attempts to dodge this girl keep failing. I didn't think much of her when we first bumped into each other, and it wasn't until I saw that look of attraction in her eyes later that day in sixth period that I told myself to steer clear. It's been difficult since she's become friends with Micah, so to avoid making it too obvious that I'm avoiding her, I pull the key from the ignition and head inside, knowing that everyone is out grabbing food.

I walk through the house to the back doors so I can take

in the waterfront view I'm not privileged enough to see every day. Opening the double doors, I step outside as the sun is setting in the distance, and a girl's voice catches my attention.

I scan the expansive yard, and find her sitting on the edge of the dock, talking on the phone. Her long blonde hair is pulled into a ponytail that hangs down the center of her back, which is barely covered by the strappy, loose top she's wearing. My chest kicks out a few hard beats, and as much as it feels good, I hate it just as badly.

I watch her.

How can I not?

Her skin is darker than it was when I met her on her first day of school, and I wonder how much time she's been spending at the beach. That thought is chased by a pang of jealousy when I consider who she would be going to the beach with. It's not like Micah has made it a secret that he likes the girl, only I don't know in what capacity.

"You haven't even called me since Mom and I moved," she says into the phone, her voice is loud with agitation. "I started a new school, and you haven't even texted me to ask how it's going."

Curiosity gets to me as I walk across the patio and down a few steps to the pool.

"Are you going to make time for us to hang out . . . just the two of us?"

Her whole tone has shifted, and I don't hear an ounce of the upbeat girl I see every day at school.

Setting the phone at her side, she braces the edge of the dock with her hands and drops her head. I feel like I'm intruding on a private moment, but I don't walk away. I don't move at all, until I do, because there's something intolerable about her being upset, no matter what the reason.

Wood creaks beneath my feet when I step onto the dock and she startles. She snaps her head up to meet my eyes and her cheeks are covered in tears.

"I didn't mean to scare you," I say, and she immediately shies away, turning to quickly wipe her face.

Kicking off my flip-flops, I sit next to her and drop my legs over the edge, alongside hers.

She sniffs and clears her throat, her lame attempt to mask what I just saw. "What are you doing here?"

"Who were you talking to?" I ask, avoiding her effort to distract me with her irrelevant question, and my bluntness catches her off guard.

"What?"

"The person who made you cry. Who was it?"

Her lips part, but she doesn't answer me right away. There's something about seeing her on the brink of vulnerability that tugs me from an unknown place. She's hesitant to talk, and I guess I can't blame her with how evasive I've been with her lately.

"I'm sorry I was a dick in my car the other week. I shouldn't have blown you off."

Her face softens with my apology as she's cast in waves of silver from the moon's reflection off the water. She still doesn't speak, though, so I go on only because I want her to trust me enough to answer my question when I ask it again.

"My parents were never married," I tell her, answering the question she asked a couple of weeks ago. The one I evaded and then gave her the cold shoulder for asking. But seeing her tonight, with tears in her eyes, the coldness is gone. "My father has never been in the picture. I've never met him."

"I'm sorry. I shouldn't have even asked you about something so personal."

"You have nothing to be sorry for. It was a simple question."

She glides her toes lazily over the water, and I give her a moment before I press on. "So tell me, who were you talking to?"

And this time, she's the one who avoids the question in order to ask her own. "Why are you so standoffish?"

"I didn't mean to be."

She arches a brow at my lie, and I chuckle at her forwardness.

"Okay, fine. I meant to be," I admit.

"Is that your nature, or is it something you reserve for me? Because I'm not going to lie, you're giving me a complex."

"I don't hold enough clout to give anyone a complex."

She smiles and tilts her head back to look at the stars.

"Last time," I state, waiting for her to give her attention back to me, and when she does, I ask again, "Who were you talking to?"

The way she looks at me knocks all the confidence I pretend to have on its ass, and I wonder if she can see through the sham.

"My dad. I'm supposed spend my spring break with him, but . . ." She shrugs and looks down at the water beneath our feet.

"But what?"

"Nothing. It doesn't matter."

"Now look who's being standoffish," I say to ease her tension, and it works when I see the corner of her mouth lift. "Why were you crying?"

"Because . . ." She fidgets her hands. "Because when he left my mom, I felt like he wanted to leave me, too. He's remarried now, and she has a son who he gives all his attention to, while I'm on the outside looking in. It's just . . . it doesn't feel good to be forgotten."

"This is the same guy who used to take you to car shows?"

She nods. "He hasn't even bothered to call me or even text since we moved."

"Why go visit him?"

"I don't want to, but my mother already bought the plane ticket. She's doing what she can to keep my father in my life, but I know it hurts her."

"When do you leave?"

"Next weekend."

I pick up her phone, which has been sitting between us, swipe the screen, and add my cell to her contacts while she watches me. When I hand the phone to her, I say, "In case you need a distraction while you're there."

"And what about you? Where will you be?"

"Working."

"You're not going anywhere?"

It's now that I regret opening myself up to this girl and giving her my number. It's the reminder that we come from two very different worlds, which she is unaware of. I've never taken a vacation in my life. This town is the only place I've ever seen, but Adaline . . . I can only imagine all the places she's already experienced in her short life.

"Not this year," I tell her before pulling my feet out of the water, and she quickly follows.

"I should probably get going."

"I'll walk you inside."

When we step into the house, Micah and Trent are already

back and scarfing down a couple of gyros.

"Food's in the bag," Trent says around a mouthful of lamb.

Adaline turns to Micah. "I'm going to head out, if that's okay?"

"You sure?"

She gives him some lame excuse about being tired, and he walks her out to her car before coming back to the table and picking up his half-eaten gyro. "So, what the hell were the two of you doing out on the dock?" he says with heavy insinuation. "Looked cozy."

I laugh him off. "Shut the fuck up."

"She's hot," Trent adds.

"Yeah, and she also lives in a big ass house that sits right on Bayshore Avenue."

"You've been over to her house?"

"I'm her fucking pool cleaner, Micah."

"Who the fuck cares?" he says, completely detached from the reality I live in. The kind of reality where girls like her have no business being with guys like me. Not to mention the embarrassment of her knowing that I don't come from this world.

A world filled with ease and prosperity.

A world where your last name and address is all you need to have respect spilled at your feet.

A world I shouldn't be a part of, but because of Micah's father, I am.

"I care. Plus, I don't want to intrude on whatever it is you have going on with her," I tell him, curious as to what their relationship actually is, even though I know better to care.

"Dude, nothing's going on. She's a down girl, that's all." He takes another bite of food and gives me a pointed look. "Plus,

I'm working on my own thing. A Tampa Prep chick."

"Sounds pretentious. Does she know what she's getting herself into?"

"Stop talking," he laughs, shoving his hand into the Louis Pappas sack, pulling out a gyro, and tossing it my way. "Eat, pretty boy."

CHAPTER
six

Adaline

I roll my suitcase out to the curb of the arrivals lane and wait for Molly to pick me up since my father *has more important things to do*. My stomach has been in knots since my mom dropped me off at the Tampa airport this morning, but dread lifts the moment I see my best friend.

As soon as she jumps out of the car, we run into each other's arms and squeal like the schoolgirls we are. Even though I only moved a month ago, it feels like I haven't seen her in forever, and I'm already wishing I could steal Molly away and bring her back to Florida with me.

"Look at your tan," she crows dramatically. "I'm so hating on you right now."

I laugh and shove my suitcase into her trunk and soon

enough we're on the road.

"I've missed you so much. Seriously, this texting relationship we have going is depressing."

Pulling out my phone, I shoot a quick message to let my mom know I've made it safely. "Tell me about it. It sucks worse on my end, so don't complain."

"Oh, please."

"It's true," I argue. "You're still here with all your friends while I'm bored out of my mind and texting you like a needy wench. It's tragic."

She rolls her eyes. "Right. Palm trees and beaches. Sounds real tragic," she mocks. "I don't feel sorry for you."

I reach over and grab her hand, and she gives mine a gentle squeeze. Our friendship stems back to elementary school. We never lived in the same neighborhood, but our moms always made sure we were in the same class every year, plus we were together every Sunday morning at our Kids' Bible Club. To say we're simply friends would be an understatement—we're more like sisters.

"So, any new updates on this Kason guy you've been pining after?"

"I wouldn't call it *pining*."

She tilts her head to me accusingly. "You spy on the guy while he cleans your pool. If that isn't pining, I don't know what is."

"I should never have told you that."

"Don't worry. Your secret's safe with me, creeper," she says with a giggle. "But seriously, did you ever get a picture? I'm dying to see what he looks like."

"Talk about being a creeper. He probably thinks I'm weird enough without him catching me taking stalker pics of him to text out to randoms."

Her jaw drops and she laughs. "Did you just call me a random?"

I throw her an obnoxious smile before adding, "And no, there's nothing new. Although, he's been nicer to me since that humiliating night when he caught me crying. Oh my god, I still want to die every time I think about it."

"I can't believe you did that," she says through her laughter.

We spend most of the day together, falling into familiar routines easily. We stop by the mall for lunch and do some shopping before heading over to her house. The afternoon flies by while we hang out in her bedroom. She catches me up on all the gossip from my old high school, but it's when she confesses that she kissed Robbie Fletcher that I slam her good with one of her pillows.

"Why didn't you tell me?" I exclaim, and she loses herself to a fit of awkward giggles.

"I just did."

"You should've told me last week when it happened."

"I know," she responds, straightening and shifting into a more serious tone. "But I didn't know what it meant. He didn't say anything afterward, and it was . . . *weird*. Plus, it was the first time I ever kissed a guy. I didn't know what I was doing, so I was embarrassed."

"You overthink things."

"Maybe to you, hooker," she teases.

"Oh my god! I've kissed one boy, and now I'm a hooker?"

The two of us fall back onto the bed and continue to tease each other relentlessly, and then I make her tell me every detail of her first kiss with Robbie. She blushes and covers her face while I secretly daydream about what it would be like to kiss Kason. We're two seventeen-year-olds who've embraced our prudish ways because boys have never been a priority to us until now, unlike some of our other friends who've been crushing like mad since puberty hit.

"So, what's going on with the two of you now?" I ask when I sit up.

"He asked me to go with him to the Spring Fling dance."

I smile over at her. "I can't believe this. I move away, and you get your first boyfriend."

"Girls, dinner!" Her mom, Suzanne, calls from downstairs.

I eye the spread of food on the dining table. "I've missed your cooking."

I've always been able to count on coming over here whenever I've wanted a home-cooked meal. With my mother's career being so demanding, restaurants and takeout have always been the main staple in our household.

I dig into the enchiladas and guacamole while Suzanne asks me about Florida, my new school, and my mom's job. When I can't put off going to my dad's house any longer, I thank her mom for dinner and get back into Molly's car.

"Call me tomorrow, okay?"

I reach over and give her a hug. "I will."

I pull my suitcase out of the trunk, and watch as she drives away before walking toward the house. You know you've become estranged from your parent when you have to knock on their front door to be let in.

"Well, there you are," Gwen says as I stand on the porch. "We were starting to wonder if you'd show up."

I step inside and she takes my bag before pulling me into a hug I don't want. This woman tries much too hard to pretend to like me, but only when I'm in her presence. Any other time,

I'm nonexistent.

"Garrison, Ady is here," she calls out to my dad, but Parker beats him into the foyer.

"Ady's here!" he squeals as he barrels into me with a big hug, and I can't help myself when I hug the little squirt back. I can't hold it against him that his mom and my dad are too self-absorbed to make any *real* effort with me.

My dad makes his appearance and wraps one arm around me in a side hug. "Hi, sweetheart."

"Hey, Dad."

"How was your flight?"

"It was fine. How was the soccer game?" I ask. Not that I care.

He takes his hand and musses Parker's hair, saying proudly, "The little guy scored three goals and made some impressive blocks."

Gwen steps behind her son and places her hands on his shoulders. "We really wish you could've been there, but you'll be able to see him play Tuesday night."

"Great," I mutter before we all fall into an unpleasant silence. I drop my eyes to my feet as I shift uncomfortably, and I almost want to thank Gwen when she breaks the tension, asking, "Have you eaten dinner?"

"Yeah. I ate over at Molly's house."

She nods before turning to my dad. "Honey, why don't you help her with her suitcase. I'm sure she's tired from the plane ride." Looking to me, she adds, "Let me know if you need help settling in."

She could easily fool you into believing she actually cares, but actions speak way louder than her words ever could. I'll always think of her as the woman my father left my mother for instead of the stepmother she sucks at being.

I follow my dad up the stairs and into the room they set aside for me to stay in for the week.

"There are towels in the bathroom for you."

"Thanks."

I lift my suitcase onto the bed before turning to face my father, who stands stiffly next to the door.

I wish he would smile.

I wish even more that he would hug me. A real hug. The way he used to before the woman downstairs came into our lives and ripped our family apart.

"I'll see you in the morning," he finally says before ducking out and shutting the door behind him. It doesn't stay closed for more than a minute before Parker comes barging in.

"Knock much?"

"What are you doing?"

I drop a handful of pajama tanks into a dresser drawer. "What does it look like?"

He walks over and jumps up on the bed. "Want to hang out?"

"Not really," I sigh as I carry my toiletry bag to the en suite bathroom, and when I walk back into the bedroom, he's messing around on my phone. "Do you mind?" I swipe it out of his hands.

"You got any games on that thing? I keep asking Mom for a cell phone, but she always says no."

"You're seven. What do you need a phone for?"

He looks at me as if I just grew a second head and exclaims, "So I can play games."

"Out," I announce, pointing toward the hall, and when he rolls off the bed with a groan and leaves the room, I lock myself in for the night.

Once I'm completely unpacked, I take a shower and get ready for bed. I pick up my cell, turn off the lamp on the nightstand, and shoot my mom another text.

Me: Gwen puts lavender in the dresser drawers. My clothes are going to smell like an old lady.

I flip through my contacts while I wait for her to text me back and come across Kason's name. My finger hovers over the icon that would start a new text thread. I want to push it and send him a message, but what the heck would I even say? His number has been in my phone for over a week now, and I still haven't used it. Not that I haven't wanted to, because I have. He just makes me nervous, and I hate that I'm so uncertain about how I should be with him.

My phone vibrates in my hand, and I click on the notification that holds my mom's return text.

Mom: We'll get everything laundered when you get back. In the meantime, try not to be too judgmental while you're there. Make the best of it.

Me: She folds the toilet paper into a point, Mom. How do you expect me not to judge a person based on that alone?

Mom: Promise me you'll try to enjoy your trip.

Me: Fiiiiiiiiiiiiiiiine.

Mom: You're my favorite, you know that?

I smile because she has always been the one person there for me no matter what.

Me: You're my favorite, too. G'night.

Everyone is already in the kitchen, dressed, and eating when I drag myself downstairs.

"Oh, you're still in your pajamas," Gwen notes when I walk into the kitchen.

I look over to the clock on the stove. "It's only eight."

"Which means it's nine o'clock in Florida. A tad late to be rolling out of bed. We need to leave in fifteen minutes."

"To go where?"

She opens the fridge and hands my dad a carton of organic milk so he can pour some into his coffee thermos. "It's the first day of registration for the summer camps at the children's museum. We need to get there early before the classes Parker wants fill up."

I look over to Parker, who's sitting at the bar top and shoveling heaping spoonfuls of some all-natural, gluten free, dye free, taste free cereal into his mouth.

"I think I'll pass on this particular family outing."

Gwen looks to my dad and then me before landing back on my father.

"Let her stay," he tells her.

She picks up her purse and keys. "You ready, Parker?"

He hops off the stool, saying, "Bye, Dad," as he runs to the garage, and I swear my hearts palpitates in the worst way possible.

When I hear the door close behind them, I turn to look my dad dead on, but he's oblivious to the reason behind the menacing sharpness in my eyes.

"He calls you *dad*?"

"Could you go easy on Gwen? She's trying to make sure you feel included."

"Like she did when she picked me up from the airport

yesterday?" My voice reeks of annoyed sarcasm before I return to the *other* situation. "Why does Parker call you dad?"

"Because I'm married to his mom. Because I'm raising him. Because we're a family. Give the kid a break, he's only seven."

"And what about me? Where do I fit into this *family*?"

Irritated, he grabs his briefcase and coffee. "I'm wondering the same thing, Ady. Because your attitude toward us makes it seem like you don't want to even try to be a part of our family."

"The fact that I have to *try* to be a part of *anything* is so messed up. It shouldn't be a matter of trying, Dad, I should just *be*."

"Then just *be* and stop making it so difficult on everyone," he states before walking out of the kitchen, and when he leaves for work, I'm determined to be gone before Gwen and Parker return from the museum.

Me: Can you come pick me up?
Molly: Be there in twenty.

The next few days pass with uneventful tension. Conversations with my dad and Gwen are artificial and underlined with unspoken discomfort. My dad has been at work every day, leaving me here with the step-family. I'm trying to stay in the background, so when I'm not hanging out with my friends or spending time with Parker, I'm hiding away in my bedroom.

Tonight, I won't be able to get away with that since my dad has insisted that I stay in for a family dinner. I scoffed when he called it that. He wasn't amused.

I can smell the roast that Gwen's been tending to in the kitchen while I lie in bed and text Micah, who's still in Tampa. He said he'd rather stay home alone than go on vacation with his parents. So they left, and he's been at the beach every day while I'm being subjected to the horrors of teenage angst.

"Dinner's ready," Parker announces when he bursts into my room.

"Any chance I can get you to smuggle a plate and bring it up here? I'll pay you ten bucks."

"Maybe for twenty," he counters with a mischievous grin.

I set my phone on the nightstand and get off the bed. "What do you need twenty dollars for anyway?"

"To buy the cell phone mom won't get me."

"That's going to cost you a lot more than twenty bucks, squirt," I tell him as we head downstairs.

My dad is already sitting at the head of the table when I walk into the dining room. Since Gwen is sitting to his left, I sit next to Parker, who's between my father and me.

"I hope you like roast," Gwen says, and I respond with a light, "Mm-hmm."

We eat, and I listen while the three of them talk about a trip to Colorado they're going on to visit Gwen's family during summer break. Plans to go hiking in Estes Park and cherry picking are discussed, without a single mention of my inclusion. At this point, I'd almost rather not be involved to avoid constantly feeling as if I'm the outcast. My time here hasn't felt good at all. It's the never-ending heaviness in the pit of my stomach, reminding me that I'm not wanted. I can't seem to figure out what it is about me that has my father distancing himself so much when we used to be so close.

After Gwen clears dinner from the table and brings out the

icebox cake she made earlier, I get an uneasy feeling in my gut when my father says, "So, there's something we wanted to tell you kids."

Gwen looks at Parker with a big smile as she serves us slices of cake. When she takes her seat, my dad covers her hand with his. The doting expression he gives her makes me want to regurgitate the roast I just ate.

While Parker inhales his dessert, mine remains untouched.

"What is it you want to tell us?" I ask.

She shoots an exciting smile to my dad again, and when he gives her a nod, she beams, "We're having a baby!"

My eyes dart to my father, and his prideful smile sickens me. "Are you serious?"

Gwen's excitement deflates as all attention redirects to me, but I can't hide the shock I wear so blatantly on my face.

"You're pregnant?" I fume with distaste in my mouth, and before she can say anything, Parker perks up at my side.

"I'm going to be a big brother!"

"Don't get too excited."

"Ady!" my father scolds.

"What? Seriously, Dad, you can barely pick up the phone to call me, yet, you're going to have another kid?"

"That's enough, young lady."

"I know this is a lot to take in," Gwen interjects, her voice needling on my nerves. "But you're father and I are very excited to be—"

"Can you stop," I bite out harshly. "I'm so sick of your fake Disney-sweet voice, talking to me as if you're *so delighted* I'm here when we both know the truth."

"Then why the hell are you even here?" My father's voice booms loudly when he stands, and I meet his stance, seething in my own anger. "You apologize right now."

"Apologize? You can't be serious." Fury for what these two have done boils beneath my skin. "She should be the one apologizing to *me* for being a home-wrecker."

"I beg your pardon."

I glare at her. "You had no right doing what you did."

She instantly turns to Parker and tells him to go to his room, and when he's out of earshot, she stands and tosses her napkin onto the table. "How dare you come into my house and talk to me with such disrespect."

"This is what I'm talking about, Dad. Her house. Not yours . . . not ours. I don't even know why I'm here when I'm clearly not wanted." I turn back to Gwen and lash out, "And I'm not some random houseguest you're hosting, I'm family, whether you like it or not. So, can we all agree that you're only pretending to like me to appease him?"

"I've had enough of this. She is my wife, and I will not tolerate you speaking to her like this. You either apologize this instant or you can find someplace else to stay."

"You're seriously going to kick me out?"

He stands cold with his fists on his hips and doesn't say another word. His silence is a knife to my heart. The realization that my biggest fear isn't some illusion I've built up in my head is devastating.

Sadness cuts through the anger, and when I blink, tears fall, but he still doesn't budge.

He doesn't want me.

He isn't affected at all.

So, why on earth would I stay where I'm not wanted?

CHAPTER
seven

Kason

The moment I walk into the backyard is the same moment I see her lying on the wicker couch that's on the covered veranda. She doesn't make a move as I walk across the yard and set my supplies at the edge of the pool. I watch her, knowing that she shouldn't be here because she's supposed to be in Texas for another two days. Yet, here she is.

Something isn't right, and the feeling unsettles me. This is the girl I haven't been able to shake for a month now, the girl I gave my number to but has yet to use it. The girl that doesn't have to do a single thing to pull me toward her. I step closer until she comes into complete view. She sleeps behind a pair of sunglasses and is wearing sleep shorts and a tank with her hair tied back.

I take a seat on the side of the stone fire pit and debate waking her, but the sound of the sliding doors opening alarms me, and I jump to my feet.

"I'm sorry. I didn't mean to startle you."

"That's okay, ma'am, I'm here to treat the pool and saw Adaline—" She tilts her head in question, and I clarify, "We go to school together."

"Oh, you're Kason?"

She knows my name?

Adaline rustles awake on the couch and sits up. "Mom?" She pushes her sunglasses back on her head as her mother walks over and takes a seat next to her. When Adaline looks at me, I see her eyes are dark, swollen, and exhausted.

"I was coming out to check on you and see if you were hungry."

"I'm fine."

Her mother gives her a sympathetic smile before standing. "Well, I'll be inside if you need anything." She then looks at me. "It was nice meeting you, Kason."

"You, too, Mrs.—"

"Cheryl. No misses or ma'am, they make me feel old," she says with a wink, and I give her a nod before shoving my hands into my pockets as she walks back inside.

"What are you doing here?" Adaline asks, drawing my attention back to her, and she quickly catches herself. "Never mind. Stupid question."

"Better yet, what are *you* doing here? I didn't think you'd be home until Saturday."

She releases a soft groan and drops her head to her palms.

"That bad?"

She nods, and I move to sit on the couch with her, leaving

space between us.

"When did you get back?"

"I took the red-eye last night."

I want to know more, but I'm cautious about asking too many questions. I don't know if her puffy eyes are due to being tired or if she's been crying.

"You want to talk about it?"

She pulls her knees to her chest, wrapping her arms around them, and it's now that I see she's visibly upset when she tenses her lips and shakes her head.

I fight the urge to band my arms around her, not only to comfort her from whatever it is that's causing her pain but also because it's killing me to know how she'd feel pressed against me. Aware that I shouldn't be presumptuous enough to cross any boundaries she may have that I don't know about, I take a chance on her when I ask, "How about a distraction?" Her brows lift. "Would you want to go hang out at the pier when I get off work later this afternoon?"

The corner of her mouth lifts but just as quickly drops with a heavy sigh. "I can't. It isn't that I don't want to, but my mom rearranged her schedule to stay home with me today. She works a lot, and I never get to see her, so as much as I really want to go, I also really want to spend this time with her."

"You don't have to explain. My mom works a lot, too, so I get it."

She gives me a nod, and as silence stretches out between us, I'm unable to stop looking at her. There's so much she's clearly hiding, which only makes her that much more intriguing. I wish she'd open up and tell me what it was that made her jump on a plane last night and come home. I want to know what happened that's too painful for her to talk about.

But also, I want to know if she feels what I feel that's making me contemplate running the risk of her finding out who I really am.

"Are you sure you're okay?"

She shrugs and her face drops in defeat. "I'll be fine."

I can tell she doesn't believe her own words, and I wish there were something I could say to make her feel better. She doesn't give me enough time to conjure up anything worthwhile before she stands.

"I should probably go get cleaned up," she says before heading inside.

She stays with me in my mind, as she often does these days, and when I finish her pool and hit the next house, it's all I can do to fight the craving that burns wildly beneath my skin. The ever-constant hunger I can't seem to fully satisfy into abeyance screams at me from the inside. I work quickly to finish at this house before jumping into the company truck and driving until I find myself tucked obscurely behind a vacant warehouse. With thoughts of Adaline and the thirst for my next orgasm, I unzip my shorts, spit a few good times into my palm, and close my eyes as I get myself off.

When my pulse slows, and I toss the wadded napkin out the window, I have to literally talk myself out of going again. Because I could—easily. Instead, I screw the cap off a bottle of water and chug the whole thing before throwing the truck in drive and getting back to work.

I do what I can to keep my mind occupied, shoving my earbuds in for the rest of the day to get ahead in the next required reading for my English class. I'm deep in the Trojan War when I drop off the truck, clock out, and hop into my car. A half hour later, I'm knocking on Krista's door, but for the first time, it isn't her door I wish I were knocking on. Because it isn't her I want to be getting off with. But I need something stronger than jerking off in the shower, so when she lets me inside, I grab her as I give in and hand myself over to impulse.

With more restless energy than I know what to do with, I leave her apartment and go for a long run before finally heading home to eat dinner and shower. I debate going to the party tonight that Trent is throwing at his house. God knows I could use a few drinks and a little fun with the constant pressures of school and work always hanging over my head, but I'm also in a shit mood for a reason I hate to admit to myself.

There's nothing more pathetic than obsessing over a girl that is light-years out of my league. And I hate that I've let myself weaken because of her when I hardly even know her. I feel like a pussy, and it pisses me off.

Time becomes my nemesis as I lie in bed and wrestle with my thoughts. I find myself going between watching mindless television, reading, and listening to music, but they do nothing for the discontent that's keeping me from calling it a night and going to sleep.

I pick up my cell and it reads 10:27PM.

"Fuck it."

I pull off my gym shorts, get dressed, and head to Hyde Park. It's teetering on eleven o'clock when I pull along the curb that's lined with cars all the way down both sides of the street.

Trent's house is filled to the max with people—some I know, some I don't. Music plays through the surround sound but not obnoxiously loud, and when I walk into the living room, I spot Micah.

"Dude, I was starting to think you bailed," he says, reaching his hand out to clap mine.

"Long day working in this damn heat."

"Keg's in the kitchen."

I follow him through the house and into the kitchen, where Trent is manning the keg with a joint hanging from his lips.

"Kason, my man! Where the fuck you been?" he shouts above the crowd of people packed in here.

Micah gives him a high five and takes the joint for himself. Trent hands me a cup of beer, and I swallow a big gulp but nearly choke when I hear Adaline's loud giggle, drowning in alcohol.

I look over and spot her on the opposite side of the large island, holding her cup out while Trent refills it.

"What the fuck is she doing here?" I question a bit too harshly under my breath.

She stumbles in her footing when she tilts her head back, downing her beer, and my first thought is that this chick flat-out lied to me about needing to stay home with her mom. Irritation ignites, and I'm pissed that I let this girl torment my thoughts all damn day for nothing.

I watch as she hangs on to Trent, laughing at whatever it is he's talking to her about, and I toss back another gulp of alcohol.

"Dude, go easy on the girl. She's had a rough couple of days," Micah defends, and my agitation spikes over him knowing more about her than I do. That she would tell him shit she denies me.

"Looks like she's really having a hard time," I sneer before turning my back to them and walking away.

A few people say hi to me as I make my way over to a couch and plop down. I lift the cup to my mouth to take an-other drink but stop when I see her enter the room. Her eyes catch mine, and she smiles big as she approaches.

I wish she weren't so fucking beautiful.

"Hey, buddy," she laughs, bracing her hand on my knee before falling next to me onto the couch.

I look at her and ridicule, "Looks like you're really taking in this quality time with your mom."

It takes her a moment before the dots connect enough for her to cut through the bullshit. "You think I lied?"

"Your words, not mine."

Tapping her finger on the tip of my nose, she pouts, "So mad."

"How much have you had to drink?"

She leans against me and rests her head on my shoulder, and the mere touch is enough to bend the hard lines of my frustration, because even though she's drunk, she's giving me a sliver of what I've been wanting. With her inhibitions intoxicated, I take advantage and ask, "Why did you lie to me?"

"I didn't," she responds without lifting her head. "My mom got called to Sarasota to meet with someone about the case she's working on." She's quiet for a second before yawning.

"Does she do that a lot? Leave you?"

"She didn't want to leave, but she had to. It is what it is, ya know?" she slurs and then sits up. Her eyes widen briefly before she slumps back into the couch, covering them and whining, "Everything is so spinny."

"You're drunk."

"Impossible. I don't even drink," she declares loudly with animation.

I look at her slouched haphazardly on the couch and crack a smile, forgetting my irritation. "You've never drank before?"

"Mm-mmm." She whips her head lazily from side to side

before losing herself to a fit of giggles. "Shh. You can't tell anyone I drank," she whispers loudly.

"I think everyone in this room already knows. You're a little on the sloppy side."

Her jaw drops. "Oh my god. You think?"

I look across the room and wave Micah over.

"What's up?"

"She's trashed."

Adaline sits up and grabs ahold of Micah's arm, insisting, "None of it's true. Don't believe him."

Micah laughs and turns back to me. "Yeah, man. She's wasted."

"I should probably get her home so her mom doesn't worry."

He reaches into his pocket and pulls out a set of keys. "Here. I swiped these from her when she started drinking."

"I'll catch an Uber back here after I drop her off."

I stand and then reach down to help her off the couch, and she falls into me. She's small and light, and it doesn't take much effort to get her out to her car. I buckle her seat belt and then slip behind the wheel of her luxury car, which is a stark contrast to my piece of shit Camaro.

As I'm driving, I sneak a glance her way and catch her staring at me with her head propped against the side window and a grin on her lips.

"What are you smiling at?"

"You," she says and then squeals, "I love this song!" before cranking up the volume. She sings loudly and way off tune, and I can't stop myself from laughing as she butchers the lyrics.

I pull into her driveway, and she's still at it, belting out another song just as badly. When I take the keys from the ignition and put an end to her personal concert, she nudges my arm. "Hey, that was a good song!"

"You're killing my ears," I tease.

"And you're killing my eyes."

"Your eyes?"

She reaches over and pinches my cheek, gushing playfully, "Because you're so cute."

"Is that so?"

"Yep!" She begins to fiddle with her seat belt, and I have to reach over to unlatch it for her because she's too clumsy to figure it out. "Seriously, though," she continues. "I mean, look at you."

"Everyone looks good when you have booze in your eyes."

She folds her feet under her and sits up on her knees. I know she's lost control when she leans over, grabs my bicep in her little hand, and squeezes, belting, "Yummm!" through more laughter.

"We have to get you under control and inside so your mother doesn't find out you're trashed."

"You're such a bore, Mister Man. And I already told you, my mom isn't home."

"She's gone for the night?"

"Uh-huh. And I have a hot guy in my car," she says in an overly flirtatious singsong voice, which has me all sorts of confused about how she feels toward me. Is this all the alcohol talking or is this her finally having the courage to hit on me.

"We really need to get you inside."

"Really? So, that's it? You're not even going to try to kiss me?"

The fear that she's going to wake up in the morning and

regret all of this is in the forefront of my mind. A part of me wants to take advantage of her current state of mind and kiss her to satisfy my urge to taste her, but that would make me a complete asshole.

"I'm not kissing you when you're drunk, Adaline."

"Oh, come on," she sulks, and before I know it, she's up on her knees and leaning over the console to get closer. She then sways, loses her balance, and topples over, falling into me.

I catch her, and in a blur, her head pops up and her hand flies over her mouth.

"Oh, shit," I mutter right before she lurches off me and is barfing all over the driveway the instant she gets her door open.

Her back convulses as her body hangs halfway out of the car. I reach over to rub her shoulder, and she hurls again. When her body calms and she's able to stop heaving, she begins to cry softly. "I hate throwing up."

"Are you okay?"

She straightens slowly and then curls into herself, entirely drained and shakes her head. Her face is ashy white and she has a few chunks of puke in her hair.

"I need you to crawl over the console," I instruct as I pull her into my arms to help her out through the driver's side. She hangs on to me with her arms around my waist as I walk her up to the front door and use her keys to get us inside. Her house is impressive even in the dark, but I don't take too much time to soak in my surroundings.

"Where's your room?"

Lifting her arm, she motions to the stairs, saying, "Up there," before letting it drop lifelessly to her side.

She grabs ahold of the banister while keeping her other

arm gripped around me. Once upstairs, she points to the door that leads to her room, I get her in and sit her on the edge of her bed.

"Bathroom?"

"Over there."

I walk across her room and into the bathroom, and the next thing I know, she's barreling past me and falling to her knees at the toilet. She heaves again, but I can't imagine anything being left in her stomach at this point. With her cheek lying on the toilet seat, she closes her eyes, and I step over to the shower and turn it on.

"I feel like dying," she moans.

I reach down and help her to her feet before flushing the toilet, closing the lid, and sitting her down.

"Do you think you're okay to take a shower?"

She nods, but just barely.

"Can you tell me where you keep your pajamas?"

"The second drawer in my dresser."

I step into her bedroom and get her some fresh clothes to change into. When I return to the bathroom, she's already pulling off her top, and I quickly turn around so I don't see anything she wouldn't want me to.

"Are you okay if I leave you alone?" I ask as I set the clothes next to the sink.

"Yeah, I'm fine."

I shut the door behind me to give her privacy, and when I'm alone, I turn the lights on to take a look around the modestly decorated room. There's something about being in her personal space that stirs an eagerness in my chest.

Across the large bed in the center of the room sits a desk with her laptop and schoolbooks. There isn't much that gives anything away about her, but then I turn and see the rows and rows of framed pictures across the dresser.

Each one is a glimpse into her life. Her with her friends and places she's visited. I scan through them and find a picture of what must be her and her dad. She's young, a little girl with a giant purple bow in her hair, and she's sitting on her dad's knee. She looks so happy in the photo, and I start to wonder what happened between the two of them that made her come home two days early.

Before she gets out of the shower, I run downstairs to see if there's something in the fridge that might help her feel better. Her kitchen is practically the size of my whole apartment, and I'm quickly reminded of all the things that separate us. I do my best to shake off those feelings, but it's near impossible.

I get two bottles of Gatorade and then head back upstairs. When I return to her room, the water is no longer running. I set the drinks on the nightstand and sit on the edge of the bed while I wait for her. The smell from her shower fills the room, and I drop my head into my hands, wondering what the hell it is I'm even doing messing with a girl like this.

After a while, the bathroom door finally opens, and she steps sheepishly into the room. Her wet hair is tied up on top of her head, and her face is flushed in embarrassment, but this is the best I've ever seen her.

"How're you feeling?"

"Tired."

I grab one of the drinks and walk over to her. "Here. This'll help you feel a little better."

"Thanks," she says, and she smells like she drank a whole bottle of Listerine. "I'm so lightheaded."

"You should get some sleep."

She walks over to the bed and crawls in. "Will you hit the lights? They're so bright."

"No problem. I should probably get going, too." I make my way over to the door and turn off the lights.

"Kason?"

"Yeah."

She lifts her head off the pillow but doesn't speak right away. The light from her pool out back paints the room in veins of light that reflect against her skin, and I can't stop staring at her. "Do you . . . do you think you could stay? Just for a little while?"

There's no way I can possibly deny her request, and I give in easily, walking back over to her. She watches me as I kick off my flip-flops. I sit next to her on top of the covers with my back against the headboard, and when she closes her eyes, she lays her head on my lap and slings an arm around me.

She's so damn close, I'm sure she can hear my heart pounding. Greedy for more contact, I drape my arms around her, and she lets go of a heavy sigh.

But it isn't only her touch I want, it's so much more. And knowing that she's running on the last remaining fumes of alcohol and her walls are down, I ask, "Why did you drink so much tonight?"

She surprises me when she doesn't hesitate before answering with so much honesty. "Because I'm really sad," she whispers, her body tensing beneath my hands.

Her admission hurts to hear, to know that under the cheerful façade there's a pain afflicting her. I want to know even more. I want to know everything about her.

"What happened in Texas?"

She tilts her head back and looks up at me with heavily

burdened eyes, which are still glossed in intoxication. "My dad is having a baby with his new wife." Her voice strains in dejection. "When they told me, we got into a huge fight and he kicked me out. He . . . he made me sit outside on the front porch while he threw all my things into my suitcase."

"I'm so sorry."

She drops her head and tightens her arm around me. Having her tucked against me and being so transparent, triggers a pang deep within my chest. It's a sharp puncture that softens me to her even more, and the feeling is so foreign that I don't know how to respond to it.

I continue holding her as I listen to her breathing as it begins to even out. Thoughts of getting under the sheets with her and pulling her closer to me run rampant through my head. But it stretches further than the physical. It's an emotional neediness I've never felt before with anyone. Never have I thought of girls beyond the idea of sex. It's all that's ever called to me. Yet, with Adaline, there's a pull she has on me that I'm unable to ignore. It's the desire to have her want me, to open up to me, and to trust me. God knows I want to be able to do the same with her, but as much as I want that, it also scares the shit out of me.

After a while, she murmurs, "Kason," as she's on the brink of falling asleep.

"Yeah?"

"I really like you."

The moment the words fall from her lips, I lose all sensibility and let go of the many reasons why I shouldn't be doing this, admitting, "I really like you, too, Adaline. More than I probably should."

CHAPTER
eight

Adaline

Sunlight pierces my eyes when I stir awake. I turn away from the window and blink a few times until they adjust. Hazy waves of wooziness swim in my head, but it's the thumping pain behind my eyes that prevents me from attempting to sit up. I weigh a thousand pounds yet, somehow, manage to roll onto my stomach and bury my face down into my pillow with an agonizing groan. The lingering taste of beer on my breath is nauseating, causing my stomach to gurgle as I curl into myself.

I reach over to my nightstand to grab my cell phone but only find a half empty bottle of Gatorade.

Remembrance strikes suddenly out of nowhere. "Oh my god."

Kason was here last night.

I turn on my back and stare up as the room spins around me. Pressing my palms against my eyes, I think back to last night but can only vaguely remember bits and pieces. Trent served me my first drink ever, but one drink turned into several, and that's where I lose track of the night. I can recall being in my car but not driving, and the more I dig to replay the night, the more memory starts serving me mortification on a silver platter.

"Oh no."

I want to die right here, right now, when I recall what I said to him in the car. How hot he was and how I wanted to kiss him.

Did we kiss?

No, I would certainly remember if that happened.

My eyes pop open.

Holy crap! I threw up in front of him!

"Oh my god. Oh my god. Oh my g-o-d," I wail in utter humiliation, pulling the covers over my head, only to be reminded of my rancid beer breath.

Tossing the sheets off me, I drag myself to the bathroom and brush my teeth. My clothes from last night are crumpled on the floor, and when I pick up my top, I see the puke dribble all over it. I drop the clothes, plop down on the seat of the toilet, and beg the good Lord above to tell me I'm still dreaming and that this didn't really happen. *This seriously cannot be happening!*

My cell phone rings from beneath the pile of clothes, and when I retrieve it, I see Micah's name.

"How're you feeling, Guppy? You drank like a real fish last night," he teases when I answer the call.

"I want to die."

"You that hungover?"

I stand and head right back to bed. "I threw up in front of Kason last night."

His laughter barrels through the phone, and I have to pull it away from my ear before my head explodes. "Yeah, you were pretty gone when you guys left."

"Well, I doubt he will ever talk to me again. From what I can remember, I acted like an idiot, and I'm scared to know what I can't remember."

"So, what's going on with the two of you anyway?" he asks on a more serious note.

"I have no idea." I sling my arm across my face. "I mean, I like him, but it's just . . . I don't know. He's so hard to read."

"Did anything happen last night?"

"I can't remember anything past the point of throwing up, but based on that alone, I would venture to say no. I don't even know how I got into my bed . . . Oh, god!"

How did my clothes get on the floor?

"What?"

"I'm in my pajamas."

"So?"

"I can't remember taking my clothes off." I panic as thoughts of Kason changing me out of my puke-covered outfit play in my head. "Did he say anything to you?"

"He came back late to pick up his car, but he didn't say anything. Only that he got you home safe. I didn't even know you got sick."

"How is this happening?" I fret.

"We've all been there, including Kase. Dude, that guy got so trashed once he stood at the side of my pool and took a piss in it."

"Are you serious?" I giggle. "Gross!"

"You don't need to feel embarrassed. We all do stupid shit."

"Well, I'm still praying that somehow he suffers a lapse in memory from last night, but in the meantime, I'm going to go back to bed."

"Call me later."

Tossing the phone, I roll over, drink the remaining Gatorade, and fall back asleep. By the time I wake again, the sun has peaked in the sky and my queasiness has subsided, although my headache still throbs.

I move slowly through the motions as I take a shower, throw my clothes from last night into the wash, and swallow some Tylenol with a bottle's worth of water and another Gatorade. It's after two in the afternoon when I step outside to find the sun has done an impressive job baking my stomach's expulsion into the concrete.

"You've *got* to be kidding me," I mutter to myself as I take in the mess.

I drop my sunglasses over my eyes, walk to the side of the house to grab the hose, and start washing away last night's disgrace.

If only it were that easy.

When Kason's work truck appears, I know this must be a punishment for doing something horribly wrong in a past life. He pulls into my driveway as I'm hosing my puke into the shrubs.

"You're alive," he jokes, shutting the truck door, and I release my grip on the sprayer.

I don't say anything in response as I stand in misery, looking like roadkill with bedhead. He hands me a bottle of

Ginger Ale. "I thought this would serve you well."

"Thanks."

He follows me over to the steps at the front of the house. We sit in the shade, and I take a sip of the soda as I muster a shred of bravery before saying, "I'm really sorry about last night."

"You have nothing to be sorry for."

"Well, apparently, I do," I say dreadfully, motioning my hand over to where the hose lies in a puddle of water.

"I would've thought you'd be more embarrassed about your singing than your puking."

"I don't know what to be more embarrassed about when I can't even remember half of the night."

He turns his head to me with an intent look in his eyes. "What's the last thing you remember?"

I shake my head as I try to think. "I don't know. Everything kind of goes fuzzy after *that*," I tell him, eyeing the driveway. "But then I woke up and saw my clothes in the bathroom, and . . ." My head falls into my hands, and I close my eyes because I'm freaking out on the inside. "You didn't—"

"No. I waited in your room while you took a shower and got changed. The door was shut the entire time."

I lift my head with a dramatic sigh of relief.

"So, you don't remember getting cleaned up or going to bed?"

I shake my head. "All I remember is being obnoxious, getting sick, and then waking up feeling like death resurrected."

He rests his elbows on his knees as he looks out over the front yard. There is a strange expression on his face, and if I have to guess, I would say he looks upset. For some odd reason, it makes me feel guilty, so I apologize again, saying, "I shouldn't have drank like that. I feel pretty stupid."

"You weren't as bad as what you're thinking. You were quite amusing for the most part."

I take another sip of Ginger Ale before he stands and offers a hand to help me up as well. "I gotta get back to work. I had a couple of houses here in the neighborhood, so I figured I'd stop by and check in on you."

I give him an appreciative smile, and his is weak in return.

I watch him as he pulls out of the driveway, and when he's gone, I finish with the hose, making sure the evidence from last night is gone so my mom doesn't see anything. When I head back inside, I can't stop worrying about what Kason must've been thinking when he was here. I go back and replay the evening while I reheat leftover pizza in the microwave, but I hit the same dead end that I hit this morning.

The only thing I do know for sure is that I want to see him again despite him being witness to my antics last night. So, with not much left of my pride to lose, I take my pizza to the bar top and find his number on my cell. For the first time, I finally get the guts to text him.

Me: You free at all this weekend?

I stare at my phone, waiting to see if he will text me back. When the screen dims, I take a bite of my pizza and think about this epic disaster of a spring break. It goes down as my worse one yet.

Kason: I get off work at 4:00 tomorrow. Why?

My hands clam up when I type my response.

Me: I was wondering if the offer to go hang out at the pier still stood . . .

Kason: I'll pick you up at 6.

By the time I finally decide on an outfit, half of my closet is strewn all over my bed.

I walk into my bathroom and step onto the edge of the bathtub in order to get a full-length view of myself. I fiddle with one of the thin straps on my flowy blue top that criss-crosses in the back before tugging at the hem of my denim shorts and then jumping down from the tub. With a light dusting of powder on my face and a little lip gloss, I tie my hair back and tell myself to stop overthinking everything. For all I know, in his eyes, this could simply be two friends hanging out—nothing more.

But what if it is something more?

My mom is standing in my doorway when I walk back into the bedroom.

"You look nice."

"I didn't know you were back in town."

"Sorry I didn't call. Sarasota was draining, and I can barely think straight," she says. "But enough about me, I love that top you're wearing."

"Does it look like I'm trying too hard?"

"You paired it with shorts and flip-flops; it looks like you're hardly trying at all, sweetheart."

"But it isn't bad, is it?"

"What has you so nervous?"

She steps into the room with a curious grin, and I tell her, "Kason is taking me to the pier."

"He finally asked you out on a date?"

"Not exactly." I walk over and sit on the side of the bed. "He asked me to hang out at the pier with him when I got back home the other day, but I told him I couldn't. So, *I* texted *him* yesterday to see if he still wanted to go. Now here I am, waiting for him to come pick me up, and I have no idea what this even is."

"I miss being young."

"Mom. Focus."

"Sorry." She sits at my side and rests her hand on my knee. "Just play it casually and see what happens. Or, you can come right out and tell him how you feel."

"No way! Mortifying much. What if I tell him and he doesn't feel the same way?"

"And what if he does feel the same way?" she counters. "I'm no expert when it comes to guys, but one thing I've learned through the years is that they are just as scared to admit their feelings as we are."

"Still. I'm not about to be the one who says it first." My spine stiffens when the doorbell chimes. "That's him." I hop off the bed and turn toward my mom. "You sure I look okay?"

"You look very pretty."

She trails behind me as I head downstairs, and when I open the door, he's the same as any other day, looking perfectly hot in a pair of cargo shorts and T-shirt. His sleeves fit snug around his muscular arms, and the sight makes me want to melt in a gooey pile of mush. I realize that I've forgotten to speak when I hear my mom greet, "Nice to see you again, Kason."

"You too, Ma'a—I mean, Cheryl."

She then turns to me, saying, "I'm going to call it an early night, so I'll see you in the morning, okay?"

I give her a quick hug. "Love you."

"Have fun," she says when we leave.

He opens the car door for me, and I slip in. "Fair warning, the AC is out."

I toss him a smile as I reach over, grab the lever, and roll down the window. "Problem solved."

And this time, when he returns my smile, it feels genuine.

He hops in, his window already down, and fires up the engine. When he pulls out of the driveway, I reach over and turn up the stereo.

"You're not going to sing again, are you?"

"Oh, come on. I'm not that bad."

"I need you to trust me when I say *you are*," he teases.

With the warm wind against my face, he drives, and I have to bite my lip to keep from smiling every time I glance over at him. He makes my stomach flutter, and it isn't only because I'm crushing on his looks. It's the mystery that's behind them that I've yet to discover. I don't know anything about him, yet I'm still drawn to him. There's an excitement that comes when he gives me more of himself and more of his time—like right now. He's giving me this evening with him, time we don't have to share with Micah or Trent—it's just the two of us—and it's electrifying.

I don't know. Maybe I'm being silly, but I can't help the way I feel when it comes to him.

Clearwater Beach is packed. Street performers dance, skateboard, eat fire, and juggle chainsaws. There are also dozens of local vendors lining the pier, selling their handmade crafts. A reggae fusion band plays a cover of an old 311 song in the distance while people bask in the setting sun and others enjoy cocktails from the many open bars.

I take in my surroundings, feeling like this is more of a vacation spot than a home, but that's what this is. This is my new home, and I've never felt so far from Texas as I do tonight . . . here at this beach . . . with Kason.

He takes me to the end of Pier 60, where I lean over the edge and watch the old man next to me reeling in a fish he just caught. For a split second, I think back to all the times my dad took me fishing as a little girl, but I don't linger on them, because the elderly man removes the hook and holds the fish out to me.

"Set him free, beautiful."

Kason watches as I take the fish and drop it back into the water. I look at him from over my shoulder, and he jokes, "He would've tasted good on the grill."

"You're heartless."

He sidles up next to me, and as we lean our elbows against the railing, I watch the pelicans glide with their wings spread over the top of the water.

"This is amazing. Is it always like this here?"

"Every night at sunset."

"You come often?"

"Not really," he says. "But I figured you'd enjoy it. It's mostly kooks."

"Kooks?"

"Tourists." He pushes back off the railing. "Follow me."

We head back up the dock and over to the sand. Kicking off our flip-flops, we sink our feet across the soft white powder toward the water.

"Where are we going?"

He points north. "Up there where there aren't so many people."

As we walk, he tells me about coming here as a kid and learning how to skimboard. I listen closely, eager to know more about him. Soon enough, the people thin out as the music fades away behind us, and he finds us a spot to sit.

I bury my feet into the sand while we watch the glowing pink sun hover above the edge of the water.

"I still can't get over how pretty it is here. I grew up around red dirt lakes that had God only knows what swimming in them."

"Do you miss it?"

I take a moment before explaining, "I miss what it used to be. Now, everything is so different back home. My dad does a bang-up job of making me feel unwanted. I used to do everything with him, but I don't have that anymore. He's given it to his new family."

He looks at me in a way he hasn't before, and when he speaks, his words cause my belly to tighten. "I'm sorry you're having to go through all of this."

I take a hard swallow, my eyes locked to his, waiting. For what? I don't really know, but the moment is broken when a soft applause sounds from somewhere behind us.

"The sun is gone," he says, turning back to the water.

I lower myself to the sand and gaze into the sky, which is growing darker by the minute. "This is my favorite part."

He looks over at me with curiosity.

"Lie down," I request.

He reclines back and shifts around until he gets comfortable. "What are we looking at?"

"Nothing right now. But soon, you'll be able to see the stars. They'll appear out of nowhere."

We lie still, not talking, only the beating of my erratic

heart clamoring inside my chest reminding me to breathe. His knuckles are touching mine, and I wish he would hold my hand, lace his fingers between my fingers, press his palm against my palm.

As the sky dims, I grow restless, worrying that the butterflies inside me will soon lose their wings because they're flapping them so fiercely.

The waves roll in and out, and I close my eyes, begging for the sound to lull the winged creatures to sleep, because I don't know how much longer I can pretend to ignore them. When my eyes open, the first star appears. Rolling my head to the side, I find Kason watching me, and no longer can I hold on to the silence when I whisper nervously, "Say something."

"I don't know what I'm doing with you."

"What do you want to do?"

He reaches over and touches his hand to my cheek, and he's so close it makes the simplest thing like breathing hard to do. I lean into his touch, and he rests his head against mine. My skin absorbs the heat from his, and never have I wanted anyone's lips on mine as badly as I want his. The ache is nearly unbearable. It radiates from the inside out, and the moment I breathe his name is the moment his lips touch mine.

My eyes fall shut, and my heart no longer beats as the whole world paralyzes. He kisses me so slowly it borders on torture, but the most blissful kind there is, and I swear I'm the only person on this planet who has ever experienced this feeling.

I shift in the sand to my side and press my hand on his chest hesitantly. I'm too nervous to do much more until he gathers me closer, and then I begin to move my lips with his. Seconds falter, throwing the metronome of time off beat, and before I know it, his mouth abandons mine, but he keeps me tucked in his arms.

"Tell me you want this," he murmurs, his breath feathering along my skin, and I nod, finally opening my eyes. "You make me nervous because I can never figure out what you're thinking."

There's uncertainty etched on his face, and it reminds me of what my mother told me earlier. So, I take the comfort he's offering me by holding me so tightly, swallow a little strength, and confess, "I feel like I could easily fall for you."

"Do you want to?"

"Yes," I breathe, and he kisses me again, fading all the layers of fear and timidity that have been keeping us from finally being able to be honest with each other.

In no rush to end this moment that's been building between us for the past month, we lie in the sand with the waves crashing at our feet. We kiss each other under the stars that cascade their reflections against the water, and I've never felt more alive than I do right now. I could stay here in this moment forever and never tire. So, that's what we do, we kiss and hug and stare up into the sky until we're the only ones left out here. When he pulls me to my feet, he takes my hand in his, palm to palm, and we walk back down the beach to his car, stealing kisses all along the way.

CHAPTER
nine

Adaline

"**P**lease don't become one of those girls who forgets about her friends because she's all obsessive over her boyfriend," Molly scolds, but I can hear the mirth in her tone.

"Oh please."

"I'm serious! I haven't heard from you since you kissed Kason, and that was over two weeks ago."

"I know. I'm sorry. I've been so distracted."

"Well, get undistracted and catch me up."

I shove my schoolbooks aside and roll onto my stomach as I lie in bed. "What do you want to know?"

"Umm, *everything*! And don't be all PG about it."

"Wait. First, tell me how the Spring Fling went with Robbie."

She huffs into the phone before saying, "Officially D-listed. We went to the dance, and everything was going great until I found out that he only pretended to like me to make Stacy jealous."

"His ex? What a jerk."

"You're telling me. I guess I'm destined to be alone forever," she sulks. "But enough about my unfortunate love life. Spill it, Ady. All the dirty details."

I laugh. "There's nothing dirty to tell."

"So, what's the update since y'all first kissed?"

I go on to fill her in about how Kason and I have been spending most of our free time together, and that the awkwardness between us is pretty much gone at this point. That we stay on the phone until the early hours of the morning most nights because neither one of us wants to hang up. So, we talk until we eventually fall asleep.

"Enough," she blurts, cutting me off. "I'm, no joke, getting sick with envy over here. But torture me more. You must have a photo of him by now."

"Hold on." I switch her to speakerphone while I scroll through the few selfies I've taken of us and text her one with the two of us at the beach that I took last weekend. I was there while he was skimming with his friends. He stands behind me in the photo with his arms wrapped around me while I hold the phone out to snap the picture. His cheek is pressed to mine, and he's wearing the most perfect smile.

"Oh my god, his arms. Are you kidding me right now?" she gushes. "It's a good thing I'm in Texas, otherwise I may kill you and take him for myself."

I take her off speakerphone and bring her back to my ear.

"Speaking of that," she adds. "I talked to my mom about

coming to Florida this summer, and she finally said yes."

"Really?"

"She's going to call your mom later this week to talk about it."

"I can't believe you're going to be here. This summer is going to be so much fun!" I squeal, more than excited to have Molly here in Florida.

"I know! It's going to be great. And I'll finally get to meet that man candy you've been kissing on."

The doorbell rings, and I jump off my bed. "I'm going to have to let you go. Kason's here," I tell her as I head downstairs. "I'll let my mom know the good news about summer."

"Hey, babe," Kason says when I open the door.

"Even his voice is hot."

"You're crazy." I laugh lightly. "I'll talk to you later."

I end the call as Kason bands his arms around me and nuzzles ticklish kisses into my neck. Giggling, I do my best to push him away, and he finally relents.

"You been swimming?"

"You're a smart one." I smirk as I glance down at my swimsuit and cotton shorts and then back at him. "Go get changed and meet me out back."

"Where'd you put my board shorts I left over here the other day?"

"In my bottom drawer," I tell him before going outside to wait for him to change out of his work clothes.

I slip off my shorts and get into water. It doesn't take too long for Kason to appear on the veranda. His shorts hang obscenely low on his hips, and I can't stop myself from watching him as he tosses a towel over the back of one of the chairs before jumping in the water. He swims over to me, and when he grabs me around my waist and backs me up against the wall, my stomach trills as it does every time we're together.

When he braces his hands on the edge of the pool, I sling my arms around his neck.

"Did you miss me?"

"Always," I tell him, even though I saw him at school a few hours ago.

Water droplets roll down his face as his electric green eyes fixate on me. I drag my fingers along his eyebrow and notice a faint scar I've never seen before.

"How'd you get this?"

He smiles.

"Tell me."

"Skateboarding accident," he says. "I was around seven years old when my mom bought me my first board. One of my babysitters had a boyfriend who skated, and they took me to a local skate park." He runs his finger along the thin marking above his eye and laughs under his breath. "There was an older kid throwing down some tricks. I watched him ollie down a small set of stairs. He made it look so easy."

"You didn't."

"I did. I crashed hard and wound up going to the emergency room to get stitches."

"You're crazy."

"That's what my mom said before she took the skateboard away."

"Did you ever get it back?"

He shakes his head. "No, but I was eventually able to talk her into getting me a skimboard."

"I used to skateboard, too."

At this he cracks a giant, disbelieving smile. "Your mom let you skateboard?"

I'm already laughing on the inside when I recall my child-hood memory. "Not exactly."

"This ought to be rich," he chuckles. "Tell me about this hidden skater life of yours."

"Well, my best friend, Molly, has an older brother that used to skateboard. We'd sit on the driveway and watch him, but every time we'd ask for a turn, he'd refuse. And when I asked my mom to buy me one, she told me no. So, I did the next best thing," I tell him, feigning as much seriousness as I can.

"And what's that?"

"I built my own," I say with pride. "There was a house being built in Molly's neighborhood, so we stole some scrap pieces of wood, unscrewed the wheels from a pair of old roll-er skates, and used her dad's tools to attach the wheels to the boards."

"You're kidding?" he laughs.

"It was pretty impressive craftsmanship if I do say so my-self. I mean, those boards were slick," I quip. "We even deco-rated them with markers, stickers, and glitter."

"And when you hopped on, did you bite it?"

I start cracking up. "I totally bit it. I fell off and scraped my arm pretty bad. No scars like you, but that doesn't mean I was any less hardcore. In fact, I think I was more hardcore than you because I built that thing from scratch."

"You can't claim to be hardcore when you admit to acces-sorizing with glitter."

"Hey," I defend. "In my defense, that glitter was gold. Like, blinged-out gold!"

"You're crazy, you know that?"

"Just saying, we've got a lot in common."

His smile is big and so is mine, and when he leans in to kiss me, I let go of a slight giggle against his lips. He swallows my jovialness, exchanging it with sincerity as he presses his chest against mine. I hang on to him, wrapping my legs around his waist as his lips move with mine, and somehow, under the heat of the sun, my skin pricks in goose bumps all over. He moves slowly, in no rush as I hold him close. I let him take the lead as I always do, but when his tongue slips into my mouth and his hand touches my breast for the first time, I tense up, not knowing what to do. He gently squeezes me in his palm, and I tighten my grip on him, self-conscious and unsure.

He's the first boy who's ever touched me like this, but I get the feeling, with his ease and confidence, that it isn't his first time. Not that it matters, but it doesn't help my nervousness, and he senses it and pulls back.

"Is this too much?"

My cheeks heat, and I hug him to hide my face.

He lowers his hand to my waist. "Can I ask you something?"

I nod, but I still can't look him in the eyes.

"I honestly don't know how to ask this, but . . ." He takes my arms from around his neck so he's able to look at me. "Have you done this before?"

I drop my head, shying away in utter mortification. My legs fall from around him, desperate to escape having to admit how innocent I actually am.

"Adaline . . ."

Too reluctant to look at him straight on, I keep my chin tucked down.

"Hey." His tone is soft, and he lowers himself into the water to meet my level. "Look at me," he requests, and sheepishly,

I do. "I don't want you to be embarrassed with me. I want to know this about you because I don't want to assume you've done things if you haven't yet."

"I haven't done anything."

"*Anything*?" He stresses the word as if my admission is too unbelievable to be real, but I'm only seventeen, which has me worried about what all he's done.

I shake my head again. "I mean, I kissed a boy I went to school with back home, but . . . not the way we kiss. You're the first guy I . . ." Awkwardness skyrockets to unimaginable levels. I cover my face and drop my head to his shoulder. "God, this is so humiliating."

His arms come around me, and with lightness in his tone, he assures, "You have no reason to feel that way . . . not with me."

"What about you?" I ask when I lift my head. "Am I the first girl you've made out with?"

His expression grows cautious. "No."

Attempting to cut through all the unpleasant tension, I poke fun, saying, "Well, aren't you the lucky one, getting stuck with the inexperienced maiden," but it does nothing to quell my insecurities right now.

"It's not what you're thinking. But you are the first girl I've ever had these feelings for. Actually, you're all I can think about."

"Really?"

The corners of his mouth lift. "Yes, really. I'm crazy about you."

"Can I ask *you* something now?"

"Go for it."

"Why do you still call me Adaline after I told you everyone

calls me Ady? You're the only one who does that, you know?"

Bringing his hands to my cheeks, he tells me, "Because I don't want to be like everyone else to you."

And this time when he kisses me, I kiss him back, and my heart swells with the love that's beginning to bloom between us. He's still so brand new to me, but I can already see myself falling hard for him. I run my hands up his chest and over his shoulders, and as soon as he moves to deepen our kiss, we're interrupted by a loud, "Get a room, fuckers."

Kason turns, and I see Trent running toward the pool and launching himself into a cannonball, splashing the two of us.

"What are you doing here?" I ask Micah as he takes a seat along the steps of the pool.

"Been trying to get ahold of this loser," he says, motioning to Kason.

"Phone's inside."

"Apparently."

Kason goes over to Micah and steps out of the pool. I watch as they talk, keeping their voices too low for anyone else to hear, and when Kason looks over to me, saying, "I'll be right back," I know he's selling Micah more pot.

He grabs his towel, and the two of them head inside, leaving me in the pool with Trent. He just smiles and winks, "Nice bikini."

I roll my eyes and splash him. "Stop gawking."

He throws his hands in surrender. "Just making a harmless observation."

"Observe elsewhere," I tease before he reaches up out of nowhere and dunks me.

CHAPTER
ten

Kason

Adaline has me trapped beneath her on the couch, and even with the sharp thorns of unrelenting desire stabbing me from within, I'd have it no other way. She lies on top of me, sound asleep with her head resting on my chest and her heart beating steadily against my abs. My arms have been wrapped around her for well over an hour since she turned on some chick flick that now drones in the background.

Being with her this past month has been perfect. School is about to be out for summer, and even though I'll be increasing my hours at work so I can continue to stash money aside for college, I'm looking forward to spending all my free time with Adaline. It's crazy how she's gotten to me. I've never felt like I needed the affections of a girl. Wanted? Yes. Needed? No. But the more she gives, the more I crave.

We've been spending a lot more time together since she told me that she struggles with feeling lonely because her mother is gone so much. So, as soon as I get off work, I come over here to be with her. There's no rules or curfews that her mom has ever set in place since she isn't around to enforce them. Not that Adaline needs anyone watching over her shoulder. She's a good girl through and through. Even with freedom in her hands, she isn't one to stay out too late or get into trouble. Hell, the girl doesn't even cuss.

As good as everything is, I'd be lying if I said being with her doesn't intensify my panging need for release. Because it does, and I've been having a damn hard time controlling myself when hunger strikes. I'm falling for Adaline, which puts me in a tough position because I want more from her—I need more. But the type of more I want, she isn't comfortable with. She isn't like Krista, who doesn't value what it means to open her legs to someone. Fuck, I don't even value what it means to have a girl open her legs for *me*.

That isn't Adaline, though, and I never want it to be. I would never use her the way I've used others, because I care about her deeply. Which is why I haven't stopped by Krista's place since Adaline and I started seeing each other.

She shifts on me, turning her head to the other side. I run my hand down her spine as she releases a small yawn and begins to stir awake. When she lifts her head, I can tell it takes her a moment to clear the fog of sleep.

"Hey." Her voice is a groggy rasp.

"Hey, yourself."

"How long have I been out?"

I push my fingers through her messy hair and away from her face. "Long enough that I no longer have any feeling in my legs."

She smiles, and I steal it away with a kiss. I roll onto my side so that she's nestled between me and the back of the couch. She sleeps hot, and when I slip my hand under her shirt, her back is slightly damp against my touch.

Each day that passes, she relaxes more and more with me. She used to be so uncertain, often tensing and pulling away when I would try to give her my affections. But now, she has both her hands under my shirt as well and her leg draped over my hip. I run my palm up the back of her thigh and press myself closer to her.

She giggles softly into my mouth when she feels how hard I am.

"Shit isn't funny, babe," I say with an air of humor. It isn't the first time she's felt me like this. I mean, it isn't like there's any controlling myself when we're this close, so I don't even bother making an awkward situation more awkward by trying to hide it from her.

Adaline pops up when the door from the garage opens.

"Fuck," I utter under my breath as the both of us sit up and compose ourselves, but Adaline can't rein in her laughter when I shove my hand down my pants to adjust myself.

"Hey, Mom."

"Hi, dear," she responds mindlessly, her attention focused on her phone. It takes her another second or two before she looks up and spots me. "Oh, hi, Kason," to which I nod and smile nervously while waiting for my dick to settle down.

"What are you doing home so early?" Adaline asks.

Cheryl sets the pizza box she's carrying on the kitchen

counter and opens a cabinet to pull down a wine glass. "I *had* to get out of the office. I'm starting to lose my mind with this case, and my mood is all over the damn place."

Adaline peers over the back of the couch toward the kitchen. "Is that pizza?"

"Yes. Are you hungry?"

"Starved!"

"What about you, Kason? Are you able to stay for dinner?"

I look over to Adaline, and she mouths *stay*.

"If that isn't a problem," I tell her mother as she pours herself a glass of wine.

"Don't be silly. Plus, it'll give us a chance to finally talk."

Even though I've been seeing her daughter for a month now and am over here more days than not, I've only seen her mom a few times, and it's always a fast exchange of hello and goodbye.

Standing from the couch, I head into the kitchen, offering, "What can I help you with?" hoping to make a good impression on the high-powered attorney. By looks alone, this woman is intimidating, but from the little encounters we've had, she seems pretty down to earth, which was unexpected.

She grabs her glass and the pizza box. "Would you mind getting the plates? They're in the cabinet to your left."

Adaline gets a couple of drinks from the fridge before we head out back to the table outside.

"The fresh air is so nice after being at the jail all day," she says, kicking off her heels and grabbing a slice of pizza. "Help yourself, Kason."

"What were you doing there?"

"I had to meet with my client. It makes for a long day when I have to go visit him. He isn't the most cooperative man, either." She takes a sip from her glass. "But enough about my life. How was school today, Ady?"

"Same as every other day—uneventful."

"Thank you, dear, for that wealth of information," her mother teases before turning to me. "Do you happen to share any classes with my daughter that you can fill me in on?"

Adaline laughs as she sits back and eats her pizza.

"We only have Anatomy together at the end of the day, but I wouldn't call it uneventful," I tell her. "Every time we have to work on our dissections, she insists that the teacher give her a mask to wear and then she drenches the thing in her body spray before putting it on."

"Those cats smell so bad. It's beyond disgusting."

"Basically, I have a slacker for a lab partner because she just stands there complaining about the smell while I do all the work."

"Ady," her mother playfully scolds as she attempts to hide her smile. "Why would you even take a class like that?"

"Because when you move at the end of the year, you get whatever classes are left over. I'm seriously doing what I can to pass. You should be proud that I'm managing a high B." She teasingly narrows her eyes at me and takes another bite of food.

I love her playfulness and feed into it when I boast, "I'm making a high A."

"You're a turd," she quips before her mother interjects, saying, "I like this guy."

When laughter subsides, Cheryl turns her focus to me. "So, Kason, what other classes do you enjoy?"

"Pretty much all of them. School has always come easily for me. I'm taking a few AP classes to help with college credits that are time-consuming, but I manage to keep my grades up."

"Already thinking about college? I'm impressed. Maybe you can encourage Ady."

"I already registered to take an SAT prep course, thank you very much."

She smiles at Adaline before asking me, "Do you have any ideas about what you want to study?"

"Not really."

"Well, it's still early. It took me a while to figure out that law was what I wanted to do." She looks at my now empty plate and serves me another slice.

"Thanks."

"What about your parents?" she starts, and I grow a little restless. "What do they do?"

Uncomfortably, I stall, unsure of how to answer. Both of them assume I come from their world since I go to the same high school as Adaline. It's the same assumption everyone around here has about me. It's the sham I've let them all believe because I'm too ashamed to let anyone know the circumstances I come from. The last thing I want is for her to know the truth about what type of guy her daughter is dating, so I do the only thing I can. "My mom works in event planning." I hate to lie. It makes me sick to my stomach, but when I see her mother's approving smile, I know she'd never accept the truth. And if she did, she'd do so with a massive scoop of pity for me.

"That sounds exciting."

I shift my eyes nervously over to Adaline, who's giving me an inquisitive look as if she's eager to know more. I don't blame her. I do my best to keep the focus on her and off me so I won't be put in situations like the one I'm in right now.

"And what about your father?" Cheryl adds.

"It's only my mom."

She looks over at Adaline. "Have you met her yet?"

Adaline shakes her head and then responds to her while looking at me. "He's never invited me over." Her tone is humorous, but I can't help feeling the sharp blade of criticism, as if she's irritated that I haven't included her in my world as much as she has included me in hers. Or maybe I'm reading too much into everything right now.

I brush her off, trying not to make a big deal about it. "Because you're always telling me to come over here."

Her mother doesn't ask anything else about my family, and I'm relieved when she turns to Adaline and says, "I keep forgetting to tell you, but I have a conference in Jacksonville that I will be at for a week in August. If you want, you can come with me. I won't be around, but you can enjoy the hotel."

"I'd rather not be cooped up in a hotel with nothing to do."

She picks up her glass of wine and says, "I don't blame you," before taking another sip.

We finish dinner, and when we take our dishes back inside, her mom calls it a night. "I'm going to turn in early and get some much-needed sleep. Kason," she says, "it was good seeing you again."

"You, too, and thanks for dinner."

She says good night and hugs Adaline before heading to her bedroom.

"I should probably get going," I tell her, needing to get some space from the deception I just threw their way.

"Already?"

"I have homework I need to finish."

She gives me a suspicious look, and I worry she can see my unease. "Are you okay?"

"Yeah. I'm fine."

She slips her arms around my waist and cranes her head back so she can look at me. "Stay. At least little while longer."

And just like that, I give in. "Come here." I take her hand, leading her back outside and over to the large hammock.

I get on first and then help her as she crawls into my arms and nestles her head on my shoulder. Holding her, I close my eyes and try to force away the anxiety that's eating away at the pit of my stomach. Shame is a vicious beast that's been tormenting me for a while now when it comes to Adaline. It's what made me want to keep her at arm's length when I first met her, but fuck if I didn't shoot all that to hell the night I kissed her on the beach.

Who am I kidding? It was shot to hell much sooner than that.

But it's when she says my name with so much uncertainty that worry cripples me.

"Kason?"

Something inside catapults, and I grow wary of why she's treading so cautiously with me.

"Why haven't you invited me to your house?"

Instinct tells me to lie, to get the hell out of here before she learns the truth and dumps me. But I stay, because I'm frozen even though she's so warm against me. However, there's no way I'm going to be able to keep this from her. Adaline's different from any other girl I've ever met, and with how close we've been getting, I'm not going to be able to keep everything a secret the way I wish I could. I know that the moment she finds out I'm nothing like the rich kid she assumes I am will be the moment she walks away. Although we've only been together for a short while, I'm already falling for her, and I don't want to lose her.

She lifts her head and looks at me from under her soft lashes, and I doubt I'll ever be lucky enough to find someone else as kind and as beautiful as she is again. Girls like her don't exist where I'm from. Those girls are hard and jaded, and if they're not those things, then they're cheap and easy.

But this girl, she's soft and good, and with insecurity in her eyes, I know I have to be honest.

"There's something I need to tell you." My gut knots, and I pull her back to my chest so I don't have to see the look in her eyes when I tell her, "I don't come from your world."

"What do you mean?"

"I don't live around here. And I don't have money like you do."

She tries to draw back, but I flex my arms around her to keep her in place. I'm too much of a coward to face her.

I take in a deep breath that doesn't serve me well and reveal, "I live in a small apartment about thirty minutes north of here. And what I said about my mom isn't true. She works two jobs, both that only pay her enough to keep a roof over our heads and our electricity on."

And this time, it's her arms that tighten around me, but I refuse to look at whatever pity she may have in her eyes.

"Why didn't you say anything?"

"Because it's easier to fit in when everyone assumes I'm a part of all this."

"*This*?"

"Money."

She presses her hands against my chest, using her strength to push up from me, and when I look at her, there's pain in her eyes. "You thought I was so shallow that I'd judge you because you don't come from money?" She's hurt and defensive.

"I know you're not shallow. I wouldn't be with you if you were."

"Then why not tell me?"

"Because I don't think you realize exactly how far I am from your world."

"It's your world, too."

"You know what I mean." I sit up and wrap my hands around her slight shoulders so she'll take me seriously. "I don't work because I want to. I work because I don't have any other choice. And I don't take advanced classes because they're fun. I do it because I'm going to need all the help I can get to have a shot at college." Her expression is stone as she takes in my words. "My life isn't easy, Adaline. It looks nothing like yours."

"The only thing that bothers me about all of this is that you felt like I would judge you. That all I care about is if someone has money." She takes a moment, and when I drop my hands from her, she slacks her shoulders. "What matters to me is that you're a good person and you care about me. I don't care where you live, and I would never look down on you because of that."

I stare at her, dumbfounded, as she tells me this. I wasn't expecting this reaction, and I'm taken aback.

"I didn't know how to tell you; I've never had to tell anyone. No one even knows except Micah."

"Why Micah and no one else?"

"Because it was his father that got me transferred into this school."

Her brows pinch in puzzlement, and I go on to explain. "When I was a freshman, I lied about my age to get the job I have now. It's one of several businesses Micah's dad owns. He found out I lied on my application, and when he sat to question me, I told him why I needed the job so badly. He couldn't officially hire me because I was too young, so he let me work around his house since they were doing a remodel. That's how I met Micah," I tell her. "After a few months of his dad getting to know me, he pulled some strings, *probably made a hefty donation*, and got me into the school."

She drops her head, and when I lift her chin, she wavers before asking, "Is this why you sell Micah weed? Because you need money?"

How the fuck does she know I sell that shit?

"What are you talking about?"

"I know you're selling it because he told me."

"I don't smoke that shit," I immediately defend.

"I know you don't. I just . . ." Her voice drifts, and she looks away for a second. "I don't like that you sell it. I mean, what if you get caught?"

God damn, this girl. The fact that she cares about what could happen to me tugs my heart down deep in my chest. I take her in my arms, and she circles hers around me as we lie back down. I have no idea what she sees in someone like me, but my heart ignores all the self-debasing answers.

"Whoever you get it from, have Micah buy it from them."

"Okay." As much as I could use the money, it isn't as if I make a lot off the deals, so it definitely isn't worth upsetting her.

Tucking her closer to me, I press my lips on to hers in an unmoving kiss, having never felt the way she's making me feel right now. She drops her lips along my jaw and down my neck, and when she nuzzles her head beneath my chin, she murmurs, "Can we hang out at your place tomorrow?"

"Yeah, babe," I respond, trusting that when she says she would never judge me, she means it.

We linger in this moment for a while longer, but when she begins nodding off, I make sure to get her inside before I head out. There's a peace that resides within me when I'm with Adaline, but it's never enough to completely snuff out the insatiable hunger I can't shake. When I'm with her, I'm needy for affection, but it only makes my struggle worse.

As I drive home, it takes everything in me not to pull off the side of the road and jerk off. My stomach twists, and I become restless. It doesn't matter how much I fight myself, I can't seem to tame whatever it is that causes me to be like this. I think back to Adaline and cringe at the thought of her knowing this about me. She may not have judged my lot in life, but she would be disgusted if she ever found out about my inner workings. That I spend most hours of the day horny as all get out, thinking of when I'll be able to get my next fix.

My dick is excruciatingly hard by the time I pull into my parking space. I run one palm over my crotch and swipe the back of my other hand across my sweaty forehead. When I get out of my car, I look over to see Krista's car parked a few spaces down.

My heart thumps against my chest, and my bones tingle with urgency. Like a bad habit, my feet lead me to the remedy, taking me to the next building over. The neck of my shirt dampens as I stand in front of her door. I think about all the highs that are waiting for me on the other side if only I could knock. God damn, I want to knock so bad as my hard-on strains against my shorts, but I can't. If Adaline ever found out, she would never see it as an emotionless release. She deserves a guy who can restrain himself better than this, but maybe I'm not better. Maybe the reason I'm about to fuck Krista is because there's something inside me that isn't right.

I shake that thought out of my head, because I can't handle the fear it brings.

Before I do something that I'll regret, I turn on my heels and walk with failure in my step all the way to my apartment.

But I didn't fail. Not entirely.

Frustration bites at my core, and I rip off my sweat-soaked shirt when I kick the door to my bedroom shut. As much as I want to pretend I don't need this, I know the truth. I know I can't live without it.

I want to do right by Adaline—I do. I want it so badly, but at what cost? If I'm forsaking sex, then shouldn't that be enough?

Lying on my bed, I open a free online porn site on my phone, and without another thought, my mind drags into a fog as I watch some chick with fake tits bouncing on top of a dude as I jack off. I cum hard and fast, but euphoria fades when I lose myself inside an unrelenting dark wave of repulsion. The fact that I had to talk myself out of fucking Krista only to come home and get myself off to cheap porn makes me sick to my stomach. My truth is so unworthy of the girl my heart has started attaching itself to. When I think about how pure she is, it only reminds me how dirty I am.

CHAPTER
eleven

Adaline

Kason's grip on the steering wheel is tense, knuckles nearly white, and I hate that he's so nervous about my seeing where he lives. His fear that I'm somehow going to look at him differently is making me feel like I should be doing something more to comfort him. But I don't want to coddle him like a child. It would probably make everything worse.

He picked me up from my house after work because he didn't want me driving alone when I don't know my way around his side of town. I try to reassure him with a silent smile when he glances my way, but I know it doesn't have any effect on him.

When he pulls off the highway, I already see the stark

difference between my neighborhood and his. Chain linked fences enclose the front yards of withered old houses. A tattooed guy, who is wearing a wife-beater and jeans slung way too low, is walking down the sidewalk, not bothering to step around the weeds that are jutting through the cracks. I peer over my shoulder at Kason, who's so clean cut in his crisp white work polo and khaki shorts, looking every bit of the part of a South Tampa kid and nothing like the guy we just passed.

The car slows as we approach the apartment complex. He drives around the worn-down buildings, and my stomach grows uneasy. I've never been in an area like this before, and I feel very out of place and skittish. Kason would be hurt if he knew, so I feign indifference when he turns into a parking spot and shuts the car off.

He lets go of a heavy breath. "So, this is where I live."

"Stop," I gently chide when I see the shame in his eyes.

He fiddles with his keys for a second and then finally opens his door. Taking my hand in his, he leads me up the stairs and down the corridor to his apartment. Bass from a nearby car thumps loudly, and when Kason unlocks the door and holds it open for me, I come face to face with his reality.

I step inside, but I'm immediately distracted from taking in the surroundings when I see his mom sitting on the couch with a stack of mail on her lap.

"Hi, Mom."

With her eyes on me, she stands and gives me the most endearing smile. There's something about the small gesture that soothes some of my nerves.

"So, this is Adaline," she says as she walks over to me, and I'm taken by surprise when she hugs me. "It's so nice to meet you."

"You, too."

She then takes a small step back and eyes me up and down. "You're a very pretty girl."

"Mom."

"What?" she defends. "She is."

"I know, but—"

She wags her hand at Kason, and I laugh as he shakes his head at her. "Well, come over here and have a seat," she invites. "Are you thirsty or anything?"

"No, I'm good. Thanks." I sit next to her on the threadbare sofa, and Kason joins me. There's no other seating in the room, only a rickety coffee table and a small television in the corner by the door.

I turn back to his mom and see she's wearing a work uniform. I spot her name tag that reads "Sharon".

"I was about to head off to work," she tells me when she notices I'm looking at her clothes, and I apologize for staring.

"I'm sorry. I was reading your tag," I explain. "Kason hadn't mentioned your name."

She touches her name tag and then smooths her hands down the front of her apron that's tied around her waist. "It isn't the best job in the world, but the people are very friendly."

I read aloud the logo on her top. "Pete's-A-Pie. Never been there."

"You're not missing much. Just an old diner that serves pizza and pies. It's a horrible combination if you ask me. But the key lime pie is made from real key limes."

"I'm more of a classic apple pie girl, but it has to be topped with a slice of cheddar cheese."

"That sounds gross."

My eyes widen in surprise when Kason says this, and I ask,

"Have you ever tried it?"

"Why would anyone want cheese on their pie?"

"Because," his mom says, "apple pie without cheese is like a kiss without a squeeze."

"Oh my god," I squeal with excitement. "My grandma used to say the same thing."

"That's because it's true." She places her hand on my knee and leans in. "Kason doesn't know what he's missing."

Looking over my shoulder at him, I agree. "She's right. It's amazing."

He shakes his head at the two of us, but he can't hide the hint of a smile on his face.

"Well, I wish I could stay and chitchat a little longer, but I need to be going before I'm late."

I stand when she gets off the couch and grabs her purse from the small coffee table.

"It was really good meeting you," I tell her and truly mean it. Getting to finally talk to Kason's mom makes me feel even closer to him, and with liking him as much as I do, I want that closeness.

She smiles and then peers around me to her son, saying, "Bring her over more often," before acknowledging me with, "And it was great meeting you, too."

"See ya, Mom."

When she leaves and closes the door behind her, I turn to face Kason, and he's smiling.

"What?"

He shakes his head, stands, and then pulls me into his arms. I can feel the relief in his hold.

"She's really sweet," I tell him, hugging him back.

He then takes my hand and walks me across the small

110

space. With a quick look around, I note the bareness of the apartment. The walls are free of photos and artwork, and there's hardly any furniture.

When I step into Kason's room, there's only a dresser and a full-size mattress that lays on the floor in the corner of the room; no bed frame at all.

I let go of his hand and take a step into his personal space. He has a number of skimboards leaning against the wall, and when I walk over to his bed, he turns on the lamp that sits on the dresser.

"What are you doing?" he asks as I kick off my shoes and crawl to the center of his mattress.

My hand runs over his sheets, and I smile. "I like it here."

He cocks his head and smirks as he kicks his own shoes off and joins me on the bed. I lie in his arms and close my eyes.

"I didn't think it would feel this good to have you here."

I cuddle in closer. "I wish you wouldn't have worried so much."

He scoots down on the bed, and we turn onto our sides so we're facing each other. When he cradles my cheeks, his brows furrow a bit as he asks, "Are you sure this doesn't bother you?"

I reach up, run my hand along his jaw, and whisper, "I'm sure."

He holds me firmly, and I wish he could feel what I feel on the inside, because if he could, he'd have no reason to doubt himself. And when he rests his head against mine, he closes his eyes and breathes, "I think I'm falling in love with you."

Sparks flare from deep within my chest, his words caressing me from the inside out, and I feel like I could burst apart at any moment.

"There's no thinking for me," I tell him. He draws back and

looks at me. "I know I'm falling in love with you."

With our walls down, I kiss him and completely lose myself as time slips away from us. As his lips drag down my neck, I gather his shirt with my fingers and slip it off him. I hold him close, soaking in his warmth, begging for more.

Being here, in his world, in his bed, I feel like I could stay forever and be content. That's how amazing he makes me feel—loved and wanted and cared for. Because in the end, that's all that really matters between two people, and we have that. He gives it freely to me, and I give it right back to him.

His hand slips under the hem of my top, and when he takes my breast in his hand, I melt a little more.

"Is this okay?"

I nod my head against his shoulder, and he squeezes me before he lifts my shirt and kisses me over my bra. My hands get lost in his hair as he moves above me, closer than what we've ever been before, but it's when his hand drops down my stomach and beneath the waistband of my shorts that my breath catches and I coil back.

He stops, and I heat with embarrassment, muttering, "I'm sorry."

"It's okay. Do you want to stop?"

Tucked beneath him, I know this is exactly where I want to be. I've never been touched the way he's touching me now, and the way he's *wanting* to, but I know it's his hands that are meant to be the first to do this, so I bashfully shake my head.

He's slow when he continues to move again, and my pulse loses its tempo when he unbuttons my shorts and slips his hand down and over my panties. Self-consciousness takes over, so I hide my face when I wrap my arms around his neck and hug him close to me.

Every one of his touches ignites bundles of burning embers all over my body. My grip on him is strong. He then pushes his hand inside the fabric, touching my bare flesh, and I swear those embers fracture into wild scorching flames.

The tips of my fingers press into his shoulders as his glide along me in the most intimate way.

"God, you're so soft," he murmurs into my ear, and I loosen my hold around him when he kisses my temple.

Never have I been as close to anyone as I am with Kason right now, but it still doesn't feel like enough.

"Kason?"

My voice is so feeble, I doubt he hears me as he keeps going, but a second later, he finally responds. "What is it, baby?"

I take a hard swallow and will myself to fight past my uncertainty. "I want to touch you."

With my words, he reaches down with his one hand and unfastens his shorts.

I don't move, and when his eyes flick to mine, I swallow another mouthful of fear and ask, "Will you show me how?"

He takes his hand from between my legs, cups my cheek, and kisses me. I blush when I smell myself on his fingers. I'm spiraled too tightly with insecurity while he's so calm and in control. Kason shifts to his side and shoves down his shorts before taking my hand in his and lowering it between our bodies.

My heart races when I touch him for the first time. I hold him in my palm while he keeps his hand wrapped around mine. His breath grows heavy as he begins to guide my hand up and down the length of him. He's insanely hot to the touch, and feeling how hard he is, I bashfully drop my head into the crook of his neck.

Every noise he emits turns me on, and when his grip strengthens around mine, I draw back and look at him. His eyes, heavy lidded and pinned to mine, transfix me.

"Keep doing it just like that," he says on a staggering breath before taking his hand off mine and slipping it back between my legs and beneath my panties.

Touching each other the way we are, I feel it happening—I feel the tug of my heart as it tethers with his. It's an overwhelming weight that takes control of me, but I don't fear it. In fact, there is nowhere else I'd rather be, so I freely hand myself over to its force field.

CHAPTER
twelve

Adaline

School is out, and I'm officially a senior. I was hoping to spend most of my summer with Kason, but he's working more hours than what he did during the school year. He doesn't need to explain why, I already know, so I refuse to guilt him with the fact that I've been missing him.

To fill in the boring gaps of hanging out at my house alone, I spend time with Micah and even sometimes Trent. My mom is busier than ever now. She does what she can to try to get home to see me before I go to bed, but those nights are starting to dwindle as the trial draws closer.

Needless to say, today couldn't have come soon enough. Molly just texted me to let me know she landed, and by the time I make it from the waiting lot and circle around the airport to arrivals, she's already standing outside.

Her familiar smile reminds me how much I've missed her, and I can't undo my seatbelt fast enough.

"You're here!"

There's no doubt everyone can hear our high-pitched excitement as we hug. She's one of the few people from back home that I truly love and miss. I can't ever remember a time when she hasn't had my back, and with everything falling apart with my dad for the last few years, she's been the only person I've felt comfortable confiding in. That is, until now. I find myself turning to Kason more and more. Not that I intentionally turn to Molly less and less, but it's hard when she lives so far away and Kason is right here. Though, I can't deny how good it feels to have a piece of my old life with me in my new life here in Florida.

We hop into my car, and when I start driving, she pegs the air conditioner, whining, "My God, it's so humid."

"You're telling me? It's awful."

There's really no point in slathering on makeup when the second you walk outside, it just melts off in the thick, stagnant air. It hangs heavily and plasters to your skin like a sticky dew, and it only gets worse after the hour-long sun showers that come nearly every afternoon. I thought summers in Florida would feel like paradise—I was wrong.

"I can't believe this is your life," she says as we cruise along Bayshore with water on one side and palm trees in front of luxury homes on the other. "I wonder if I could convince my mom to let me transfer here for senior year."

"I wish. I haven't made a single girlfriend since I've been here."

"Are you serious? Why?"

With a shrug, I respond, "I don't really know. I mean, I don't want to come across as a snot, but my best guess would be that they're jealous."

"Of what?"

I turn into the front drive of my house. "I somehow wound up making friends with a group of guys that are all pretty popular. But popular here is different from popular back home. They kind of do their own thing, but they've always included me, and we've become close."

"I take it Kason is one of those guys."

"Yeah." I park the car but leave the AC running. "You'll meet him later when we go over to Micah's. They're all down at the beach right now," I tell her. "But the thing is, he's a pretty quiet guy, so I don't want you to think he isn't being friendly. He barely even talks to anyone at school."

"Oooh, the quiet type," she teases, wagging her brows.

I grab her suitcase from the trunk as she steps out of the car, and when I take her inside, her voice echoes through the open space when she says, "This is amazing."

"Oh stop. My house back in Texas was nice, too."

"Yeah, but you didn't have this view," she exclaims, holding out her arm toward the back of the house, which is covered in floor-to-ceiling windows that offer a perfect view of the veranda and pool.

I roll her suitcase over to the foot of the stairs and give her a quick tour before we head to my room.

"So," she says, dragging out the word as she walks over to the large window, "this is where you stalked Pool Boy?"

I roll my eyes.

"You still watch him?"

I throw a pillow from my bed at her.

"You do, don't you?" she teases. I do, but I'm not about to admit that to her. She embarrasses me enough as it is and doesn't need more ammo.

We spend the afternoon lying around and catching up. She fills me in on all the latest gossip at my old school, and I gush about Kason while I paint her toenails. When I get the text that the guys are heading back from the beach, Molly freshens up, and we drive over to Harbour Island.

"Guppy's here!" Micah calls out when I let myself in.

"*Guppy?*"

"It's a size thing," I tell her as we walk into the kitchen and find the guys devouring a huge bowl of chopped fruit.

They're all shirtless, sun kissed, and in their board shorts.

Kason walks straight to me and lifts me in his arms, giving me a strong hug. "Hey, babe."

I plant a kiss on his neck and then lick the salt from my lips when he sets me back down on my feet.

"Kason, this is Molly."

"Hey, Molly," he greets, and then I introduce her to Micah and Trent.

Everyone exchanges hellos and then we all head out back so I can show Molly an even more impressive view than the one at my place.

"I would never leave my house if I lived here," she says as she rounds the pool and walks down closer to the water. "Is that your boat?"

"Yeah," Micah tells her. "If you want, we can take it out while you're here."

"I'd love to."

Trent then jumps into the pool and finds himself a raft to lie out on to deepen his already dark tan while the four of us hang out under the shade.

"So, what do you two have planned tonight?"

Sitting on Kason's lap, I tell him, "No plans. I thought we'd take it easy for today."

"Dude, your best friend, I mean, second best, comes out to see you, and you're going to bum it at home?"

Molly eyes Micah. "Second best?"

"Tell her, Guppy."

"I'll let you two battle that one out," I say.

"Until you're able to make this girl laugh so hard she pees her pants, there's no way you're trumping me."

"Oh my god! Molly!" I shriek as I swat my hand at her, but all she can do is laugh at me.

"You peed your pants?" Kason chuckles.

Molly gives an exaggerated nod. "Luckily my car has leather seats."

Kason's face is slathered in amusement, and I throw him under the bus right along with me when I say, "And what about the time you pulled down your pants and used Micah's pool as your own personal toilet?"

"Dude!" he shouts at Micah. "Is nothing sacred?"

"Besties share everything," he teases in response and then shoots an antagonizing air kiss to Molly.

But Molly likes retaliation, and as quick as lightning, reaches over and pinches his nipple.

"Holy fuck!" Micah jumps in his seat and covers his chest as she and I burst out in a barrel of giggles.

"What the hell's going on?" Trent questions when he walks over to us as he's toweling off.

"Girl just attacked my nipple, man."

"Nice. She's feisty."

Trent drags a chair over to where we are and sits next to Molly, and I already see it in his eyes—he thinks she's cute. But I have nothing to worry about as I slack into Kason's arms a little more. Molly isn't attracted to boys with foul mouths, and especially ones who drink and smoke pot. So, I sit back and watch him as he proceeds to flirt, enjoying the entertainment as the evening plays on.

"This humidity is killing my hair, literally," Molly fusses as she gives up on the flatiron.

"Tell me about it."

Molly stands in front of the mirror in my bathroom as I sidle up next to her, dab on a little gloss, and toss my hair back into a ponytail.

"So, what kind of party is this?"

"Pretty much like the ones back home, except there might be pot there."

Her eyes bulge. "You mean, like, marijuana?"

I nod, wondering if my reaction was as dramatic to Micah when I first saw Trent smoking. "It doesn't seem to be a big deal around here."

Twisting the cap back on the gloss, she leans her hip against the sink, asking, "Have you smoked it?"

"God no!"

"Do your friends?"

I shrug passively as I walk back into the bedroom. "Trent and Micah do, but they're not obnoxious about it." I slip on my sandals as she stares at me from the bathroom, still half-shocked. "Molly, relax. It's fine."

"I can't believe you're being so . . . *whatever* about it."

"Trust me, I was as stunned as you, but honestly, it's different from how it is back in Plano."

"I guess," she succumbs as we head out.

Molly and I have been keeping busy this past week. We've hit the beaches, explored the port, and have spent a lot of time with the guys, swimming and hanging out. Tonight, we are going over to Trent's house. His parents are away on a week's vacation in Montreal, so he's throwing a party with his older brother, who's home from college.

When we arrive at his place, the house is already packed with people. I recognize a lot of faces from school, but there are even more I've never seen.

"This is crazy," Molly says as she holds on to my hand while I navigate my way through the crowd.

I raise on my tiptoes to try to find Kason who texted me a little bit ago to tell me he was already here, but even on my toes, I'm still shorter than most.

"Adaline!"

I turn around, and see Kason weaving through everyone to get to me.

"Did he invite the whole town?" I joke, and he takes my hand.

"We're all out back."

Molly and I follow him out to the backyard where a group is gathered around the large stoned-in fire pit. Everyone is drinking, and when Trent offers, both Molly and I decline. It doesn't take long for him to strike up a conversation with Molly, and when Kason leans down to my ear and asks to sneak away, I get an approving nod from her.

"I've been missing you," he says when we are far enough away from the crowd that it feels like we are alone.

I soften into him. "I'm right here."

"You know what I mean."

And I do. With his busy work schedule and Molly being here, we haven't spent any real time together. Since both our moms are always at work, we're used to being alone with each other and we spend more than our fair share of time kissing and making out. Kason is an extremely affectionate person, more than what I would have guessed when I first met him, so I don't doubt him when he tells me this.

After a few more steps, he takes a seat next to a palm tree and pulls me down with him so I'm sitting between his legs. I scoot and angle myself toward him, and when he threads his fingers into my hair, I slip my hand around the back of his neck and kiss him.

We kiss until our lips grow tired and then he holds me against him. A simple touch that consumes me, and I find that there's really no place else I'd rather be than in his arms. I've come to know them well, and often crave them when he isn't around.

Somehow, he's found the hidden path straight to my soul, a path not even I was aware of. But here he is, my body absorbing him in fractions as he continues to slowly hand himself over to me, piece by piece. He isn't one to open up quickly, but when he does, with every small bit he hands over to me, I fall that much deeper.

"I love you," I whisper up into the stars, but he grabs hold of my words before they travel too far and gives them right back to me, saying, "I love you, too."

We stay tucked away from everyone for as long as we can

until we're dragged back into the chaos.

"Where's Molly?"

"She went inside with Trent," Micah tells me.

When I leave Kason to go find my friend, I'm shocked when I see her dancing with Trent and a few girls. Girls that go to my school. Girls that have never spoken a word to me. They only stare and whisper, never outright rude, but it's clear they have something against me. But here they are, dancing and laughing with Molly. I can't help the tinge of insecurity that spills over me, wondering what it is about me that keeps them from wanting to talk to me.

It isn't until dawn reaches the horizon and Molly and I crawl into bed that I find out.

"I heard something tonight that I feel like I need to tell you," she says in the darkness of the room, and the uncertainty in her voice is apparent.

"What is it?"

She props her head on her hand, and the seriousness on her face has me worried about what it is she's going to tell me.

"You know the girls I was dancing with? Well . . . I later overheard them talking about you."

"What did they say?"

"Those girls are cows, just so you know."

"Tell me what they said," I press, anxious to know but also scared.

She stalls for a moment before revealing, "They were saying really gross things about you."

"Tell me."

She sighs heavily. "They were calling you a slut. Saying that the only reason Kason is with you is because you must be an easy lay."

The chill of shock spreads through my chest. "Are you serious?"

"Apparently, the one girl, Katy . . . she and Kason . . . they've slept together."

"You mean sex?" I blurt out.

She nods, and my stomach drops. I instantly feel sick. Waves of sadness crash over me, and I can't even speak. I had asked him if I was the first girl he's been with, but I meant it on my level, as in dated, kissed, made out with. Never did I even consider sex, so when he told me no, it was easy to accept. But to think of him being so intimate with another girl, more intimate than he is with me, it feels like a punch to my gut. My throat tightens with so much hurt as I struggle to hide it from Molly, but she knows me better.

How could he not tell me?

How could we be at the same party with her and he not even say anything?

I roll over and turn my back to her the moment I feel my eyes water, and I want to cry so badly. I want to fall apart the way my body is begging to, but I force down a painful swallow, take a deep breath, and do my very best to speak on an even tone when I say, "He already told me that I wouldn't be his first," even though I didn't know that was what he meant when he said it.

CHAPTER
thirteen

Adaline

Anger.

That was what I felt when I got out of bed this morning. After Molly told me about Kason and that girl, I couldn't clear my head and calm my thoughts long enough to fall asleep. Tossing and turning is how I found myself for most the night. I hardly got any rest at all. How could I with the images playing in my head. My mind tormented me all night as I pictured him with her, over and over in various scenarios: in his car, in her bed, in a random room at a party. With each scene, I imagined him on top and then her on top. Clothes all the way off. Clothes halfway off. Slow. Fast. Sweet. Rough. And when it was over, did he hold her in his arms or get up and walk away? And then my heart cracked a little when I started wondering if he talked to her lovingly the way he does with me. What did he say? What were his words? How did he touch her? I drove myself to the brink of craziness last night with tears that refused to stop.

I'm still going crazy.

Crushed.

That's what I am under the anger that's working as a mask for the sadness beneath. It's too tender of an emotion for me to touch right now, so I bury it under feelings that are strong enough to keep me from falling apart. At least on the outside. My outward appearance is intact. But on the inside, I feel like Kason took an ax to my heart.

"We don't have to go," Molly says while I drive.

"I'm fine." Lie. "Like I said, Kason and I had already talked about that stuff." Another lie—kind of.

She shoots me an *I-know-better* look, but I sluff it off and muster the best smile I can. Honestly, I'd rather be at home sulking and throwing darts into photos of Kason's face—his perfectly perfect face—but this is Molly's last day here. The last thing I want is to subject her to my misery. Besides, there will be plenty of time for me to sulk when she leaves tomorrow.

I can't even begin to explain how it feels when I walk into Micah's house, knowing Kason is here. It's a mixture of so many things that settle low in the bottom of my gut. I don't want to spoil this day for anyone here, but my temper is already flaring.

The three of them are out back on the dock, and I trail slowly behind Molly as she rushes outside. I drop my sunglasses over my tired eyes while I watch Trent take Molly's hand and help her step onto the impressive sports boat.

My first glance over to Kason is all it takes for another

agonizing image to appear in my head, and I want to run back home. But I don't. Instead, I walk inside in hopes to pull myself together with a moment alone.

As I'm rummaging through the fridge for a can of coke, I hear the back door open and close.

"What are you doing?"

I snap open the tab and take a quick sip. "Just thirsty."

He walks over and pulls me into his arms. I want to push him away, knowing these are the same arms that held Katy. My embrace is weak at best, and he senses it.

"Everything okay?"

"I'm tired, that's all."

He pushes my sunglasses back, and when he sees the dark circles under my eyes, I duck my head and walk away, going back outside before I break down in front of him. I make my way straight to Micah, knowing he'll be able to distract me enough from my brewing emotions.

"Can you hold this line for me?" he says when I hit the dock, and I'm happy to be put to work.

Micah shows me what to do, and a few minutes later, he shouts out to Kason, who is still inside.

"Let's go!"

Kason comes down to the dock and takes the line from me. Trent then helps me step onto the boat. I don't look back when I grab Molly's hand and lead her up to sit with me in the two-seater bow cockpit.

Micah starts the boat, and Kason jumps on before kicking us off the dock. Once Trent is in the water on the jet ski, we start to move.

"You didn't know, did you?" Molly asks as she leans in close to me.

I look back and see Kason and Micah talking as Micah steers us through the channel that leads out to the bay before turning back to her.

"It's obvious you're upset."

Again, shielded by my sunglasses, I can hide the sadness in my eyes, but I know she sees it all over my face. I quietly admit, "I'm so mad at him."

"Did you say anything yet?"

"No. I didn't want to make today any more awkward than it already is."

"But you are going to say something, right?" she questions, and when I don't answer her, she presses, "Ady, come on. You have to say something."

"I will. It's just . . . I really love him."

"Which is why you need to say something. If it's bothering you this much, he should know and at least have a chance to talk to you about it."

"I feel stupid, though," I admit. "It isn't as if he cheated on me or anything. He didn't do anything wrong."

"No one is saying he did. But you're still upset, and he should know."

I shake my head and let the wind whip through my hair when we hit the open bay and Micah speeds up. "Not today." I take a deep breath and fill my lungs before tilting my face to the bright sun. "It's your last day here. I don't want to ruin it with stupid boy drama."

She gives my cheek a peck, and when I finally crack a smile, she tosses her arms up, and hollers back to Micah, "Faster!"

He cranks it a gear up, and Trent lets out an excited, "Yeah, man," as he speeds alongside the boat.

We fly across the smooth water of the bay, and I'm so

thankful to have Molly here with me today. I take her hand and try not to think about how sad I'm going to be when she leaves tomorrow. Instead, I do what I can to focus on the here and now as we toss our cover-ups aside, lie back, and soak in the blazing rays from above.

Molly takes my mind off the guy who's at the back of the boat when she begins reminiscing, bringing up funny memories from our past. I can't even count how many times we bust out laughing as we go on and on with, "Remember when," stories. We stay on the bow because there are only two seats up here, preventing Kason from joining us. But when the heat becomes too much, and we're sweaty and dehydrated, Molly heads to the stern to grab us some drinks from the ice chest.

"Molly, hop on," Trent calls from the water, and I see the excitement in her eyes, I take the bottle of water from her, saying, "Go."

"You sure?"

"We came to have fun. So, go have fun. I'll be fine."

Her laughter fills the space around us as Trent throttles hard across the water with her arms wrapped around his waist. I guzzle the water before Kason's shadow casts over me.

He takes the seat next to me, vanquishing the levity Molly was able to throw my way. I attempt a smile, but it doesn't fool him.

"What's going on?"

"What do you mean?"

He leans forward with his elbows braced on his knees. "You won't even look at me, Adaline."

"I'm just hanging out with Molly." I sound like a total brat, and I hate that, but I don't know how to talk to him right now. I'm still so irritated. The mental images that won't leave me alone are stomach churning.

He huffs in defeat before standing and going back to the cockpit with Micah without saying another word. Guilt needles on my nerves, and I silently chastise myself for acting this way. But how am I supposed to act?

Frustration brims, and I grab Molly's phone and earbuds out of the small beach bag we brought and tune out everything around me when I open her music folder and spike the volume.

Deep into one of her playlists, I startle when a hand lands on my arm.

I yank out my earphones and look at Kason as he clips, "Come on."

"What are you doing?"

"Just come with me."

Even though I don't want to, I let him pull me up, and I see Trent and Molly are back from their ride. Looking over at Micah, he nods his head toward the jet ski, encouraging me to go with Kason.

Clearly, Kason mentioned my pissy mood to Micah.

"We'll be back later," Kason tells him as he holds my hand and leads me to the stern of the boat.

Kason gets on the jet ski first, and Molly whispers, "Be honest with him," before he reaches out his hand and helps me onto the back.

The minute my arms are secured around him, he cranks the throttle, and I hang on as we fly across the glassy water. My heart grows heavy having him so close to me. It's a conflict of emotions battling inside, and I wish knowing this about him didn't affect me as much as what it is, because I love him. I press my cheek to his smooth back, and he takes one of his hands to hold on to mine that are clenched to his chest.

We ride for a long time before he kills the motor, hops off, and drags the jet ski onto the sandy shore of a tiny island.

"Where are we?"

He ignores my question as he steps back from the water and sits in the sand. Squinting against the hard sun, he looks at me and says, "Don't lie to me and tell me everything's okay when I ask you what's wrong."

I go sit next to him.

"Have I done something to upset you? Because you were fine last night."

I pull my knees to my chest and look down as I sink my toes into the sand.

"Adaline, just talk to me."

I'm struggling in my head with what to say. I grasp on to a word, but it fails me before I can even utter it. So when I turn to him, I take Molly's advice and speak honestly, saying, "Molly overheard a couple girls talking really bad about me and you last night."

"What did they say?"

I shake my head, not wanting to say the words aloud.

"Who was talking about us?"

"A girl named Katy," I tell him and then watch his eyes to see his reaction. When they drop away from me, it feels like a boulder landing on my chest. "She said the two of you slept together. Is that true?" I hate how weak my voice sounds.

He hangs his head for a moment before admitting, "Yeah."

His arm wraps around my shoulders, and I tense against his touch.

"Adaline . . ."

"When?"

"I don't want to hurt you."

"Just tell me when."

He takes a pause, and it's evident that he doesn't want to talk about this, but I do, so I push again and he reveals, "Sophomore year."

My eyes widen. "Sophomore year? When you were sixteen?"

He doesn't say anything.

"Was she your first?"

He still doesn't speak, and my stomach knots. I shrug his arm off my shoulders and ask again, "Was she your first?"

Finally, he gives me a cowardly headshake, and I can't even look at him. Dropping my head to my knees, I take in a long deep breath to keep myself from crying, but God this hurts.

"Adaline, please. I don't want this to upset you."

"How many girls have you had sex with?"

"I don't want this to be something you're thinking about."

"How many?"

"What does it matter? It isn't something that can be changed."

"Because it matters." My voice pitches and cracks. "Because you say you love me, and I thought that meant something, and now I just feel stupid."

"God, babe, don't feel that way. You're the only one who has those words from me, and that's the honest truth."

"So, you didn't love them, but you slept with them?"

"Please, I don't want you worrying about this."

And then it happens, a tear slips and falls down my cheek. "What are you even doing with me? Because if that's what you want, you're with the wrong girl. I'm not like that."

"You are exactly what I want," he insists. "I swear to you,

you are all that matters to me, and when I tell you that I love you, I mean it. You are the only one I've felt this way about." He takes my hand and holds it firmly in his. "I never had any interest in having a relationship with anyone until you came along. And if that makes me an asshole, then fine. I was an ass to use them. But none of them matter to me, only you. You're the only one I care about, and I don't want to hurt you with the things I did before I met you."

"They're calling me a slut for being with you."

His jaw clenches when I tell him this. "They're jealous. That's all that it is."

"It doesn't feel good. Aside from you, Micah, and Trent, I have no friends here. None of the girls will give me a chance, and now I find out that this is what they're saying about me behind my back. That I must be easy if you're giving me attention."

His hand comes to my cheek, and he catches another tear. "Fuck what they think about you. Katy and her friends are desperate for attention, and everyone knows that. They line the shore every time we hit the water. They're bunnies, Adaline. That's all they are and no one takes them seriously."

With my hips in his hands, he pulls me over the top of his lap so my legs are straddling him. Banding his arms around my waist, I hold on to his shoulders as he looks at me. "You're the only person I've ever felt safe enough with to open up to. You're the only one who's seen where I live and who's met my mom." His lips press to mine, and I melt against him. "I don't ever want you to feel insecure with me, because you are exactly what I want. Because when you touch me, it means so much more than what anyone else could ever give me. I love that you're untouched and that you value yourself."

His words make me blush, but he doesn't let me shy away when he cups his hands along my face, forcing me to look at him.

"I love you, Adaline. I swear to God, I do."

His eyes are more sincere than what I've ever seen them before. "I'm sorry," I tell him, dropping my head against his.

"Don't ever be sorry with me, babe. If something's bothering you, I want you to come to me."

"I don't want you to think that I ever *truly* doubted your love for me," I tell him. "It's just hard to know that there are girls that have more of you than what I have."

"They don't." He then takes my hand and presses it against the bare skin of his chest. His heart beats into my palm. "You have so much more."

CHAPTER
fourteen

Adaline

Molly left, and saying goodbye to her, knowing I most likely won't be seeing her until spring break, was tough. Nine months is entirely too long to go without my best friend. Thankfully, I had Kason there that day. We didn't do much, but we didn't need to. Simply having him around was enough to help me feel better.

But that was nearly two months ago, and since then, I've been taking advantage of the summer. We've gone out on Micah's parents' boat a few more times, luckily without any more unwanted tension. Kason and I are closer than ever, and I'm settled in the fact that he's the one holding my heart because I wouldn't trust it with anyone else—only him.

That isn't to say that my skin doesn't crawl when I cross

paths with Katy, which only happens on rare occasions. But senior year is starting next week, and those occurrences will surely multiply. Kason and I have done what we can to link our courses, and when the emails came with our schedules, I was thrilled to find that we have three classes together.

I'm also finding myself over at Kason's apartment more often. I've been able to spend time with his mother, too, which has been nice. She's an easy person to get along with and makes me feel as if I've been going over there for years instead of just months. Without Kason having to say a word, I can tell he appreciates my effort to get to know her better.

But Kason is at work today, Micah is out with his parents, and my mom is at a conference in Jacksonville for the week. So, before I lose my mind to boredom, I call Sharon to see if she's home and decide to go hang out there while I wait for Kason to get off work.

The other week, she wanted to know how I get my hair so soft, and when I told her about the homemade keratin treatment I use, she asked if I could bring over a little the next time I made some. With as much time as I've been spending at the beach with Kason, I'm due for a little hair TLC. So, I grab all the ingredients from my house and hop in my car.

I know it bothers Kason when I drive over to his place alone, so I feel a little bad for not calling him to let him know I'm headed that way. I just don't want him to worry. Plus, I'd like to surprise him when he gets off work.

I park my car, which sticks out like a sore thumb next to the old, rusted Buick that's propped up by two cinder blocks in the next space over. Grabbing everything out of the front seat, I head up the stairs and knock on the door.

"What's all this?" Sharon says when she lets me in.

"Beauty day." I set everything on the small kitchenette table. "How long until you leave for work?" I ask, taking in her old sweats and oversized sleep shirt.

"A little over an hour."

"Perfect." I start to unload the bags, and she comes to stand by my side to see what all I've brought. "The sand and salt haven't been good to my hair, so I figured we could both do one of my treatments today."

She picks up a box and gives it a puzzled look. "What are these?"

"You'll love them. They're charcoal pore strips."

"Charcoal?"

"Trust me, you'll thank me later."

She helps me in the kitchen while I measure out the olive oil, coconut milk, and other ingredients to make the hair treatment. I notice her eyes are sunken in and her skin has a weird sickly color to it. When I ask if she's feeling okay, she shrugs it off, claiming lack of sleep. Something tells me it isn't exhaustion, but I let it go and pull out a chair for her to sit.

"I'll do your hair first and then you can do mine."

I stand over her with the plastic bowl and start brushing the mixture onto her coarse hair.

"Are you excited about your senior year?"

"I am. It feels weird since I only started at the school two months before last year ended. I still feel like the new kid, and I *hate* that feeling."

"You're a sweet girl. I can't imagine it being difficult for you to make friends."

I slather on more conditioner and opt not to tell her about the unwelcoming girl committee I try to avoid. "Walking in last year without knowing a single soul was horrible. At least now I have Kason."

"I'm sure he feels the same about having you. It's always been a little hard on him knowing he doesn't belong at that school. It's a huge gap between here and there, but you've been able to help mend that for him."

On the outside, Kason fits in well. He's popular and gets perfect grades, but his mom is right; I can't imagine how uncomfortable it must be for him to immerse himself in a world that's nothing like the one he lives in. No one would ever suspect *this* to be his life. But that's what I love so much about him. He doesn't let fear stand in his way of bettering himself. He understands that he will be afforded more opportunities graduating from South Shore High than what he would at his neighborhood school, and he doesn't take that for granted.

When I finish applying the treatment, I cover her hair in plastic wrap, and we switch spots.

"Have you two made any plans to do something for his birthday?"

"He never mentioned his birthday," I respond in total surprise. "When is it?"

"He hasn't said anything?"

"No."

I sit still as she dips the brush in the bowl before returning it to my hair.

"August twenty-third," she notes. "I can't believe my baby will be eighteen."

My mind starts racing with ideas of what I could do for him, but then again, maybe he doesn't want me to do anything. I wonder why he hasn't told me yet, but before I can dwell on the reason, Sharon distracts me, saying, "I can remember when he turned six. His favorite thing to eat was buttered toast, so when he woke up that morning a year older, he wanted to make his own breakfast. I was still in bed, but I could smell the toast. He rushed into my room with two pieces, one for him and one for me." She starts to laugh while she continues working on my hair. "I should first tell you this, if the butter melted on the toast, he would always want more because he had to be able to see it. Well, I took one bite into his birthday toast and nearly choked."

"Why? Too much butter?"

"Too much Crisco!"

"Eww, gross!"

"He thought the tub of Crisco was butter. I don't even know how many layers he spread on that had melted, and for some reason, he didn't notice the taste."

"You didn't tell him?"

She can't stop laughing at this point, and I'm giggling right along with her. "Adaline, if you could've seen his proud smile for fixing the toast, you wouldn't have had the heart to tell him, either. So, we sat there and ate the toast."

I picture him in my head, a little Kason celebrating his birthday with a slice of toast and wonder if that's why he hasn't told me he's about to turn eighteen. I wonder if his birthday has ever been celebrated beyond toast in bed. The thought alone weighs on my now sullen heart.

After she finishes, we tidy the kitchen and set the timer. With our hair wrapped in plastic and pore strips stuck to our noses, we sit on the couch and chat. She tells me more silly memories about Kason when he was a kid, but with each funny story comes a little bit of heartache. Hearing about his childhood and how vastly different it was from mine isn't easy. It only brightens the spotlight on how rough he's had it.

I can tell from how his mom speaks about their past that she doesn't see it the same way I do. Probably because she doesn't know any other way. This is the only life she's lived, and although these are happy memories for her, I wonder if they are for Kason. Because Kason sees the difference every day. He may live here in this apartment, but his life is mostly lived in South Tampa. It's where he goes to school and where all of his friends are. His mother isn't involved in that world at all. And knowing how hard it was for him to open up to me about this part of his life he keeps secret only goes to show that he's probably more affected by all of this than his mom is.

A key rattles in the lock, and when the door opens, Kason looks at the two of us in both horror and amusement.

"What the hell are the two of you doing?"

"Beautifying," I respond simply.

"I love you, babe, but nothing about this picture is beautiful." He walks over and gives me a gentle peck, which is followed by a sniff. "Why do you smell like Italian food?"

Sharon laughs. "That's the olive oil. Adaline shared her secret hair treatment with me."

He looks at me with an adoring smile. "She did?"

The timer goes off, and I pop off the couch. "Time to rinse, but first, let's take the pore strips off."

Kason follows us into the kitchen, asking, "Why didn't you tell me you were coming?"

"Because you would've told me to stay put until you got off work, and I didn't want to sit at home any longer."

"I hope you set your car alarm," he teases.

"It's set, Mister Boss Man."

Sharon and I peel off the pore strips, and Kason cracks up when her eyes start watering.

"You'll get used to the sting after you've used them a few times," I tell her before I start washing her hair in the kitchen sink.

Once it's clean, she runs her fingers through the wet strands, and smiles. "Wow, it's so soft."

Kason looks at his watch. "Mom, you need to get ready for work before you're late."

"Shoot, you're right," is all she says before disappearing into her bedroom.

"When she leaves, you can wash your hair in the shower with me," he says, tugging on his sweat-soaked shirt.

I pinch his side. "I don't think so. The sink will be fine."

He helps me unwrap my hair, and then takes his time washing it with the shampoo, all the while making jokes. When he's done, I grab the towel he offers and twist my hair in it. As I finish wiping drops of water off my neck, his mom emerges from her room with her waitress uniform on and her hair dried.

"I cannot believe how much better my hair feels," she exclaims, and when I turn to Kason, he's looking at her in amazement.

"I'm shocked."

"Me, too," she says and then gives me a hug. "Thank you, dear. I really needed a girl's day."

She rushes to grab her purse, and with a goodbye and another thank you, she's out the door.

I boast my proud smile to Kason. "Like I said, it's called beautifying."

He walks straight to me, lifts me in his arms, and hugs me. "You made her whole year, babe."

"It was only a little hair treatment. No biggie."

"I can tell she likes spending time with you."

"I really like spending time with her, too." He buries his face into my neck and starts nipping playful kisses. "Eww, you stink."

After setting me back on my feet, he peels off his work shirt and heads to the bathroom. "Give me ten minutes."

The door is cracked when I hear the shower start, and I head into his bedroom to towel-dry my hair a little more before tying it in a bun. I lie on his bed, always feeling close to him when I can smell him on his sheets, but I'm not able to get too lost when he hollers, "You took my towel."

I step into the bathroom, and when I modestly hand him the towel through the shower curtain, he rips it wide open, making me jump back in surprise.

"Kason!" I turn around and cover my eyes.

He chuckles for a moment. "You can look now. I'm covered."

Peeking over my shoulder, I find him stepping out of the shower with the towel in his hand instead of wrapped around his waist. "Oh my god."

He grabs my arm before I can run out of the bathroom, picks me up, and sets me on the counter. With his towel now wrapped around his waist, he wears a mischievous smirk. "Why are you so shy? It isn't like you haven't seen me naked."

"That's different, and you know it," I chastise.

"So, it's okay if we're in my bed?" His hands run slowly from my knees to my thighs as he steps between my legs, taunting me. "It's okay if we're touching each other?"

My cheeks heat, and I give a tiny nod.

His voice drops. "Touch me then."

I slip my hands over his shoulders and then wrap my arms around his neck, his skin is still wet from the shower, and he kisses me. There's hardly a day when we're together that we aren't physical with each other, and a part of me is starting to question if he needs the affection more than I do, even though I find myself needing it a lot.

It's unexplainable, the way he makes me feel when we can share moments like this. Lately, when we come down from touching each other, it almost seems as if he needs more. I don't deny him, because I love him, but I wonder if he wants more of the little we share since he's experienced and used to getting more out of girls.

My lips spill all along his neck, and when he whispers, "Can we try something new?" I grow timid.

"What do you mean?"

He picks me up, and I wrap my legs around his waist as he carries me into his room and lays me on the mattress.

We continue to kiss as his hand slips down to my shorts and unbuttons them. He's sits on his knees and pulls them off my legs, and then I watch him as he tucks his fingers beneath the hem of my panties and starts dragging them down my legs. I close my knees bashfully and sit up.

"What are you doing?"

"I want to taste you." His words come out with confidence, contrasting my nervousness.

"No!" It's one thing for him to touch me, but to have his mouth on me—*like that*—for him to see me so up close, it rankles my self-consciousness.

Kason crawls over me, lowering me back onto the bed, and I stare into his eyes with trepidation, muttering, "I don't know."

"Tell me why you're so nervous with me."

"Because . . ."

"It's me, Adaline. It's just me."

"I know."

"I want to be closer to you." He runs his hand down the side of my neck. "Are you scared?"

"A little."

"Because it's new for you?"

I nod, mildly embarrassed, but I know he understands me, and when his hand drags down lower and squeezes my breast, he asks, "Were you nervous when I first touched you like this?"

"Yes."

He palms me. "And does it make you nervous now?"

"No."

"And what about when I touch you like this?" he says when he parts my knees and gently rubs me between my legs.

I gasp, clutching on to his arms and shaking my head.

He lowers his chest as he continues to move his fingers along me. "Close your eyes."

My breathing struggles to keep cadence with my increasing pulse, and when he spreads my thighs wider and his head drops to me, I battle between wanting to push him away or to pull him closer. I reach down, needing his comfort, and he holds my hand tightly, lacing his fingers with mine before I feel the warmth of his tongue sliding along my seam.

His breath is hot against my flesh as he loves me in this new way, and I completely give into him, melting and splintering all at once. I squeeze his hand in mine as my eyes fall shut, and I've never felt more in love with a human than what I feel for Kason. When he touches me like he is right now, I just don't feel it on my skin, I feel him in the blood that's racing in and out of my heart as it pumps wildly for him. He's in my veins, claiming me with his love, and there isn't a single part of me that wants to deny him of that right.

CHAPTER
fifteen

Kason

S he's fucking perfection in my mouth the way I knew she would be. She has a death grip on my hand right now, but I also know that if she didn't want this, she would have let me know. So, even though I feel the hesitance in her thighs she's clenching against me, her tiny gasps tell me she's okay.

I bury my tongue inside her and imagine it's my dick when I reach down, pull the towel off me, and touch myself. Normally, just the thought of Adaline is enough to get me hard, but for some reason, I'm not. I jerk off while I continue licking and sucking. Her body squirms, and she has me so worked up right now. My balls ache, screaming for release. The intensity is so strong that I can feel it crawling under my skin, but frustration taunts as I try to get an erection.

"Kason."

God, she sounds so fucking sweet when she moans my name.

After a few more strokes, I give up and use my hand to pleasure her. The second I slide my finger inside her, she arches her back off the bed. I watch her from between her legs and imagine what it would be like to have sex with her. Would she move beneath me the way she is right now? Would she make the same sounds? But no matter how much I fantasize, my dick remains limp and useless even though I'm horny as hell.

She's so sincere with me, trusting that I'll take care of her with each step forward we take in our relationship. She isn't like most of the girls who've hit on me at school, eager to make out because somehow they're misinformed, thinking physical and emotional intimacy goes hand in hand, so they're quick to give it up.

Not Adaline. This girl threw her heart at me before she ever considered the physical stuff. And it doesn't matter that I have her legs spread open right now, she isn't one who would give herself flippantly to me. That's how I know she truly loves me in return. She gives beyond what a guy like me deserves, and she does it so perfectly.

I love that I'm the one who gets to witness her learning what her body likes and discovering her sexuality. My girl is so innocent and sweet, never faking her pleasure to appease me. She's always honest. The first time I fingered her, she wasn't able to orgasm, and since then, she still has a difficult time. So when she pulls me up to her right now, I know she can't get there. Only once have I made her come. I've jerked off to that memory so many times because it's the hottest thing I've ever seen.

She lifts her lips to mine and kisses me, moaning into my mouth as her tongue tangles with mine, tasting herself on me. Without thinking, I settle my hips into the cradle of her thighs, and her whole body freezes at the skin-to-skin contact.

"Kason," she panics.

"Sorry."

I back off the bed, grab a pair of athletic shorts from my dresser, and pull them on. When I return to her, she already has herself under my sheets. Her cheeks are flushed pink, and she's timid as I wrap my arms around her and tuck her in close to me. She's the same way after each time we try something new, but it doesn't usually take long for it to pass.

Scooting us down on the bed, I turn to my side and meet her eyes. Her smile is soft, and I kiss it, greedy to taste her happiness. We linger in closeness for a while before she eventually drags her lips from mine and nestles her head under my chin. I pull her still damp, bright blonde hair down and run my fingers through it.

"Can I ask you something?" she murmurs.

"You can ask me anything."

Her hand trails across my abs. "Why haven't you mentioned your birthday coming up?"

"How did you know?"

"Your mom."

I tuck a lock of hair behind her ear. "It isn't that I didn't want you to know. It just isn't a big deal to me."

"Has anyone ever made it a big deal?"

"You mean like giving me a party or something?"

"Yeah."

She tilts her head back, and when she looks at me, I shake my head. "No."

There's a hint of sadness in her eyes, and it comforts me to know that she cares about the fact that I've never had a birthday party—something so trivial. It isn't anything I can say I'm upset about, but clearly she finds it important.

"It doesn't bother me."

"Maybe not now," she says gently. "Did it when you were younger?"

"I guess I didn't know anything other than what I had, which wasn't much."

She sits up and looks at me with wishful optimism. "Would it be okay if I wanted to do something for you?"

"You don't have to. It's nothing special, really. Just another day."

"Maybe to you it isn't special, but it is to me."

I couldn't possibly tell her no, so I don't, and when she returns to my arms, we allow time to drift with the setting sun. She finds contentment as she lies next to me, but I ache. The tightness between my legs only gets worse the longer I ignore it, and as much as I hate having to send Adaline home, I need her to go.

"It's getting late, babe."

She picks up her cell that's on the floor next to the mattress. "It's only nine."

"I don't want you driving by yourself around here late at night."

She groans, and I give the top of her head a kiss before getting out of bed and grabbing her shorts from the floor. When she's dressed, I walk her to her car.

"Call me when you get home, okay?"

With another kiss, she closes her door, and drives away the same time I see Krista pulling in.

"I was beginning to wonder if you fell off the planet," she says when she gets out of her car.

"I've been around."

"You want to come over?"

The offer is tempting. My body craves the release sex offers, but my heart is too wrapped up in Adaline to allow me to give in. "I can't. I'm kinda seeing someone."

"Oh. Okay, well . . ." She digs around in her purse, but her keys are already in her hand. "You know where to find me," she says as she walks away.

Before I change my mind, I rush back to my apartment, lock the door, and head straight to my room.

With my phone in my hand, I lie back down, and open the internet porn site I've been frequenting lately. It only takes a short second for me to get hard, and my whole body electrifies. My head swims in currents of complete indulgence, and I no longer feel anything other than intoxicated delirium.

All I can see, hear, and taste is the hunger I feed over and over again, but never into abatement. I watch the two girls on the screen of my phone as they get each other off, and I lose myself.

Everything drops out of focus.

The phone falls from my hand, but I can still hear the girls in the video moaning as I surrender all control. My body gives in, shooting its release onto my stomach while my head spins in utter haziness. With my eyes clenched shut, I see her innocent smile, and when I let go of myself, the weight of shame bears down on my ribs.

Taking in deep breaths, my vision clears, and I come

crashing down fast, feeling like a total asshole.

"What the fuck am I doing?"

I stop the video and toss my phone aside when I get out of bed to clean myself off. I grab a drink of water from the kitchen and then fall onto the couch with immense guilt for pushing Adaline tonight for my own selfish reasons.

I knew she probably wasn't ready for what we did, but I talked her into it, and I feel like the biggest piece of shit for doing so. My need to get off took precedence over her, and I hate myself for that. This girl isn't ready for all the things I need but have deprived myself of, and I wonder why I can't just be satisfied.

I don't know what to do with the urgency that taunts me throughout the day, and it's beyond my tolerance of frustration. I've always thought of myself as a typical horny teenager, but I'm beginning to wonder if there might be something wrong with me.

I'm starting to think that the feelings I have for Adaline are making my cravings worse. It's hard to be around her and not be turned on, so I douse her in as much affection as she'll let me give, but I'm probably coming off needy. If so, she hasn't mentioned it or told me to stop, so I'm not sure it's a problem.

The ringing of my cell in my bedroom drags me away from my thoughts.

"Hey, did you—"

"Kason!" Adaline's voice is strangled with horror. "Someone broke into my house!"

"What?"

"The glass in the front door is shattered."

"Get out of there," I shout in my own panic as I search for a pair of shoes.

"I'm back in my car." The fear in her voice causes my heart to pound, and I can hear her struggling to breathe. "What do I do?"

"Hang up and call nine-one-one. Do not get out of your car, okay? I'm on my way right now."

I pull on my shoes, toss on a T-shirt, and fly out the door. Driving as fast as I can, I weave through town and slam on the gas when I hit the interstate. Adrenaline courses through my veins as the fear in her voice replays in my head. I can't get to her fast enough, knowing she's there all by herself with her mother away on a business trip. I fucking hate that she's always alone.

When I turn the bend on Bayshore, the night glows in flashes of red and blue from the handful of cop cars that line the street in front of her house. I throw my car in park and bolt down the sidewalk and up the driveway where I see her sitting on the front steps, crying.

"Whoa, whoa, whoa, son," an officer shouts as he rushes toward me with his arm outstretched. "You live here?"

"This is my girlfriend's house." I barely get out the words before Adaline runs into my arms. Her entire body shudders as she bursts into tears, and I can't hold her tight enough.

"Are you okay?"

"The house is destroyed."

"Have you called your mom?"

"I left a voice mail." She lets go of me, covers her face with her hands, and drops her head against my chest as she starts to cry again. "She's going to be so mad at me, Kason."

"This isn't your fault."

"I didn't set the alarm. She gets on to me all the time because I'm always forgetting to set it."

"Miss Rees."

The both of us look up as another officer approaches.

"I need to ask you a few questions."

She holds on to me as we follow the police officer up the walkway to the front steps. There are a few other officers walking around the perimeter of the house, photographing the damage, and when we sit, he begins asking Adaline about where she's been, what time she got home, and if she has any ideas on who could've broken in.

"I don't know," she tells the officer. "We just moved here not too long ago."

"Where are your parents?"

"I live with my mom. She's in Jacksonville for work right now."

She gives the officer her mother's cell number, and after a few more questions, he heads over to his squad car.

"I feel like I'm going to be sick," she says, dropping her head to her knees, and as I'm rubbing her back, her cell begins to ring. "It's my mom."

Obviously scared to take the call, her eyes dart to me in an unspoken plea for help. I take the phone from her and answer it on speakerphone.

"Cheryl, it's Kason."

"Kason, is everything okay? Where's Ady?"

Fear chokes Adaline again, and another tear falls down her splotchy face. "She's right here. You're on speakerphone."

"What's going on?"

I nudge Adaline to talk, but she cowers. "The house was broken into tonight. Adaline's pretty shaken up."

"Oh my god. What do you mean the house was broken into? Have the police been called?" she rattles off in disbelief.

"Yeah. The police are here," I tell her. "They just got done questioning Adaline."

"Is she okay? Where is she?"

Hearing the alarm in her mother's voice, I urge Adaline again to talk to her, and she gives in, saying, "I'm okay, Mom."

"Ady, what happened? What's going on?"

"I don't know. I came home and freaked out when I saw the glass on the front door had been shattered. I don't know how bad it is because they won't let me inside."

"I can't believe this," she says, her voice in panicked shock. "But you're okay?"

"I'm scared," she tells her mom, and I tuck her under my arm.

"I know, dear. I feel awful that I'm so far away." She takes a pause before asking, "Is there an officer I can speak with?"

"Yeah. Hold on." I drop my arm from around Ady's shoulder and walk over to the cop that was just questioning us. "Her mother's on the phone."

He takes the call, and I return to Adaline, doing what I can to help calm her, but her nerves are shot. I watch as the two officers who were taking pictures of the house head inside, and after a few more minutes, I'm given back the phone.

"Ady?"

"Yeah, Mom."

"Do you have a girlfriend you can stay with for the night?"

"All my friends are guys."

Her mom releases a heavy sigh. "I don't want you in that house until I can get home."

The way Adaline is clinging to me tells me everything I need to know. "Adaline can stay with me."

"This is a mess," she mutters to herself.

"I can promise you have nothing to worry about," I try to assure and then skate the line of honesty when I tell her, "She'll be there with me and my mom. Everything will be fine," because I know the only place Adaline is going to feel safe tonight is with me.

She's hesitant to respond, but when she does, she agrees. "Ady, I'll call you as soon as I book a flight back home, okay?"

After a couple more minutes, we hang up and ask the officer if we can go inside to pack an overnight bag. He calls one of the officers inside the house and instructs them to gather the evidence from upstairs first so they can allow us up there.

It takes about an hour until we are let inside, but we are told not to touch anything we don't have to and to be quick. Adaline gasps when we step inside and take in the destruction. The house is ransacked and artwork and electronics are missing.

Adaline reaches for my hand, her face veiled in fright as I lead her up the stairs.

"Kason," she utters the moment she sees her room has been destroyed.

"Let's get your things and get out of here."

I go to her closet and grab a duffle bag as she begins pulling clothes from her dresser with petrified tears falling down her face. Her whole room is a mess—her television was ripped out of the wall and all her picture frames are shattered on the floor. I grab a few of her toiletries from the bathroom, and when she zips the bag, she turns to me, banding her arms around my waist.

"I'm so sorry, babe."

"What if I would've been here?"

"I don't even want to think about that." I take the bag from the dresser. "Come on. Let's go."

We have to wait around until the officers collect all the evidence they need, and it's after midnight when they board up the door and we are able to leave. I pull Adaline's Mercedes into the garage, and she sets the alarm before we get into my car and head back to my place. Exhaustion settles in and the drive is silent.

It isn't until we walk into the apartment that she finally speaks. "Ironic that I feel safer on your side of town."

I give her a weak smile.

When we're changed for bed and she's back in my arms, I'm unable to loosen my hold on her. What if she had been home? I go to the worst-case scenario and pull her in even closer.

"Did you lock the door?"

"Yeah, babe. I did."

This girl has found a way to burrow herself inside my soul, and the very thought of something bad ever happening to her jolts my heart into arrhythmic poundings. I never thought I would depend on someone the way I find myself depending on her. Her love is the reason I'm stronger, but she's also the reason I'm getting weaker.

She's soft and gentle but so damn powerful. It's only after she's finally able to fall asleep, her body relaxing against mine, that I slip on that weakness. I close my eyes and try to think about anything other than her, but like fangs in flesh, there's no hiding. The craving overpowers me, and I'm so damn frustrated that I'm unable to tame the monstrous urge that gnaws through skin and bone, eating straight to my nerves.

I slip my arm from underneath her, and I feel sick to my

stomach when I sneak out of the room to go jerk off in the bathroom.

When I return, I watch her as I stand in the doorway, and I'm nowhere near close to feeling satisfied. All I want is to spend the night with her in my arms, but the very thing I want is the very thing that tortures me, and it makes me want to throw my fist through a wall. The closer I get to her, the worse I feel, but the better I feel, too. It's a goddamn web of heaven and hell I'm trapped in.

I go back to the bathroom and lock the door, determined to expel the poison that's keeping me from enjoying this night with her. I get myself off for the third time tonight, but I don't stop there. With my getting to spend an entire night with her in my bed, I feel manic and restless. Since I'm still hard, I keep going and beat off until I cum again. Emotions swelter as the room caves in on me, and I pull my shorts up, sit on the lid of the toilet, and allow myself to recover before I keep going.

My body breaks out in a cold sweat as I battle with myself to find another release. But this time, there's no orgasm that comes with it, which only furthers my frustrations, and I swear to god, I feel like crying as I clench my teeth and work to get myself hard. I need to get this out of me, but I'm trapped in an unrelenting labyrinth. My head falls into my hands, winded breaths wreak havoc on my system, and I hate myself for not being able to get my shit together enough to go sleep next to her.

When I finally open the door and go into my room, I pick up my phone to see I've been locked away in my festering prison for almost two hours. I slip back into bed with Adaline, and my dick aches so badly you'd think it would be impossible to crave another orgasm, but I do. This time, I'm able to restrain myself because I'm so sore that the thought of jerking off makes me cringe. In my pain, I'm able to find a small sense of relief as I curl my body around hers from behind, close my eyes, and silently love her through the dirty shame that stains me from deep within.

CHAPTER
sixteen

Adaline

I t's been two weeks since the break in, and even though only a few remnants of that night's devastation remain, each creak of the house is more unnerving than the last. I never noticed all the noises this place makes until after the break in, but now, I hear everything. The shift in the air vents each time the AC kicks on, the running water from the fridge when another slat of ice cubes is made, it all piques my awareness and forces a jump to my heart rate.

My mother arrived the following morning. I didn't want to come back home, but I knew she wouldn't be okay with me spending another night with Kason, so I wound up sleeping in her bed a few times before I was able to return to my own room.

Still, every now and then, I have a hard time sleeping. Kason will stay on the phone with me those nights, although I'd rather be at his place. Never in my life had I been so scared as I was the night of the burglary. It wasn't until Kason came for me that my sheer panic started to settle. I didn't think I'd be able to sleep that night, and even though my nerves were rattled with fear, when I was in his arms, I was eventually able to get some rest.

All the electronics and broken goods have been replaced, new front doors installed, and the holes in the walls patched up. Investigators were able to locate a couple pieces of my mother's jewelry that ended up in a pawnshop in Fort Meyers. Three men were later arrested. It turns out they were retaliating against the man my mother is representing who's about to stand trial for first-degree murder charges.

Everything hit the news yesterday, and it's now known that my mom is the one who will be defending this man's case. It wouldn't have been so bad if her client hadn't made his way into the media over a year ago when the murder happened.

My mother has never been in the public eye, but she explained to me that she's never worked a high-profile case before, either, so it was bound to hit the news as the trial drew near.

"*Do you believe he did it?*" I asked, not liking that my mother would defend a murderer.

"*It doesn't matter what I believe, sweetheart.*"

"*How can you say that? How can you defend someone if you know they're guilty?*"

"*It's a complicated thing for some people to understand, but whether he's actually guilty or not has no relevance on the case.*"

She went on to explain, *"In the courtroom, there's a difference between factual guilt and legal guilt. The only thing that matters is legal guilt, and that's up to the prosecution to prove. It's my job to defend my client no matter what I think. It's more than my job—it's their right. In the end, I don't hold the gavel, the judge does."*

I still don't know how she could stand behind a man she knows is a killer.

I decided to stay home from school today because I'm scared to find out if anyone knows about this. And if they do know, have they made the connection that the lawyer being interviewed is my mom?

Trying to keep myself busy, I find a movie to watch until Kason gets out of school. When the doorbell finally rings, I turn off the security alarm, which now has a small video screen linked to several cameras around the property.

"Hey," Kason says when he steps inside. "What've you been doing all day?"

"Nothing. I've been so bored."

We make our way to my room, and he tosses his backpack next to my dresser before settling on the bed.

"Why are you smiling at me like that?"

"Because," I tell him. "I got you something."

"I thought I told you no gifts."

"It's your birthday, Kason. Did you really expect me not to get you a gift?" My smile grows. "Close your eyes and no peeking."

He shakes his head, and when he closes them, I walk into my closet and pull out the Victoria custom Poly skimboard that's hiding in the back.

"Your eyes still closed?" I call out.

"They're closed."

I'm full of excited anticipation when I crawl onto the bed next to him, holding the board in my hands.

"Okay. Open them."

His reaction is priceless, and I can't help but giggle.

"Happy birthday!"

"Are you kidding me?" His eyes gleam in disbelief, and when I give him the elite board, he runs his hand over the smooth carbon fiber finish.

"Do you like it?"

"How did you . . .?"

"Micah helped me with the customizations."

He takes in all the upgraded detailing, and I know he's probably thinking I overdid it, but I don't care. He works so hard for everything he has that he deserves to have a top-of-the-line board.

"No one has ever done anything like this for me. I don't even know what to say or how to thank you."

"You don't have to say anything. I just wanted to get you something you'd love."

He sets the board aside and pulls me over his lap. "If that's all you wanted, you didn't have to get the board." Running his fingers through my hair, he draws my lips down to his, murmuring, "There's nothing I could possibly love more than you," before kissing me.

It's a kiss laced with gratitude and humility, and I'm happy that I could do something special for him on a day he's always considered unimportant.

"I don't deserve this."

"The board?"

His hands cradle my cheeks. "Any of this. The board. You."

"Me?"

"Sometimes you feel too good to be true, and I wonder what I did so right to have someone as incredible as you in my life, loving me the way you do, because you do it perfectly."

"You have it all wrong." I drop my forehead to his. "I'm the undeserving one."

The two of us slip down into the bed, eager as always to be as close as we can with each other. Knowing we have time on our side before my mom is supposed to be home, we take advantage. With hands exploring, I relax into his touch—the only touch I ever want on me.

I reach to unbutton his shorts, but he stops me. Before I can ask him why, he kisses my lips, nudges my legs open, and grinds himself against me. We move this way for a while, making out and kissing so deeply, I no longer know whose breath I'm breathing.

Needy for his touch, I raise my hips to him, and he's quick to give me what I want when he slides his hand beneath my unbuttoned shorts. My fingers press against his back, and he watches me as I ride on how good his love feels when we're as close we are right now.

One hour melts into another as we slow down and cuddle into each other. I'm finding it harder and harder to keep myself from going further with him. There's hardly a day that passes that we don't find ourselves lost in the affections we share. A few times lately, I've had to stop him from touching me before I do something I'm not sure I'm ready for. He's temptation to the nth degree, and my feelings for him are unbounding, which makes it difficult not to go the final step.

After a while, Kason and I go out back and sit along the edge of the pool.

"Was anyone talking about me today?" I ask as I hook my ankle around his from under the water.

"A couple of people."

"Seriously?" I fret.

"You can't skip another day, Adaline. It's only going to make them talk more."

"What if they say something to me?"

"Ignore them." He reaches over and holds my hand. "You have me, and no one is going to talk shit if I'm with you."

"And when you're not with me?"

"Then you have Micah and Trent to fill in the gaps. You don't have anything to worry about."

I shoot him an unbelieving side glare.

"I'm home," my mom announces as she pokes her head outside. "I picked up dinner from Jackson's."

When we go inside, Kason is quick to tease, "I was hoping you'd cook for me, Cheryl."

"You've known me long enough to know better," she quips back, because her idea of cooking is pasta with sauce from a jar. My dad was the cook in our family, not her.

She pulls out the salads and an array of sushi rolls as Kason helps by grabbing plates and silverware. I love that, after spending so much time over here, he blends right in with my mom and me as if this were his home, too.

"Did you get the cake I ordered?" I ask.

"I put it in the fridge, dear."

"You didn't have to get me a cake."

I look at him like he's a crazy man, exclaiming, "That's the best part about birthdays—the cake!"

"She's right, Kason. What's the point if there's no cake?"

"What kind did you get?"

"Italian cream."

We carry all the food into the dining room, and after we sit, there is nothing but silence and the soft *clinks* of our silverware as we eat.

After a few minutes, my mom looks between us. "So, did you two get signed up to take the SATs yet?"

"We registered for next month," Kason tells her before popping a bite of sushi into his mouth.

"As if the hundreds of tests we take in high school aren't enough, they make us stress out and pay for this one."

My mom smirks. "Stressed? Really?"

"Okay, maybe I'm not stressed, but everyone else is."

"Because everyone else is taking it seriously, babe."

My mom laughs.

"I'm taking it seriously," I defend. "I'm just not freaking out about it." I stab a piece of lettuce with my fork. "I'm not kidding, Mom. It's all anyone can talk about at school."

"Speaking of, are you going back tomorrow?"

"Yes," Kason answers for me.

"Why do I feel like the two of you are ganging up on me here?"

They both chuckle and shake their heads as I chomp down on a crouton.

"They're already talking about me, you know?"

She sets her glass of wine down and drops the humor, saying, "I know this is hard on you, dear. And if there were anything I could do, I would. But this is a high-profile case, one that could do a lot for me if I can win it."

"I know. I just . . ." I sit back in my chair. "The man killed his own child, and now everyone knows you're the one defending him." As soon as she opens her mouth, I cut her off, saying, "And before you start with all that *allegedly* stuff, the last thing I want is to be singled out at school."

She looks to Kason. "How bad is it?"

"A few kids are already talking, but I don't see it getting bad. There's new gossip every week. This week happens to be about this."

"That's easy for you to say. You aren't the one they're talking about."

"They aren't your friends," he says, softening his voice. "So, what does it matter what they say?"

I shove another crouton in my mouth.

We continue chatting as we eat our dinner. Kason begins asking my mother questions about various trials she's worked. Long after we've finished eating, they are deep in a conversation about one of her previous cases where her client had hired a hit man to kill her husband, only to find out it was all a sting operation. He's entirely enthralled by the story, asking her one question after the next while I revel in contentment for the relationship they've forged this summer.

My mother's cell cuts into their conversation when it vibrates against the table. She silences the call as soon as she looks at the name on the screen.

"Who was that?"

"Nobody." She takes another sip of wine and returns her attention to Kason.

Her screen lights up and buzzes once more, and when I look over the table, I see she has a new voice mail from my dad.

"Why is Dad calling you?"

"We'll talk about it later, dear."

"Why can't you tell me now?"

There's reservation in her silence, which only amplifies my curiosity.

"Mom?"

"I've been trying to talk to him about reaching out to you," she says.

"He's a jerk," I lash out in irritation. He hasn't bothered to call me—not once—since the night he threw me out of his house.

"That may be true, but he's also your father. And that relationship is important to me."

"Why?"

"Because *you're* important to me. You're my favorite," she stresses. "It hurts me to see the two of you at odds when it was never supposed to be this way."

"He made it this way when he chose her over us. He hurt you, too, Mom."

She sits back and fiddles with the stem of her wine glass, and I hate him for walking out on us. My mother never let the divorce affect the lifestyle we had been accustom to living, but even years later she's still working her butt off.

"So, what did he say when you told him to call me?"

When she takes her eyes off the glass and looks at me, she tilts her head, and Kason's hand comes to rest on my knee when I press, "I want to know what he said. His exact words."

"That he didn't see a point," she answers warily, and even though I'm still so angry with him, I can't deny the agony that punctures through my heart when she tells me this. "And with the baby coming, he feels it's best that your holidays be spent here."

Kason's hand leaves my leg when he wraps his arm around me, but I shrug him off with an aggravated, "I'm fine."

I'm far from fine.

How could he just cut me off like that?

It feels like my heart is caving in on itself and sinking in my chest. I'm so mad at him, and I wish that was all I could feel because being furious *at* someone is so much easier than being hurt *by* someone.

"I'm sorry, Ady."

I don't even try to speak around the emotional knot lodged in my throat. I know if I try, I'll lose control of my façade and cry, and that's the last thing I want to do. So, I sit here, stone-faced as the two of them look at me as if I'm a broken doll. I do what I can to swallow the bitterness of my father's rejection, but when I start to teeter on the brink of falling apart, I scoot my chair back and abruptly excuse myself before rushing up to my room.

My legs won't move fast enough, and the first tear falls before I can close my bedroom door behind me. Bracing my hands on to my dresser, I take in a trembling deep breath and attempt to calm myself. But then my eyes catch the stack of photos from the frames that were destroyed in the burglary, and I look into my dad's eyes as I sit happily on his knee. Memories of how close we once were crumble from all around, and when I cover my hands over my face, the pain I've buried erupts out of me in an agonizing sob.

I fall apart.

My body hunches over, and I cry because the one man who was never supposed to break my heart is the man who completely shattered it.

Warmth covers me from all around as my tears free fall, but his strength never wavers as he holds me with everything he has. I cling to Kason as my sadness dampens his shirt. He grips me tighter. Needing his comfort, I let him take care of me, and when my eyelids start to get heavy, he walks us over to the bed.

My head rests over his heart, and I let the steady beats lull me until I find a semblance of peace. We're wrapped in each other, and it's here where I've come to find my safety. It's wherever Kason is. He's where I can be my most vulnerable when I'm so used to keeping everything bottled inside.

His lips fall on top of my head in a still kiss before he finally speaks. "What can I do?"

I lift my shoulders and drop them just as quickly.

"Have you thought about calling him?"

"What's the point? I shouldn't have to force my own dad to talk to me."

"I know." He drags his thumb across my salt-covered cheek. "I hate seeing you hurting so badly. I wish there were something I could do. Just tell me, and I'll do it."

"This is all I want," I respond as I squeeze my arms around him. "You're all I want. Only you."

"You have me. I couldn't possibly imagine giving myself to anyone else. You're everything, Adaline."

I close my eyes, and within the sadness flooding this room, I find pure happiness. He never loosens his hold on me, and when night paints the sky with a peppering of stars, I feel myself dozing. A shadow crosses the room, and I sit up as my tired eyes focus in on my mom. Kason sits up next to me, and after she sets the cake box on top of the covers, she crawls onto the bed with us.

With only the moon casting its glow into the room, I open the lid as we all grab a fork. And without a single word spoken, so much is said as the three of us eat Kason's birthday cake straight from the box.

CHAPTER
seventeen

Adaline

I walk into last period photography and catch a ridiculing look from the teacher as I pass by his desk. The trial for my mom's case started a few days ago. Most people's reaction toward me is pretty much the same: long, judgmental stares, and mild whispers. I wish everyone's despise for my mother would remain just that—for her. But she isn't here facing the swamps of high school fodder. I am. It's me they talk about, as if I'm the one in the court room defending one of Tampa's most hated men.

We're nearly halfway through the school year, and I've been dodging condemning side-glares this whole time. Surprisingly, most of the negative attention comes from the teachers, not the students. I guess teenagers have better things to do than sit at home and watch the evening news. Thank God, because if they knew half of what the media has been reporting on this case, they'd be treating me a million times worse than the staff.

"He's a middle-aged prick," Micah mutters when I drop my books onto my desk, having seen Mr. Berrystine's reaction to me.

"I'm so ready for Thanksgiving break. I'm sick of this place."

Micah gives my shoulder a supportive squeeze when I slump in the seat next to him. I glance up to the head of the class to find that old Berrystine is still looking my way, but he's distracted when Trent strolls in with a loud, "First one done, losers!" and drops his mid-term project portfolio loudly on the teacher's desk.

"I said not to turn projects in early."

Ignoring Mr. Berrystine's irritation, he makes his way to the back of the class, responding carelessly, "Shit'll get lost if I hang on to it."

"Language!"

"Sorry, sir." He slings his bag over the back of his chair, claps hands with Micah, and turns to me with a smirk.

"You know he can't stand you, right?" I say.

"Can you blame him? He's expired and still has to show up here every day. Dude's life *has got* to suck."

When the bell rings, we head back into the darkroom to waste away the last hour of school. I was thrilled when I found out we all got this class together. It's the easiest A senior class that's offered even though the teacher has the crotchetiest attitude ever.

While other students are soaking their photos in the

developer, the three of us sit on the floor in the back corner of the room.

"Bunny alert," Micah says while I'm laughing at the story Trent's telling me.

Within the dim red glow of the room, Katy walks over to the developer station, eyes me as if I'm some gross leper, and sets her film canister on the counter.

"Is that seriously all you're going to do today?" she sneers my way, but only my way, because she cares too much about maintaining good graces with the boys in this school.

I ignore her. It's hard enough looking at her, let alone actually speaking to her. Knowing that she and Kason hooked up still needles on my heart, and I think it's even worse since after all this time together, we've yet to have sex. Not that Kason doesn't want to. He does. And I do, too. But I'm nervous and scared. Every time we edge closer to crossing the line, I panic and make him stop. So, having to see Katy every day is far from ideal.

Micah slips his arm around my shoulders. He understands why I'm so tense around her. Apparently, she made it no secret of what happened between her and Kason during their sophomore year.

"I can't stand her," I mumble under my breath.

"She's only a bitch because she's jealous. Don't take it personally."

She stands over the soaking trays with such arrogance in her too-short shorts, and Micah grimaces when he hears my teeth grind.

"What the hell are you guys doing back here?" Kason says when he walks in, opening the door without warning and exposing all the developing paper to light.

"Dammit, Kase," Katy snaps at the same time I jump to my feet and throw my arms around him.

"What are you doing here?"

"We had a sub and the teacher didn't leave her with any work to give to us, so—"

"Pretty boy is ditching," Micah teases. "There's a first."

Katy turns on her heels with a huff. "Do you mind? You just destroyed my photos."

"Your pictures suck anyway," Trent says as we walk back out to the classroom.

"What's all the commotion?"

Micah approaches the teacher's desk and distracts him while Trent and I grab our bags and sneak out the door with Kason. Running down the hall, we turn the corner and wait. A minute later, Micah's rushing toward us. "Let's go."

Kason grabs my hand, and we make a run for it when we hear Mr. Berrystine holler, "You kids better get back here."

I burst out laughing as Kason pulls me through the halls, and the moment we hit the parking lot, my feet drag as I try to catch my breath.

"Hop on." Kason turns and bends so I can jump on his back.

"Where are we going?"

"Beach," Trent calls out to me.

Kason sets me on my feet when we get to our cars. "You two have fun."

"You're not coming?"

"Another day, man," Kason tells them, still eager to spend as much alone time with me as he can while my mom's at work, and before Micah and Trent can give us a hard time, we both hop into our cars.

Trent flips us the bird as Kason and I pull out of our parking spots, and I blow him a kiss in good fun.

When we make it to my house, the alarm is already off.

"Mom?"

"In here," she answers from her office.

"Let's go to my place," Kason teases, and I nudge him in the ribs.

"She already knows we're here. Plus, I still haven't talked to her about Thanksgiving."

The two of us walk into her office and find her buried behind a stack of files as she taps away on her laptop.

"What are you doing home?"

"Judge called an early recess," she responds without looking my way as she continues typing at a million miles an hour. "I swear, that lead prosecutor is raking on my last nerve. It's taking everything in me not to have an outburst in the courtroom." She stabs her keyboard a couple of more times with her fingers before giving up and closing the lid down.

"Bad day?"

"You have no idea."

Kason and I walk over to the leather couch in the corner of the room where the sitting area is.

She takes a look at her phone, and then eyes the two of us suspiciously. "What are you doing home from school already?"

"We, uhh . . ."

"Think twice," she warns Kason with affection, to which he responds with nothing but a devious smile.

"You two skipped out, didn't you?"

"Thirty minutes early on the last day before Thanksgiving break. You can't possibly get mad over that."

"Even if I wanted to get mad, I don't have the energy. But it's fine."

"I've been meaning to ask you, but you've been so busy that I keep forgetting. Can Kason hang out with us for Thanksgiving?"

"What about your family?" she asks him.

He shifts next to me, having not expected to be questioned since I was supposed to have already asked my mom. And now that he's here, I know he's caught off guard.

"My mother has to work."

"Work? On Thanksgiving?"

"Yeah," I pipe in. "So, it's okay, right?"

"Of course it's okay," she tells me before looking back at him. "You're always welcome here, but surely your mom isn't working all day, so you should invite her over for a little bit. It'd be nice to meet her."

With his arms braced on his knees, he wrings his hands nervously. I can tell by the look in my mom's eyes that she knows something is up. With her job, she's a pro at reading into body language.

"Yeah, I can ask her if she'd want to stop by."

She comes over and sits in a chair next to the couch. My stomach somersaults when she crosses her legs.

"Why do I get the feeling you have no intention of asking her?"

"Mom," I chastise. "Why are you being so rude?"

He leans forward and hangs his head, and I grow anxious for him because I remember how much it upset him when he originally lied to my mother about what his mom does for a living. He isn't a deceitful person, but it was hard enough for him to open up to me with the truth about his life. Now, here's my mom, fishing around where I don't want her to be fishing. I know how much he fears her finding out the truth, and I would be lying if I were to say I didn't share the same fears. I'm scared she'll judge him, even though I can't imagine her being that way, but what if? What if she doesn't want me seeing him because she doesn't think he's good enough?

"Kason?" Her tone is of concern. "I'm pretty good at knowing when someone is hiding something."

He lifts his head, and his muscles tense when I touch his back

"Mom, please. Just drop it."

"You're right," he says to her, ignoring me, and I go still. He releases a defeated breath through his nose. "I haven't been completely honest with you."

He's painted in apprehension and insecurity, and I slip my fingers through his, offering what little support I can.

"My mother doesn't work in event planning. I lied to you."

"Why?"

His palm sweats against mine.

"Because I was embarrassed, and I hadn't even told Adaline about my mom at the time. The truth is, I don't live around here." He shifts uncomfortably and clears his throat. "My mom and I live up north in a small apartment. I don't come from money like your daughter. We don't have any money at all, and my mother works two jobs. At night, she waits tables and during the day she works at a call center."

When he stops talking, he's squeezing my hand hard. My mother then stands, steps over to us, and sits on the other side of Kason. She takes a moment as the two of them look at each other before saying, "My daughter loves you. It isn't something she even has to tell me because it's written all over her. And when I met you, it was easy for me to understand why she felt the way she did about you. You're a young man who works hard, you're polite and respectful, and I see how much you love Ady in return. In the end, that's all that really matters to me." Her eyes skate around the room and then fall back on the boy I love. "And all of this . . . this is my life. Ady will choose her own life, though. A life that may or may not look like this one. As long as she is happy and content, then I'm happy and content."

Leaning in, I rest my head against his arm, and I can feel his body slacken in relief along with mine.

"This is my daughter, Kason. She's the most precious thing in my life. With that said, moving forward, I need you to be honest with me."

"I know. I'm sorry."

She lays her hand over ours, which are still clutched together, and says, "I understand. I do. And I'm sorry that this is something you felt you couldn't share with me."

"Adaline is important to me, and I worried you wouldn't want me around her if you knew," he admits.

"And you're important to me as well. I hope you know I would never judge you, Kason." She then stands, smiles, and lifts the tension when she says, "But just so you know, if you're coming over for Thanksgiving, your butt will be in that kitchen helping me cook."

"We're not ordering out?" he quips as the two of us get off the couch.

"Don't tempt me."

Solaced with the truth exposed and relieved that there is nothing but understanding in return from my mother, I give her a hug. "Thank you, Mom."

She whispers her love for me and tells us to get lost so she can get some more work done. We leave her office, and when I shut the door behind us, I can't kiss him fast enough. I taste contentment and relief, which is a flavor that follows us into the next day when he kisses me after helping my mother clean the kitchen after Thanksgiving dinner.

This holiday was so much better than any in the past because of him. Nothing but laughter and happiness fills this house. And as I lie in his arms while we swing in the hammock out by the pool, I trace the lines of his face with the tips of my fingers, determined to engrain everything about him in this moment into my soul. Because I've never seen him as happy as he is today.

"This feels like a dream," I murmur peacefully. "*You* feel like a dream."

He takes my hand from his face and presses his lips to the inside of my palm. "Then let's never wake up."

CHAPTER
eighteen

Adaline

I t's the middle of winter and I'm in my bikini, drinking the warmth of the sun. It's New Year's Eve as I lie face down on my beach towel in the sand. Salt clings to my skin, and a bead of sweat trickles down my neck as I listen to the waves bend and fold against the shore. My love's laughter can be heard in the distance, making my heart flutter.

Our final semester of high school is about to begin. The days seem to slip by faster and faster, but I cling to them, needing time to slow, because it's days like this that I wish would last forever.

I turn my head toward the water and squint my eyes open in time to see Kason release his board, jump on, and glide effortlessly across the water before kicking it into a spin beneath his feet. Micah and Brogan shout their enthusiasm while a few more of their friends are out in the water. I peer up and see Trent down a ways, talking to some girl, but I'm distracted when a bead of cold water lands on my back.

Kason stands over me for a second before dropping to his knees, winded. "Did you doze off?"

"For a little bit."

He reaches over to my bag, grabs the sunblock spray, and reapplies it all over my shoulders and back. "You're pink."

I sit up and smile at his beautiful face, pushing my fingers through his wet hair. It's unreal how, by simply being near him, butterflies take flight within my stomach. He hands the bottle to me so I can spray him as well, but a second later, I catch the girl Trent was talking to slapping him across his face.

"Dude," Kason chuckles as Trent jogs back our way.

"What was that all about?"

"I didn't know we had already met, but according to her, we hooked up last year," he says as he flops down on my towel next to me.

"You were hitting on her as if you'd never met?"

"How am I supposed to remember every single person who crosses my path?"

Kason laughs at him, and I scold, "She didn't just cross your path, Trent. You hooked up with her."

"Your point?"

Micah joins us. "Why are you all sitting up here like buoys?"

"Taking a breather," Kason tells him.

"Throw me a water, Guppy."

I do, and he sits with us, downing the water in a couple

gulps before twisting on the lid and tossing it into my open bag. "I can't wait to be in Miami next year. I'm sick of these weak-ass waves."

"You got in?"

"Not yet," he tells me. "But I don't see why I wouldn't."

College applications have all been sent, and now we're waiting to see where each of us are going to be next year. So far, Kason has been accepted into three colleges here in Florida, all with scholarship offers, but he's yet to tell me which one he's going to accept.

"What about you, Trent?" I ask.

"Honestly, I can't even think about college."

"Have you even applied anywhere?" Kason questions.

"Nah, man. What about you? Where are you going?"

Kason's arms wrap around me as I lean back against his chest. "Looking at all my options, I'm thinking staying here in Tampa and going to USF is probably my best bet."

I tilt my head back against him. "So, you're going to stay?"

"Compared to the other schools, it's the cheapest tuition, and they're offering me the most money, so yeah. I mean, I'd love to go to Miami, but . . ."

"What about you, Guppy? You coming to Miami with me?"

"I was kind of thinking USF, too."

Micah slicks his fingers through his long blond hair. "You guys are dopes, man."

"I don't want to be too far from my mom," I lie, and they all know it.

"It's a five-hour drive," he defends before Kason drops his head to the side of my face, muttering into my ear, "You never told me you were considering USF."

"There's nothing to even consider if it's where you're going to be."

He doesn't say anything in response while Micah does his best to convince Trent to get off his ass and apply to the University of Miami. I expected Kason to be happy to know that I have no plans to go away to college, but his silence has me a little uneasy.

The sky has begun to darken by the time I grab my towel and bag and head over to the beach showers with Kason. I should have left him out by the water, because the boy can't keep his hands off me as we wash away the salt and sand. He tugs on one of the strings to my bikini, and I laugh, swatting him away. His playfulness eases my worry about the whole college talk from earlier.

Once we're rinsed off, we head to my car to put everything in the trunk. As he holds a towel up to cover me while I change out of my bathing suit and into some dry clothes, he wears a lustful smile.

"Stop," I warn with a facetious smile as I shimmy out of my bottoms and kick them aside.

"Let's ditch everyone and go to my place."

I slip my panties on and step into my shorts. "I want to watch the fireworks."

"We can watch them next year."

When my top is on, and I'm fully clothed, I snatch the towel out of his hand and toss it into my trunk. Kason turns me in his arms and pins me against the car. He runs his nose along the length of my neck. "I love the way you smell." I shiver, and he chuckles before kissing me behind my ear.

After everyone finally gets out of the water, we head over to Frenchy's, which sits right on the beach, for dinner. I can tell

Kason is over being with the group, so I don't protest when we finish our food and he pulls me away. With my hand in his, we walk in the dark down to the shore and sit.

The water is black ink, rippled in silver from the moon above as it ebbs and flows. A small group of people to our left light a firework, which soars right above us. It pops into a thousand shimmers of blue, mirroring off the water below.

I smile and lie back with Kason, excited to be spending New Year's Eve with him.

"Do they do this all night long?"

"Yeah. More people will come out the later it gets."

Nestling my head on his shoulder, I watch as the sky illuminates in purple fractals. A few people clap in the distance.

"Fireworks are illegal back home," I tell him. "I've never been this close to them before."

Kason stares into the sky, and I watch his face light up in different colors with each explosion above. I could stare at him forever and never tire of the fluttering in my chest.

"I need to ask you something," he says. "Earlier when you mentioned going to USF, I need to know that you're not just going there for me."

"Why?"

He exhales a slow breath before turning toward me. "Because I don't want to be the reason you hold yourself back."

"You don't know, do you?"

"Know what?"

"How much I love you," I tell him, slipping my hand around the back of his neck.

"It couldn't possibly be as much as the love I have for you, which is why I need you to make this decision for yourself and not me."

"Because you're worried that if I stay here with you, I'll regret it?"

He nods and another spray of shimmering light bursts from up above, staining us in brilliancy.

"The only thing I'd regret more would be walking away from you."

"Why does it feel like I have nothing to offer you?"

I shake my head and deny his words with whispered fervency, assuring, "You give me everything," and then pull his lips to mine in an open kiss, hoping my truth spills into his mouth so that he won't have to second guess anything when it comes to the two of us.

He kisses me in a hundred ways, stealing the breath from my lungs. Each passing minute does nothing but solidify that he's what I want in my future, because when I close my eyes, it's him I see.

How could I possibly love anyone more?

No one else exists in this moment as my heart surges, and all I can think about is how badly I want to show him just how special he is to me.

Breathless, I beg, "Take me to my place."

He grabs my hand when he helps me to my feet and doesn't let go until we're back at my house and he has me in my bed. His lips cover me entirely, leaving no spot unkissed until he has me naked. He holds me in his arms, and when I reach down and pop the button on his pants, he grabs my wrist.

I look into his eyes, knowing he's all I will ever want. "I don't want to stop tonight."

"Are you sure?"

"There's nothing I could give that would ever be wasted on you."

I reach to tug his pants, and he's quick to pull them off. For the first time since I fell in love with him eight months ago, there isn't a single part of me that wants to tell him to stop.

Kason rolls on top of me and takes his time as he drags his mouth from my lips to my breasts. I close my eyes as he suckles and kisses, his tongue melting against my soft skin. As we move in this new way, working toward something we've both wanted for so long, I feel my heart beginning to falter in rhythm.

There's no doubt inside me, because tonight, I'm right where I want to be, safe and covered in his touch. A touch that loves and heals, and I know it's him that will be the one to forever hold my heart.

"God, baby, I love you so much," he breathes between my legs, and my vision blurs as I reach down and hold on to his head. Time spins into negative space, and when sweat beads from behind my knees and my flesh becomes too tender, I pull him back up to me.

His mouth falls to mine, and I bow into him when I taste myself on his tongue. It's beyond intimate to be this close, but I crave more.

I slip my hand between our bodies, and I'm surprised to find that he isn't hard yet. He shoves my hand away, and begins stroking himself while continuing to kiss me. The feel of his hand as it brushes back and forth against me is electrifying. I'm so lost in the moment, I grow eager. My hands press against his back, but he breaks away from my mouth in frustration.

"What's wrong?"

His eyes clench shut, and his sweaty forehead presses against mine as he jerks himself off more aggressively. His other hand slips between my legs, but as good as it feels, I don't give in as I watch him in utter dismay.

His body goes rigid on top of mine.

"Kason, stop." I push against his hand, and when he stops touching me, he sits back on his heels and lets go of himself, still soft.

"Fuck," he strangles harshly under his breath, dropping his head into his palms in a storm of aggravation before getting off the bed.

I watch, mortified that I couldn't even turn him on enough to have sex with me, and fight not to cry. Covering my body with the sheets, I want to die of humiliation as he throws on his clothes.

My god, he won't even look at me.

"I can't do this," is all that's left of this night as he rushes out of my room without a single look my way.

The second I hear the front door slam, hot tears stream down my cheeks, and I curl into myself. Confused and hurt, I can't believe I misjudged him so much. Never did I think he could treat me so badly when I was about to give him everything. I swear it feels like he ripped a canyon in my heart as I fall against my pillow, naked with tremendous insecurity coming at me from all angles.

If he says I'm the only one he's ever loved, then what is it about me that just sent him running?

I feel so stupid.

What just happened?

How could he leave me like that? So cold and mean?

How did this night turn from something so beautiful into *this*? Whatever feelings I have for him are suffocated under the unbounding embarrassment of being naïve enough to actually believe he wanted this when it is so clear he doesn't.

He just gashed the heart I trusted him to take care of, and the pain only becomes worse as hours pass, one by one, slipping me into the new year without a single text or call. And for the first time in a long time, I feel completely unwanted.

CHAPTER
nineteen

Kason

Silence is agonizing.

With every call that goes unanswered, another knot yanks, taking up residence in my gut.

I'm an asshole.

I took my own frustrations and embarrassment out on Adaline when I stormed out the other night. There she was, doing everything perfectly, about to hand herself over to me entirely, and I threw it in her face when I couldn't keep my shit together. I was so wrapped up in my own head—so unbelievably pissed off that my body wouldn't allow me to be with her—that I lost it.

The fucked-up thing is that I had no problem getting hard a few hours later once I had calmed down. I jerked off that night numerous times, feeling like a total piece of shit and wondering how much I had hurt her. I couldn't call her, though. There was too much shame and confusion roiling through me. It took a solid day for me to pick up the phone, only to be sent straight to voice mail. I've been calling daily, but she declines every single one of them. I would've gone over to her house, but if she refused to talk to me on the phone, I knew I'd be crossing a boundary with her if I showed up on her doorstep.

So here I am, sitting in my car that's parked next to hers in the school's lot while storms plague the city and beat down on metal and glass. It's our first day back after Christmas break, and it's been three days since the night I walked out on Adaline. I hate that the first time we are going to see each other again is going to be so public, and it's terrifying to think about how she's going to react to me.

Trent slams his hand down onto the hood of my car, knocking me out of my daze.

"What the hell's your problem?" I snap a bit too harshly when I sling the door open and get out.

"Dude, chill. Don't get all hormonal with me. Save that shit for your girl."

I shrug my backpack over my shoulder and silently brace myself as we walk inside. I scan the halls, looking for her as I make my way to first period, but she's nowhere to be found. We don't have class together until third hour, so I suffer in panging regret and worry through my first two classes.

I walk in right before the bell rings, but her desk, which sits next to mine, is empty. As I go to take my seat, she catches my eye from across the room, and my heart free falls, hitting every rib on the way down.

Her eyes find mine for only a second before she turns away,

as if the pain of seeing me is too much for her to bear. In a new desk on the opposite side of the room, she might as well be on the opposite side of the planet. I watch her, I can't take my eyes off her, but she uses her long hair to shield herself from me. Everything on the inside is screaming for me to go to her, to rip her from her seat, to hold her, and to tell her how sorry I am. I don't. Instead, I'm paralyzed by my own misery of being the self-aware culprit I am.

How could I be so selfish to walk out on her the way I did?

The bell hasn't even finished ringing when she's out of her seat.

"Miss Rees," the teacher calls after her, but she's already gone, and I'm next to follow.

She's out of sight when I step into the hall, and I don't know how I'm going to make it through the day like this. We've been so close for so long, inseparable, and now I walk the halls feeling more alone than I ever have before. Knowing I need to get out of here and figure out how to resolve this with her, I stash my stuff in my locker and head out to my car.

With dark clouds sunk low in the sky, I duck my head against the rain as I make my way through the parking lot. I stop short when I find her sitting in her car, which is still parked next to mine. Her head is down against the steering wheel, and I tap gently against the passenger side window. She looks at me through the rain-slicked glass and then clicks the lock, giving me permission to slide in next to her.

I can tell she's been crying by the red in her eyes. All I want to do is make her feel better, but I'm scared to talk as she stares blankly out the windshield. There's a heaviness in my chest, and a big part of me is terrified that this may all be over. I fist my hand through my wet hair as I struggle to figure out what

I could possibly say to her when I land on a tormenting, "I'm so sorry."

Her face pains before she hides it away from me when she looks out her side window.

"Adaline, please."

Slowly, she turns to face me, and it feels like a boulder slamming down on my lungs. When sadness slips down her cheeks, she strains to speak. "Is it me? Because it really feels like it's me."

"God, babe, no."

"Then why?"

I wish I could give her an answer, but I can't because I'm just as confused as she is. And with confusion comes monumental embarrassment to admit what I've been hiding from her.

Balling my hands against my forehead, I battle with exposing the lewd impulses that have taken control of me. If she knew about this, she'd be sickened, so I drop my hands and give her a cowardly shake of my head.

"So that's it? You don't know why you can give yourself to other girls but not me?"

"I don't know what to say. I was a total dick to you the other night, but I never meant to hurt you, I swear."

"None of this makes sense to me." She wipes the tears from her cheeks and fixes her eyes straight ahead as the rain hammers down on the car. "I thought you wanted this with me."

"I do," I stress, wanting to tell her the truth, but I can't—I don't know how.

She's quiet, unmoving, unspeaking, but by the look in her eyes, I know insecurities are mocking her.

"You don't think I notice, but I do," she says cryptically

before adding, "All the times you won't let me touch you because I don't turn you on."

"Adaline, don't. You're perfect, I swear to you. You're everything to me."

But my words aren't enough for her as she stares down into her lap and weeps, "I just want to be left alone."

The last thing I want to do is step out of this car and away from her, but I give her the space she's asking for even though every move I make comes with the painstaking worry that it'll be the wrong one.

Standing in the rain, silently screaming my regrets as they claw at me from every corner of my body. I grit my teeth when she drives away, pissed beyond measure at myself, replaying in my head all the ways I should've handled the other night. But I can't go back. I can't change how horribly I treated her when she was at her most vulnerable with me. I took something so precious and shit all over it.

That night spits its ugly venom through my veins, and I slam my palm against my car. I swear to God, I'll do anything to fix whatever the hell is going on with me. It kills me to know she thinks my not getting hard has anything to do with her, but I can't tell her that I'm the one with the issue.

I shut myself in my car, barraged with a million and one thoughts of how to remedy myself, when the realization that maybe this is due to the fact that I've been robbing myself of what my body truly fiends for. I automatically hate myself for thinking of doing what I'm considering. But I never had this issue until I started depriving myself of sex. I used to be able to get an erection at the drop of a dime.

Throwing my car in drive, I tell myself I'm doing this for Adaline. Because if I don't fix this, then I'm scared this issue will only drive her further away if it continues.

I love Adaline, and I never want to do anything to hurt her, but the emotional fulfillment she gives me is extrinsically disjointed from my physical contentment. Movies and books would have you believe the two go hand in hand, but they don't for me. They never have. I've always been able to be sexual with a girl without any interference of emotions. They never came into play because they never existed for me.

Until now.

The confliction is sometimes unbearable because of how much I've fallen in love with Adaline.

I've gone without sex for eight months, and I feel lost and out of control. Most hours of my day are spent wading in the waters of anxiousness. It's as if I'm constantly trying to fight against impulses that won't leave me alone. It's the idea that if I starve myself, eventually the urgency will lessen. I push and push until I can't anymore. And when I give in, it only makes everything worse. All I seem to be doing is encouraging the craving instead of stifling it into dormancy.

I pull up to the apartment, but her car is gone, so I keep driving to where I know she'll be. Every muscle wrapped around my bones ache for what I'm about to do. The anticipation alone has my dick coming to life. Maniacal adrenaline swims through my veins, causing a cold sheen of sweat to break out all over me.

Thoughts cloud into a dense fog when I turn in to the grocery store parking lot, and when I spot her car, a frenzy breaks through my pores. I can already feel the rush tingling to the surface as I walk inside the nearly empty store.

Lane three—lucky number three—poisonous redemption three.

"Kason, what are you doing here?" she asks before her face falls. "Are you feeling okay? You don't look so good."

"I need ten minutes." I shake my head in an attempt to clear the haze, my voice not sounding quite right.

She takes a quick look around the barren space, and gives me a nod with a flick of a smile. Grabbing my hand, she leads me down an aisle to a set of double doors. Passing through the break room, Krista pulls me into the single-stall employee bathroom, and I can't grab the condom from my wallet or rip my pants off fast enough. She shoves down her panties with a giggle and lets me lift her onto the rusted sink. When I slam inside her, everything fades into blackness as I give myself away to the toxicity I pray will cure.

She clings to me, but hers are the wrong arms.

She moans with the wrong voice.

She smells of the wrong perfume.

Stop fucking thinking, Kason.

My eyes clench shut, I flex my jaw, and I screw away any goodness I thought I possessed.

"Harder."

"Don't talk." I nearly hiss the words while giving into her request.

She hangs on, and I come quickly.

I can't even look at her as I yank the condom off, toss it in the toilet, and pull my pants up.

"I didn't realize how much I've missed that," she says as she tries to catch her breath, but her acidic voice kills the smokescreen I came in here with.

What the fuck just happened?

Realization of what I just did crystalizes and shatters all around me, and I'm out the door before she can put her pants on.

I fly through the store and bolt into the rain that should cleanse, but there's no hope for my rotten soul. My heart pounds through ribs, splintering them with every debilitating pump, reminding me over and over and over that I just cheated on Adaline.

"Fuck!"

When I walk into the apartment, I can't even recall the drive that got me here as I tear off my clothes and throw on a fresh pair of gym shorts. My skin is clammy to the touch, my vision flickers in a wave of lightheadedness, and I fall onto my mattress.

Like a weak little boy, my eyes water when my lungs fill with the scent of Adaline, which lingers on my sheets. I shove my face into the pillow her head last rested on, and my stomach convulses. Tucking my knees under my chest, I grind my teeth so hard they just might break under the pressure, and I release the most agonizing wail as I scream.

Vocal cords strain, bleeding around the jagged knives that force their way up my throat, and I cry out for some sort of relief. But I don't deserve relief, and I don't deserve Adaline. I'm a goddamn scumbag, and it's only a matter of time before she figures it out for herself. But at the same time, I can't lose her. I'm a selfish bastard, but fuck it, I need her because I know I'll never find a love as pure and virtuous as hers. She's perfection, and I pissed all over everything we shared.

Tears come, and I don't have the strength to fight them off. I'm sick to my stomach, needing to purge the sins I know will pollute everything.

In a break between my suffering cries, I hear knocking, which is followed by her frantic voice.

"Kason, open the door."

No part of me can deny her when I rush to let her in, but she takes one look at me and is horror-stricken.

"My god, what's wrong?"

The answer comes too quickly, too clearly, too fucking painfully, and I crack, dropping my head and backing away from her. She meets me step for step, refusing the distance she'll be begging for the moment she finds out. God damn, I can't even look at her, and when my back meets the wall, she reaches for me before I drop to my knees.

"Kason, you're scaring me," she cries and then lowers herself to the floor in front of me.

"I'm so fucking sorry."

Her hand touches my skin like a lick of fire, and as much as I want to take this to my grave, I love her too much to ever deceive her. I look into her eyes, and like a cleaver to my ashen heart, I persist in desperation, "I love you. You have to believe me. Tell me you believe me."

"What's going on."

"Tell me you believe me."

She trembles under tear-streaked cheeks. "I believe you, Kason. I know you love me. I love you, too."

She takes my hands in hers, and the touch is so undeserved. Bending into myself with the dagger of the truth on the tip of my tongue, I tighten my hands around hers, choking on the bitterness of my words. "I'm fucked up, Adaline."

"What do you mean?"

And in a single breath, I strip away all the faith she ever had in me when I make my confession.

"I cheated on you."

CHAPTER
twenty

Adaline

Pain. Sadness. Misery. Heartbreak.

None of those words come close to describing how I feel.

Kason speared a hole through my heart, and I've been bleeding out ever since.

It's been two days since I drove to his apartment. I had wanted to talk to him about what happened New Year's Eve, which was why I had unlocked my car door that afternoon. I tried, but there were too many emotions swarming me, and I needed space. The smell of him alone strangled me. I could barely breathe.

Driving away, I cried.

But when *he* drove away on New Year's Eve, it was so much

worse. He took a noose, secured it around my heart, and then slammed his foot down on the gas.

I didn't know when I showed up at his door that my life source had already been torn from my chest.

In the time it took me to realize that I didn't want what happened between us in bed to end our relationship, Kason had already cheated on me. He destroyed all the trust I had foolishly given him.

Stupid me. I can't believe all the times he told me he loved me, I actually believed him.

The doorbell rings, and I hesitate to answer, but it's Micah's truck in my driveway and not Kason's Camaro. I haven't returned to school since I told Kason I hated him and never wanted to see him again. Knowing how close he is to Micah, and how many times he's tried calling me these past few days, I'm pretty sure Micah's here to relay Kason's attempted apologies.

"I know you're in there, Guppy. I can see your shadow through the glass."

"I'm not in the mood to talk."

"No shit. You've been ignoring all my texts. Now open up."

My reflection in the entryway mirror is far past dreadful. With swollen eyes, hair piled on top of my head, and homely sweats, there's nothing quick I can do to improve my ghastly appearance.

He begins ringing the doorbell in rapid repetition, hollering, "I can be annoying about this or you can just open the door."

"Okay, okay," I grumble and let him in. It only takes him two steps to stop in his tracks.

I turn my back, embarrassed that he's seeing me like this

and head into the living room. He trails behind me and joins me on the couch when I plop down.

"So, what is it? Why have you been avoiding me?"

With a pausing breath of confusion, I wait a beat too long to respond when he pushes, "Ady, what's going on?"

"Kason didn't tell you?" My heart constricts the second his name touches my lips.

"Tell me what?"

Dropping my head, the intensity caged inside grows, and it takes everything I have not to let the tears fall—the same tears that have been falling incessantly for the past two days. But strength abandons me, my chin trembles, and Micah's arm reaches around my shoulders.

I've become so accustomed to touch because Kason gave it in abundance, but I've been without when I've needed it the most. I slump over and another arm comes around me. And somehow, even though Kason shattered me into ruins, I manage to crack once more.

"Ady, what happened?"

Covering my face with my hands, I cry into my palms, fearing the pain that will come when I try to speak around my emotionally seized throat.

"What did he do to you?"

"He cheated on me." And like a switchblade to a vein, I'm forced to endure the pain of Kason's betrayal all over again.

Micah lurches back, in shock. "He did what?"

Curling into myself, I wipe my cheeks with the sleeve of my sweatshirt and struggle to look at him through my wounded spirit. "I feel so stupid."

"Why?"

"Because I trusted him and—"

"Yeah," he bites, cutting me off. "You trusted him to keep his dick in his fucking pants. You have no reason to feel stupid."

I shrug in defeat, because no matter what he says, I can't help the way I feel, which is foolish and embarrassed, because I wasn't good enough for Kason to want me so he had to go cheat.

"No. Don't fucking do that. He's the one who should feel stupid. There's nothing you could've done that would justify him fucking another girl."

"Then why?" I cry as the blood from the rip in my heart seeps out, but I already know the answer. I was too much of a prude for him, and he lost interest. I sensed it this past summer when he started struggling to get an erection with me. In the beginning, it barely took a touch from me for him to get hard. But then he started pushing my hand away because he didn't want me feeling that I no longer affected him that way. It's so beyond mortifying when you can't even turn on your own boyfriend.

Micah pulls me back into his arms, and I cry on his shoulder, wishing I could expel the heartache and humiliation. Wishing I didn't still love him when I hate him so much. Wishing I never got involved with him in the first place. I knew better than to trust some guy when my father showed me first-hand what jerks men are.

I'm two for two for being hurt by a man I loved.

I take the comfort Micah is offering, but it doesn't comfort at all. He lets me cry until I tire, and when I'm nothing more than stingy eyes and a stuffy nose, I exhale deeply.

"So, this is why you haven't been at school?"

"What am I supposed to do? We have three classes together."

"Fuck him," he says. "He's the one who should be hiding out, not you."

I draw back and rest the side of my head against the back cushion. "Easy for you to say."

"It should be easy for you, too. He's a dick wad."

Micah's right, he is a dick wad. I'm hurt and I'm angry, but I also miss him. I hate myself for missing him as much as I do. I hate myself more than I hate him because I can't seem to simply *hate him*! That hate is tangled with so many other feelings that I get confused, and that's when I find myself breaking down and crying.

"I'm in one of those classes you have with him. You and I can sit somewhere else, then all you have is two classes with him to get through."

"Two feels like a million."

"But it's not. It's only two."

I'm completely drained as I stare at Micah, and when he takes my hand, his voice is sincere when he says, "You want me to talk to him?"

"No." My response comes instantly. Closing my eyes, I shake my head, repeating, "God, no. That would make everything worse."

"You want me to kick his ass?"

A sliver of a smile cracks my lips for the first time since Kason left my bed on New Year's. "He's your friend, Micah."

"Is he?"

"Micah . . ."

"You're my friend, too, Ady," he says, opting to ditch his nickname for me.

"Still. I don't want to be the one to throw this drama between the two of you."

"He did that, not you," he stresses. "Why are you blaming yourself for something he did? This is all on him. The guy didn't even have enough balls to tell me what happened when I asked why you weren't in school. Dude knew why and didn't say shit."

I don't blame him for not telling Micah. It's human nature to avoid acknowledging when we do something wrong. But this is another thing that I find so conflicting: Kason could've easily avoided telling me the truth, but he didn't. He told me right away, knowing that I would break up with him.

He cowered on the floor, cried out in his own misery, and told me the truth.

Why?

Why not lie to keep me?

Did he even want me?

But if he didn't want me, then why did it kill him to lose me? Why did he bleed his tears and beg me to love him, not to leave him before I turned my back and walked out the door?

I can't make sense of any of this, and that makes everything so much worse. I wish it were simple, that he was just a prick. At least then I would be able to understand.

"We'll park in the lot behind the auditorium tomorrow so you don't have to see him before your first class together."

"Who says I'm going to school tomorrow?"

He pushes his fingers through his long hair and, with the slightest hint of a smirk, tells me, "You're going to school tomorrow. I'll walk in with you. We'll leave campus for lunch. Whatever you need."

"Like a babysitter?"

"Like a friend."

And that's exactly what he does when I show up to school

the next day. He's already there waiting for me in his truck. With way more concealer under my eyes than what I typically wear, I step out of my car, dread rifling inside my every cell. I wanted to bail on him today, but I knew he'd only find his way back to my house and ring my doorbell until I couldn't take the dinging anymore and let him in.

"You ready?"

"No."

He smiles, and I thank God that at least I have him so I don't have to bear this day on my own.

Micah slings his arm loosely around my shoulders. "Come on, Guppy. Time to swim with the big fish."

CHAPTER
twenty-one

Kason

I t took her two weeks to start smiling again.

It hurt to breathe that day.

It was yet another sign that she was moving on. First, it was her eyes, the puffiness subsided and the red slowly started to fade. I've been watching her come back to life little by little, while I remain in my self-created purgatory.

After countless attempts of calling, texting, and knocking on her door, I finally had to face reality—it was over. It still is. She hasn't spoken to me in almost three weeks. Every now and then, I'll catch her glancing my way from across the classroom. I strain to see if I can find a shred of hope in her eyes, but who am I kidding? There's no hope for the hopeless.

I fucked up, and I've been paying for it ever since. Most

days, I don't even want to attempt to do anything that would make me feel better. I don't deserve relief. I hurt the only person I've ever loved. The one person who trusted me with her heart, and I let her down in the worst way possible. I never wanted to cause her pain. As fucked up as it sounds, I did what I did to avoid all that.

I thought that if I could get myself back to where I was when I first met her, when I had a little more control over my body, then I'd never again have to put her through what happened the night we were about to have sex. The last thing I wanted was to disappoint her again or to make her feel that she was the reason why I couldn't get it up.

The thing is, I'm confused. I'm confused and angry and stressed the fuck out because I don't know why I'm so messed up. I don't know why everything revolves around sex and my constant craving to get off. It's irritating as shit, and all I was trying to do was fix myself so that I could fix *us*. But in the end, I broke us—I broke her.

And here she is, looking healed with a semblance of happiness as she walks into the classroom with Micah by her side. The two of them now sit up front and away from me. Aside from the casual "What's up?" when we pass each other in the halls, Micah and I don't talk. It doesn't bother me as much as I would have thought. I'd rather Adaline have him as friend than for her to be alone. After all, I'm the one who put the fracture in our small group, so I'm the one who should be ostracized.

She wears her golden hair down today, and I can still remember how soft it felt between my fingers when I would drag my hands through it. I can still remember how her heart would beat against my chest when she'd fall asleep on top of me while watching television. And I can still taste the little bit of what's left of her in my mouth.

I have to look away when my stomach pangs in remembrance of how good it felt to be with her, to have someone like her love me and care about me when I'm so undeniably worthless.

I always knew she was too good to be true.

I flip open my textbook and pull out a pen when the bell rings. Chatter subsides from around the room when Mrs. Wexler instructs us to pass forward our homework, and for the next fifty minutes, I steal glances over to the girl who was once mine. I don't know how I'm still managing to keep my grades up, when she's all I can think about.

As the final seconds of class tick by, I'm overwhelmed with the same sinking feeling that comes every time she walks out of a class we share. It's the definable divide that now separates us. Texts no longer tether us during the school day when we aren't together. Nothing tethers us anymore—only memories.

"Yo, Kase. What's up?" Rhett, a buddy of mine, shouts when I walk out into the crowded hall. He shoots me a high five and starts talking about the party he's throwing this weekend.

I only half pay attention when I hear Trent's voice from a few lockers down. "So, you guys coming tonight, or what?"

I peer over my shoulder to see Micah sling his arm around Adaline. His touch on her twists my gut. Whatever he just said causes her to laugh, but it's when he kisses her cheek, that I uncoil.

In two quick steps, I slam my hands against his chest and push him away from her, with a gritty, "What the fuck, man?"

"Dude, chill."

"Don't fucking touch her."

"Kason, stop!" My Everything snaps, grabbing my arm and pulling me back from completely losing it with my so-called friend.

Everyone around us stares as Micah steps up to me with a sneering, "What's your problem, man?"

"Leave him alone, Kason. He was only kidding around."

I look to Adaline and my chest seizes. "Are you two together?"

Too quickly, she lets go of my arm. A touch I wasn't ready to lose. A touch that heals and wounds all at the same time; its absence only antagonizing my anger for everything I've lost, and I spit it out on Micah, because I wouldn't dare accost Adaline. "Keep your fucking hands off her!"

"Why? You think yours are any better?" he goads me with a shit-eating grin. "You treated her like a piece of shit."

And with everything I did wrong, I know I loved her the best way I knew how. In a flash of a second, I have my fist reared back, but Rhett pulls me away.

"She isn't worth it, Kase. She's just some chick."

Jerking out of his grip, my neck flames when I get in his face, temper lost, and fume, "What the fuck did you say? Just some chick?"

"What is going on out here, Kason?" Mrs. Wexler scolds as she steps in. "You want to explain this outburst in the principal's office?"

"It was a misunderstanding. Kason didn't do anything wrong." Adaline immediately defends, and I'm in shock that she would even care enough to keep me out of trouble.

"I suggest you all get to your next class and keep yourselves under control."

"Yes, Ma'am," I respond, and when Adaline turns to look at me, I want to say something, anything, but I can't. My heart won't let me.

Before I know it, Micah's pulling her away, and I want to fucking scream at him for putting his hands on what was supposed to always be mine. As they walk away, leaving me emotionally stalled in the middle of the hall, students begin to move about. Life resumes for everyone but me, and I wonder when it'll be my turn to be able to move on like Adaline's been able to do.

Rhett claps his hand over my shoulder. "Forget about her, man."

With my heart in my throat, I don't say another word as I turn my back and go about my day.

"You going to be at the Battle of the Bands tonight?" Rhett asks as we head down the hall.

"After what just happened, I don't think it's a good idea."

"So, what the hell happened between you guys?"

"Nothing," I grumble before turning down another hall and leaving him behind.

"If you're hard up for her, she's going to be there," he calls out. "Trent's band is playing."

I spend the last two classes of the day wrapped up in my head, debating whether I want to show up at the school tonight for the annual Battle of the Bands contest. I figured that was what Trent was asking her about in the hall before I lost my shit, but Rhett just confirmed it.

I hate that, after all we shared, we're so incredibly detached from each other. There's nothing I wouldn't do to have her back, to have her understand that my heart was in the right place even though my actions were the wrong ones. How do I even begin to try to explain that fucked-up logic to her when it's anything but logical?

When the final bell rings, urgency takes me by the throat as it does at the end of every day. I can't get out of the school fast enough, and as much as I want to fight this off, I know I can't. The more I deny myself, the worse I become. But at the same time, the more I give in, the worse I become. No matter what I do, it's a losing battle. With each month, I'm more and more dependent on the rush that comes with each release.

Weak and powerless, I drive to the nearest gas station, lock myself in the stench-filled bathroom, and beat off. For the moment, I'm transfixed by the intoxication of pleasure that races through my bloodstream. My whole body singes in excitement as I work myself closer and closer. Gripping my hand on the edge of the sink, I close my eyes and imagine Adaline in the obscenest way and shoot my load into a wad of toilet paper.

With my dick still out, I try to catch my breath as shame devours the buzz of gratification. I look at myself in the mirror and curse the guy staring back at me.

What the fuck is wrong with you?

When I imagine all the possible responses, they all come up null. Because what the fuck *is* wrong with me? Why am I holed up in a skeezy bathroom, getting myself off to indecent thoughts of the girl I love? Nothing about this feels okay anymore.

Is it because I've never had to consider anyone aside from myself, so indulgence was always easy? It wasn't until Adaline came into the mix that I started to see how corrosive this craving was. It's made me lose the one thing I never wanted to lose.

Disgust snakes around me, and I zip my pants before bolting out of the bathroom. Every step is a battle to clear my head of my own tormenting thoughts. But torment lingers on, because it's her day on my work schedule.

I was sure Adaline's mother would've requested another employee to maintain their pool after she found out what I did to her daughter, but I haven't been given a different route. It should be me to request the change, but, as pathetic as it sounds, I'll take any thread that ties me to Adaline, even if it is cleaning her damn pool.

She's my second to last stop of the day, and from behind the protection of my sunglasses, I sneak a peek up to her window. She's tucked behind the wide slats of her shutters. She thinks I can't see her, but I do. It isn't the first time I've caught her watching me, but where there was once hope, now dwells dejection.

Maybe if she knew this side of me, the side I'm too ashamed and embarrassed to tell anyone about, she'd listen to me. I doubt I'll ever be able to muster enough courage to expose my truth to her. I'm caged and locked up, imprisoned from the one person I want most of all.

I want to talk to her, if anything, to simply remind her of how much I still love her.

She continues to watch me as I gather all my supplies and head out to my work truck. And I know that even if I showed up tonight and found a way to corner her, it wouldn't be enough. I don't want to force her to listen to me. I don't want to force her to do anything she's either not ready to do or that she simply doesn't want to do. All that would serve is my selfishness, and it isn't me I'm concerned about—it's her.

If she's to listen to me, it needs to be because she wants to. She deserves far better than some thoughtless, persistent asshole. She's so damn delicate but so significant that she's able to bring the sun to its knees every night. I just wish it were me still sitting next to her as it happens.

CHAPTER
twenty-two

Adaline

I touched him.

It was a little over a week ago, but my skin still radiates from the contact.

He lost his temper with Micah at school, and I had to pull him back before he did something stupid. I grabbed his arm. I even said his name after promising myself I wouldn't utter it again. But I did, and I immediately felt the effects.

Like air flowing with a vengeance through the punctured holes of my heart, it stung and reminded me that I still missed him.

I didn't need the reminder, though. The loss is ever-present.

My laughs are forced. My smiles are fake. But the loneliness that follows me around is so very real.

It's February now. A solid month has passed since we broke up, and I still can't seem to get over him. Although the initial anger and shock have worn off, what I'm left with feels far worse. It's the exposed wound beneath the madness that I must deal with. Sometimes at night, I lie in bed and think about the same things I used to when I found out about him and Katy. I never asked who it was he cheated on me with, but I wonder how it happened and where it happened. Was it loving? Was it fast? Was it slow? Did he hold her when it was over? I make myself sick with the million questions that plague me, mock me, and remind me that no matter how much he claimed he loved me, his hands never touched me like they've touched others.

And then there's the vile of jealously. It's a putrid cocktail I'm forced to swallow every day, and I'm so far beyond ready to move on. He destroyed my self-worth, and the aftermath has been a detrimental slap in my face, and I need to find a way to let go of him.

In an attempt to do just that, I called his mother a couple days ago to make sure she'd be at the apartment after school today. Several of my belongings are still over there, and it's time I pick them up. Knowing Kason would be working, I told her I'd be stopping by.

It's strange to be sitting in this parking lot, staring up the stairs that lead to the apartment I used to love coming to. There was no better feeling than to be in Kason's space, a world he kept private from everyone but me. It felt special to see the side of him no one else got to. But all of that is gone now.

Needing to get this over with, I take a deep breath, step out of the car, and head up the stairs. When I knock and no one answers, I wait for a moment longer before knocking again. Still, no answer. I stare at my feet as they shift nervously beneath me, and when I turn to leave, the door finally opens.

All it takes is one look to see that Kason's mom isn't well. Her skin and even her eyes are . . . *yellow.* I've never in my life seen a person look this way, and I'm immediately concerned.

"Adaline?"

"I'm sorry. Did I wake you?"

She's disheveled, in her pajamas, and when I peer over her shoulder, I see all the lights are off in the apartment.

"What are you doing here?"

"We spoke a couple days ago, remember? You said I could stop by before you went to work."

Her eyes shift down in confusion, and she widens the door to let me in.

"When did we speak?"

"On Sunday," I mutter. "Don't you remember?"

She blinks a few times as she tightens her bathrobe around her.

"Are you feeling okay?"

"I think I need a little breakfast."

"It's after four."

"Four?"

"Are you not going to work?" I ask, because she's normally dressed and getting ready to leave at this time.

"I just got off work."

"From the call center?"

She looks around the apartment, completely disoriented. "I think so."

"Are you sure you're feeling okay?"

Dragging her feet, she takes a few steps away from me

before asking, "Are we supposed to be doing something?"

Everything coming out of her mouth is disjointed, and I'm worried something is very wrong. She looks ill. She's always been on the thin side, but after a month of not seeing her, she's dropped a lot of weight and her belly is protruding as if she were pregnant. But more than anything, it's her confused state of mind that's so alarming.

"No. Remember I told you that I needed to pick up a few of my things."

"I think we have some eggs in the fridge," she mumbles as she staggers into the kitchen, not making any sense whatsoever.

Uncertain of what is going on with her, I start walking back to Kason's room when I hear a loud *thud*. I rush back to the kitchen and panic when I see her lying on the ground.

I run to her and drop to my knees. "Sharon, are you okay?" Her eyes are closed, and she doesn't respond. My heart races in sheer fright as I jostle her shoulder. "Sharon, can you hear me?"

Oh my God! What do I do?

Rolling her on to her back, I drop my ear to her chest to hear that her heart is beating. Franticly, I pull my phone out of my pocket and dial nine-one-one.

As soon as the call connects, words fall from my mouth at a million miles per hour. Hysterical and wracked with chills, I pace back and forth, terrified to touch her as she lies lifelessly on the floor. It isn't until I hear the sirens that I realize I'm crying.

In a wild madness, the apartment fills with a stretcher and paramedics, but I don't even remember opening the door to let them in. They hover over her, and I sink to the floor in the corner of the room—petrified beyond comprehension that something awful has happened. My skin breaks out in a cold sweat as tears coat my cheeks, and somehow, I manage to find Kason's number on my phone and call him.

"Adaline?"

"Kason, something's happened to your mom." I choke out the words and struggle to take in a decent breath.

"What are you talking about? Where are you?"

"I'm at your apartment. She was really confused and not making any sense and then she passed out."

"She what?"

I gasp for air, but my lungs refuse to inflate, and I fight so hard just to draw in little jagged breaths.

I'm freaking out!

"Adaline! Are you okay?"

"I can't-I can't breathe-I-I . . ." My whole body erupts into prickling tingles, and the phone slips out of my fingers.

Everything dims, and all the commotion in the room tunnels far away.

"Can you talk to me? Tell me your name?"

I look up to find a man, but he's static behind the blur in my eyes. Kneeling in front of me, he slips a mask over my nose and mouth as he instructs me to take in a couple of deep breaths. "I need you to look at me, okay? What's your name, dear?"

I watch them strap Sharon to the gurney, but she swims out of focus when more tears flood my eyes.

My attention shifts back to the paramedic. "Ady Rees."

"Ady, you're experiencing a little bit of shock." I look to my arm to find a blood pressure cuff. "I need you to take some deep breaths in through your nose and out through your mouth, okay?"

I take a slow blink and then bend to the side to lie down. "I don't feel so good."

There's a bustling in the room seconds before Sharon is wheeled through the doorway. Then another paramedic comes to my side, and the two men help me to my feet and down the stairs.

"Where are we going?"

"We're taking your mother to the hospital," they tell me as they help me into the back of the ambulance.

I don't correct them. Instead, I sit on the bench next to her and hope to God nothing life threatening is happening. My stomach churns as I watch them shove a needle into the top of her yellowed hand.

"Is she going to be okay?" I ask, but my voice doesn't sound right.

"Can you tell me your mother's name?" the same man that was asking me questions says, and again, I don't correct him. I simply respond, "Sharon Stratton."

"Is she allergic to any medications?"

"I don't know."

"Is she currently taking any medications?"

"I—I don't know. She's my boyfriend's mom," I stammer, instantly realizing my slip, but my head is all over the place.

"That's okay," he assures calmly. "Just sit back and relax. Your blood pressure is coming back up."

I close my eyes, and when the ambulance comes to a halt, the doors fly open and she's immediately pulled out and wheeled in to the ER. One of the paramedics tends to me, checking my blood pressure once more before removing the oxygen mask and escorting me inside.

"Are you feeling better?"

I take a seat on a couch in the waiting area and nod, because I do. Warmth has returned to my skin and the dizziness has subsided. The paramedic walks over to the attendee sitting at the desk, and I reach for my phone, but it isn't in any of my pockets. I must've left it back at the apartment in the middle of all the chaos, and I don't know what to do because I don't have anyone's phone number memorized. Not even my mother's.

"Adaline."

As soon as I see Kason rushing in, I'm flooded with emotions all over again, and without a single thought, I pop off the couch and run to him. The moment his arms are around me, I burst into tears as he holds me tighter than he ever has before.

I know I should pull away. I shouldn't be this close to him, but after what just happened, I need the sliver of safety I find in his embrace. He doesn't linger in it for too long, though, and I want to shrink away completely when I hear the fear in his voice. "Where's my mom?"

I step back and away from his hold. "I don't know. They rushed her in before I was allowed out of the ambulance."

"Wait right here."

He walks over to the desk, and I sit back down, confused by the maniacal feelings that are running rampant through me right now. I don't know what to think or how to feel—about anything. It's a swarm of intensity that has me frightened, and deep breaths do nothing to grant assuagement. And now, seeing Kason, hugging him . . . I shouldn't have done that.

A nurse comes out to speak to Kason. I wish I knew what she was telling him. He looks in my direction for a second before turning back to her. After a few concerning nods, he comes over to me.

"Is everything okay?"

"They're going to take me to see her. Will you wait until I come back before you leave?"

"Of course," I tell him when I see the worry for his mother etched all over his face.

"Promise me, you won't leave."

"I promise. I can't go anywhere anyway. I left everything back at your place."

It's easy to see his reluctance when he walks away from me, but he shouldn't worry about me in this moment. He needs to focus on his mom.

I watch as the nurse leads him past the double doors, leaving me all alone as I try to process what could possibly be going on with his mother that would explain everything that just happened. Curling my legs up to my chest, I rest my head on the couch cushion and close my eyes, burdened by the urge to stay and hold up my promise when I know I probably shouldn't. Because this isn't my life anymore. It's his, and the last thing I want to do is give him any remnant of false hope by staying.

CHAPTER
twenty-three

Adaline

I slowly stir awake as Kason gently whispers my name. Blinking the fog of sleep away, I slowly push myself up from the couch. Kason sits next to me, and it takes me a moment to collect my bearings.

I look out the windows to see it's dark outside. "What time is it?"

"Around seven. I'm sorry I kept you waiting so long."

Stress stains Kason's face as he stares at the floor, and I'm conflicted over what I should do. It's clear he's in need of affection, but I'm not sure I'm the one to be giving it to him.

"Is your mom okay?"

He nods, but his hands are clenched so tightly over the edge of the couch cushion his knuckles are white.

"What happened?"

"She's just a little sick," he tells me, but I don't believe him.

"Kason . . ." When he turns his head to me, I add, "I know we're not together, but it doesn't mean that I don't still care about you. I care about your mom, too. But I know what I saw, and it scared me. I want to know what's wrong with her."

He lets go of a tense breath before saying, "She has liver disease. She's been sick for a long time, and now it's failing her." He chokes on the last two words and then clenches his jaw to keep his emotions at bay, but his pain is evident.

"What does that mean?"

"They said they are going to start her on several medications that will give her relief from some of the symptoms so that she won't feel so sick. But they can't fix her liver."

"So . . . I guess I don't understand what . . . I mean . . ." My words fumble because there's no easy way to ask what it is I'm trying to.

Kason doesn't let me falter when he answers my unspoken question. "It means that . . . eventually . . ."

There's no debating myself when I slip my arms around him. His head falls to my shoulder as every muscle in his arms flex hard as he tries to hold himself together. With fistfuls of my shirt gripped in his hands, he doesn't need to say another word. I hold him with as much strength as I can, but I find myself cracking too when I think about how hard this must be for him. Kason has no other family aside from his mother, and I can't stomach the thought of him one day being all alone in this world.

A couple of tears slip down my face and seep into his shirt as we both cling to each other. But in our case, instead of our touches soothing, they only serve as reminders that loss comes in many forms—not just death. It's heartbreaking as we try to seek comfort from each other, and even though I feel it failing, it doesn't stop us from trying. So that's what we do. We hold on to each other with the hope that the sadness will diminish as the minutes tick by, because what other choice do we have?

Eventually, energy drains, and we naturally fall away from each other as our bodies slack in exhaustion from the day's intensity.

"Come on," he eventually says as he pushes off the couch. "I'll take you back to your car."

Words abandon us on the drive to his apartment. It's uncomfortable being in his car again after all this time. His scent surrounds me, taking me back to when we were so happy. And now, we're lonely and broken. But my brokenness is insignificant compared to Kason's. My heart aches for what he must be going through, and I feel guilty that I'm here, adding to whatever sense of loss he must be feeling.

He parks next to my car, and when I follow him up the stairs to find his door unlocked, I apologize. "Everything happened so fast."

"It's okay."

This time, when I step inside, flashes from this afternoon come rushing back. I can see his mother lying on the kitchen floor.

"Adaline?"

Kason steps up behind me as I look down to where she collapsed. "I didn't know what to do. I was so scared."

"I don't even want to think about what would've happened if you hadn't been here." He pauses with a questioning expression. "What were you doing here anyway?"

"I'd left a couple things in your room that I wanted to get."

Defeated, he heads to his bedroom with me trailing behind. I stop at the door. I'm too overcome by the memories this room holds. He goes straight to his dresser where he has my sweatshirt folded next to a couple pairs of my earrings. He doesn't pick them up, though, rather he braces his hands next to them and hangs his head, and I've never felt so confused.

I want to run to him, scream at him, kiss him, slap him.

More than anything, I simply want to go back to when we were good.

I look at his bed, and I can still remember how it felt to be wrapped up in his sheets with my head on his shoulder while he talked so sweetly to me.

"I miss you," he says before facing me, and suddenly, I'm reminded why we're no longer together.

My heart can't take the weight of all this, and I walk away.

"Adaline, wait."

"You hurt me!" I snap when I turn around to see him following me.

He stops in his tracks, his chest rising and falling with disappointment in his stance. "I never wanted to."

"But you did." Tears well up, turning him into an iridescent obscurity. I blink. Tears fall. And he comes back into clarity. "I trusted you."

"I know you did. I know I fucked up, and I'm so sorry. God, Adaline, I am so sorry."

"Why did you do it?"

He opens his mouth but fails to speak.

"Just say it. Put me out of my misery and tell me what I did wrong. Because all I can do is go back and forth, picking apart everything I ever did, trying to make sense of it all," I tell him, my voice trembling with tears on my tongue. "I don't get it. If the only reason you cheated was for the sex, it doesn't make sense, because I was ready to give you that. I was ready to give you everything. But for some reason, it wasn't enough for you."

"It was," he responds fervently as he steps toward me.

"Then why? Tell me. Help me understand what I did."

"You did nothing. I swear to you." With his brows cinched, his face pains, and his voice cracks. "It's me." He turns away, pressing his palms against his eyes, and paces a few times back and forth before muttering, "It's all me." He drops to the couch, head in hands. "I'm so lost."

And he looks like it, too. Like a lost child, desperate for someone to save him, but from what? What is he not telling me?

Warily, I go and sit next to him, and when he lifts his head, tears flood his eyes. My ribs crumble, exposing my heart to the wild elements, no longer protected.

I touch him, hand on knee, and he grabs it quickly. His fingers tense around me. Whatever it is that's causing him this much anxiety, I wish he'd tell me.

"Kason, please," I beg. "Just talk to me."

"I don't know how."

"Why is this so hard for you?"

"Because . . ." A tear rips down his face. "There's something about me . . . and it's embarrassing . . . and I'm scared to tell you. And as much as I want to keep hiding this from you, you deserve the truth."

What could he possibly be hiding that he's this terrified to tell me?

"Kason." I wrap my other hand around his that's still

holding on to me. "It's only you and me here. No one else," I assure. "You can tell me anything."

"Can I?"

"Like I told you before. Even after you did what you did, I still care about you. Whatever it is you're scared to tell me, don't be."

With uncertainty, he wavers, but I don't push him as my stomach flips around in worry.

After a long pause, he squeezes my hand a little tighter and finally speaks. "I cheated on you because I thought it would fix me. I never did it to hurt you. I did it because I thought— God this sounds so fucked up—but I thought it would help me *not* to hurt you."

His pain-ridden eyes meet mine, and my head shakes in confusion.

"What does that even mean?"

There's no question how badly he's struggling, but I'm scared to say anything for fear he'll shut down, so I wait until he eventually says, "I've been dealing with these . . . compulsions." He stops for a moment, his brows furrowing in discomfort as he pinches the bridge of his nose. "I never really thought much of it because I've always felt them. I can't think back to a time when they didn't exist for me. It wasn't until a couple of years ago that it started getting worse."

"What started getting worse?"

His head drops, and he won't even look at me when he mutters, "My need to umm . . ." He hesitates. "My need to get myself off."

His words catch me off guard, but I see how uncomfortable he is right now, so I keep my bearings when I ask, "What do you mean when you say that you've always dealt with this?"

He wipes his eyes with the back of his hand and then sits up with an unparalleled amount of shame in his eyes, which still refuse to turn my way.

"God, I don't know how to talk about this."

"I've never given you a reason not to trust me," I say to try to reassure him. Whatever this is, it's eating him up on the inside, and I want to help him. "Will you look at me?" It takes him a moment, but he does. "There's nothing you can't tell me and nothing that you can't trust me with, okay?"

With a subtle nod, his eyes drift away, and he keeps them downcast when he swallows hard and explains, "I used to touch myself a lot when I was little. It's been something that has always followed me. And when you found out about Katy, I didn't know how to tell you that I only used her to satisfy this urge I can't seem to get rid of without you thinking I was a complete asshole." I listen to him speak, not knowing how to even react to what he's revealing. "But that's exactly what I was."

And as much as I don't want to know, I ask anyway. "Is that who you cheated on me with?"

"No."

"Who was she?"

"Some chick who's okay with meaningless sex."

"So, you and her have . . . I mean . . . you've been with her before?"

He nods. "She never made me feel guilty."

I want to be a supportive friend, but we've shared too much, and hearing about this side of him rips at the tear he's already put in my heart. With each word he speaks, the wound grows. And like razors down my cheeks, I cry.

"How many are there?"

"For the past couple of years, just her and Katy."

"And before them, how many?"

"Only three."

Oh my god.

I hiccup against a cry that threatens to break free, and he quickly starts to defend himself, saying, "It's not what you're thinking. In the moment, it's like I'm not even inside myself. All I'm after is the release, nothing else."

"I don't understand why you cheated, though, because you had me."

"I did, and you have to know how perfect you were—how perfect you *are*. And I never pushed you to have sex, because you're so much more to me than that. But everything got really out of control for me, and I started freaking out when we would be together, and I couldn't . . ." His words drift, and I can tell he's uncomfortable with what we both know. There were several times that I would touch him, and he'd push me away because he didn't want me to feel that he wasn't hard. I never said anything because I didn't want to embarrass him, but it embarrassed me more that I couldn't turn him on.

"Was it because of me? Something I was doing?"

"No, I promise, babe. You're more than perfect. You're everything." He takes a second, and then goes on. "I don't know why sometimes I'm fine when we're together and other times I'm not. It's definitely not because of you; it's something with me, I just don't know what. But it killed me to disappoint you when you wanted more and I couldn't give that to you." He turns to me on the couch, takes both my hands in his, and looks me straight on. "I never should've stormed out on you like I did, and I am so sorry. I tried so hard to be with you that night, and when I couldn't . . . I felt worthless. I was embarrassed and angry, and I acted like an ass."

My insecurities from that night are still with me, I cried for hours, blaming myself for not being enough for him. But it still doesn't make sense, so I ask, "Before me, had that ever happened to you?"

"You're the most beautiful girl I've ever met."

"Has it?" I press.

"I don't want this to hurt you."

"Tell me."

His jaw flexes and he shakes his head. "You are the only one that I ever truly wanted, though. The only girl I've ever loved. And when I say that it has nothing to do with you, I mean it. This is me. This is my problem."

"So, is this just sex?"

"Most of the time it's me getting myself off."

"Is it a lot?"

"It's starting to feel like it," he says as his palms sweat against mine, and I know I shouldn't pry, but I ask anyway.

"How much?"

He avoids my eyes and fidgets his hands out from mine. "Three . . . maybe five times a day. Sometimes more."

Oh my god.

I try my best to hide my shock when he tells me this, but the moment he looks at me, he sees it and breaks. "I'm sorry I'm not what you thought I was."

"Don't say that," I respond urgently. "I'm not judging you at all. It's just . . . this isn't easy for me. And I know it isn't for you, either. I just . . . I had no idea you were dealing with all of this while we were together."

"I know you hate me, and you have every right to, but you need to know that even though I crave this every day, there is nothing I will ever want more than I want you."

"Then why did you do it?" I ask, as new tears form.

"Because I was desperate to save us. I thought that maybe the fact that it had been so long since I'd had sex was the reason I was struggling to get hard. I know it doesn't make any sense, but I thought it would fix the problem, and then we could be together. I never wanted to disappoint you like I did that night ever again."

"And what about now? Have you been with anyone since we broke up?"

After a slow blink, he nods, saying, "I never want to lie to you."

I lose composure in the devastation of his truth, drop my head, and weep quietly into my hands.

I know he wants to be truthful with me, but that doesn't lessen the brutality of the honesty. Even when he cheated, he could have easily hid it from me, but he didn't.

And the thing is, he doesn't owe me anything right now— we're broken up. I've given him no reason to hang on to any hope that we could get back together, so it shouldn't matter if he's had sex. We're both free to do what we want, but for some reason, I don't want him to be free. Never has it been more clear than right now.

I continue to cry for so many things. For everything he just admitted to me, for walking away from him, for being betrayed, but most of all, for loving him and hating him all at the same time. He wraps me in his arms and holds me as my cries grow louder. It's then that I feel the staggering heaves of his chest against my face, and I pull back to see he's crying, too.

The two of us stare into each other's brokenness, and I swear I can feel him breathing through the holes of my wounds when he begs, "Tell me what I can do. Tell me how to fix this, because I can't keep pretending that I don't need you."

"I'm so confused."

"Do you still love me?"

And this is what has me so conflicted, because I do still love him. And now, after everything he told me, I'm not even sure how I feel about the cheating. He's crying and telling me that it was never something he meant to do to hurt me, but only to fix us, and a big part of me believes him.

After all he opened up about, giving me his deep secret, I feel I owe him the same in return when I admit, "Yes. I still love you."

CHAPTER
twenty-four

Adaline

"You will never believe what came in the mail for my parents yesterday," Molly says. "An invitation from Gwen and your dad for Harlow's dedication."

Flipping mindlessly through a magazine as I lie on my bed, I wonder aloud, "Harlow?"

"Earth to Ady. Hello? Their new baby."

I push the magazine away and sit up, feeling the exclusion return. I haven't spoken to my father in nearly a year, not even after the baby was born. I count back in my head and resolve that she must be around four months old by now. As much as I don't want to care, the mere mention of my father's life—the life I'm no longer a part of—is enough to trigger all the feelings of abandonment I've done a good job avoiding.

"Why would they send you guys an invitation?"

"Apparently, Gwen is on the Junior League with my mom, and they've been working on a couple of charity events together."

Hearing Molly say her name makes my skin crawl. "As if she hasn't taken enough from me, now she's making friends with your mom. Before I know it, you'll be babysitting for them or some crap."

"Not a chance. Your enemies are my enemies," she declares, and as silly as it sounds, it makes me feel a little better. "Speaking of enemies, how are you dealing with the breakup? Is Kason still keeping his distance?"

"I don't know. Things got a little weird last night."

"What happened last night?"

I go on to tell her about going over to Kason's to pick up my things and his mother being taken to the hospital.

"Oh, my god. That's so scary."

"I saw him at the hospital." I still can't say his name without feeling it's effect on my heart, so I avoid it when I can.

"Did you guys talk?"

I grow quiet, still overwhelmed by everything he revealed to me. I barely slept at all last night as I tried to make sense out of it all, including my feelings toward him. It's a hard confliction that still has me wading in the depths of confusion. My head tells me to feel one thing, and my heart screams the opposite.

"Ady?"

"I really miss him," I confess.

"Are you forgetting that he cheated on you? That guy is an ass."

The moment I told Molly that Kason cheated on me, he went to the top of her hate list, and she's had nothing good to say about him ever since. Her anger helped get me through all the times I wanted to call him. All I had to do was talk to her, and she would be more than happy to remind me of all the reasons why I needed to stay away. But now, knowing what I know, I don't think there's anything she could say that would cut through the magnetic pull toward him that I'm starting to feel again.

"What he did was really bad," I tell her. "But he isn't a bad person."

"What did he say to you, Ady?"

"It isn't something I can really talk about."

Her voice pitches in annoyance. "I'm your best friend. You tell me everything."

"I know, but . . . He just explained some things that helped me understand him a little better. It was a very private conversation, and I don't want to betray him by telling anyone about it."

"So, he can betray you, but you can't betray him?"

"Molly, don't be mad. I'm not trying to be mean or anything."

"You're not thinking about getting back together with him, are you?"

If only she could see the side of Kason he allows me to see, maybe she'd be more understanding of him and my feelings toward him. But to her, he's a jerk who didn't care about me enough to stay faithful. But I know he cares, and I trust him when he tells me that. And now knowing his issues with sex and how much his urges torment him, it's hard for me to continue being mad at him.

"He's not a bad guy," I contend.

"You seriously expect me to agree with you on that? Really?" She releases a frustrated sigh. "What's going on with you?"

"What do you mean?"

"The Ady I know would never put up with a guy treating her the way Kason has. I still can't believe that you almost slept with him!"

And I get it. Molly and I grew up conservative, vowing to each other when we were fifteen that we'd save ourselves until marriage. It probably sounds stupid to some since it seems everyone in high school is having sex, but to us, it was a pact we took seriously. Then I fell in love with Kason, and even though I held off for as long as I did, I always knew it was him I wanted to give myself to.

"I feel like you let this guy change you."

"People change all the time, Molly."

"I know that. But I can't even begin to understand why you'd even consider giving him another chance."

"Because I love him," I affirm without any doubt. "And he loves me."

"He has a strange way of showing it."

"I'm not defending what he did. It was wrong, and he knows it." I do my best to speak confidently, because I don't want her disapproval. "There are reasons why he cheated, reasons I can't tell you, but you have to trust that I'm not some stupid, love-struck girl who can't be alone so she takes back her loser boyfriend. That's not what this is."

"Well, it's what it sounds like. And if you can't tell me whatever it is you're keeping secret, then you can't expect me to see it any differently," she snips before quickly adding, "Look, I have to run. I'll talk to you later," and then ends the call before I can say anything else.

I drop the phone from my ear, feeling as if I'm the one responsible for Molly being so upset with me. There's no way I could ever tell anyone what Kason fought so hard to tell me. His compulsion is a pain that harbors so much shame and condemnation that he hides so deeply within the fibers of his being just to make it through the day. I'm the only one he's ever told, and I would never reveal to anyone what he's trusted me to keep safe.

The *clank* of the wrought iron gate closing jerks my attention to the window. Slipping off the bed, I walk over and see Kason down below. I wasn't expecting him to show up since he didn't go to school today, but here he is. Just like every other time he's been at my house since we broke up, I watch his every movement as he works. Loneliness makes its mark on me the way it always does whenever I see him or think about him. After a while, the disconnect becomes too much, and I decide to make my presence known.

Kason never misses school, but with everything that happened yesterday, it didn't come as a surprise when he was a no-show. Concerned for him and what he must be going through, I step outside as he's pulling the skimmer out of the water, and give him a somber, "Hey," as I stand on the veranda.

He looks up from across the pool and acknowledges me with an equally somber, "Hi," before dropping his attention back to his job.

I hesitate to move any closer to him or to say anything else for fear he's embarrassed by what I now know about him. Awkwardly, I watch as he moves about his business, and I can tell he's as uncomfortable as I am. It's a strange feeling to be out here with him after I've been hiding away all this time. I'm tangled in uncertainty about how to act around him when more than anything, I long for the ease to return between us. Then the thought that it may never return with all we've been through hammers on my already heavily battered heart.

When he rounds the pool to my side and kneels down to the water, I slowly walk over to him with a timid, "I didn't see you at school today."

"I was at the hospital." After checking the chemical balance, he dumps the water from the vials back into the pool and places everything back in the case.

"How's your mom doing?"

Latching the box shut, he stands and finally looks at me with exhaustion in his eyes. "Better. They think she might be able to come home tomorrow."

"And how about you? Are you doing okay?"

"I'm trying."

I should reach out and touch him. I should give him a hug. I should be able to show him some sort of affection, knowing that he must be starving for it so badly. It was always something he was hungry for when we were together. It was as if survivorship was dependent on nothing more than touch alone, and I was always happy to give it to him. I have to wonder if it was the fact that he'd been denied physical compassion his whole life that has made him unconsciously needy for it to try to make up for all he's been deprived of.

"Will you thank your mom for me for the flowers she sent to the hospital. I doubt she'd want to hear from me, so if you wouldn't mind—"

"I never told her why we broke up," I say when I cut him off, and his face twists in what looks to be regret.

"I don't deserve that."

"You do," I assure him, because even though he hurt me, he doesn't need to be publically disgraced by everyone knowing. I told Micah and Molly because I had to. As much as I wanted to hide from my own humiliation, the pain was too much for me to deal with on my own. "You're not a bad person, Kason."

He shakes his head, refusing my words. "I should get going."

"Okay," I murmur. He turns to walk away, and I drop my shoulders, wanting nothing more than for him to stay. "Kason?"

Stopping, he turns back around.

"You, umm . . . you want to hang out some time?"

I hold my breath, rankled with the same nerves that used to plague me when we first met, but he grants me relief when he nods, saying, "I'm going back up to the hospital after work, but I should be home around eight."

My lips lift in a subtle smile, and so do his. When he leaves, I return to my room, fall back onto my bed, and pick apart the last twenty-four hours. Last night it felt as if I had become an intruder upon his soul, unworthy of the glimpse into the crux of who he is. But what's at his core is enigmatic beyond my comprehension.

What exactly was he trying to say?

Does he even understand it himself?

In the absence of clarity, I grab my laptop and open the lid. Words rattle around as I stare at the empty search bar. Thinking back to our conversation and the way he described things to me, I type in "uncontrollable need for sex" and hit enter.

The screen floods with websites, highlighting words like

hypersexuality, uncontrolled masturbation, compulsive sexual disorder. Seeing these words so blatantly in black and white edges on alarming, and I grow upset when I think about how much I never knew about Kason.

How could we be so close and so disconnected all at the same time?

I click on one of the websites and am taken to an article about sex addiction. My chest tightens as I read some of the same things that mirror what Kason was trying to tell me. I continue to scroll down until I hit a passage that explains:

> Sexual addiction has nothing to do with love, intimacy, or emotional connection with another human being. Rather, it involves an uncontrollable craving for the euphoric high that is associated with the sexual fantasy or actual activity. Many experts believe this intense high is different from the normal pleasure non-addicts experience from sexual activity. The intense craving drives the addict to do whatever it takes to satisfy it.

I don't realize I'm crying until a teardrop falls onto my hand, which is trebling above the keyboard.

> Sex addicts, like alcoholics, gamblers, and drug addicts, typically use sex as a way to alleviate stress and numb painful or unpleasant feelings. In some cases, the addict's sexual activity may not directly involve another person, for example, masturbating excessively or viewing pornography. However, when it does involve someone else, the addict

generally views the other person as nothing more than an object.

Many experts believe that sex addicts have problems with intimacy as well as close relationships in general. This may be due to the deep-seated self-loathing, shame, and sense of unworthiness that often accompanies the disorder.

Visions from the day Kason admitted that he cheated on me reappear in my mind. He was on his knees, shaking and cowering against the wall as his own tears streamed down his face. The anguish he felt must've been excruciating as he confessed what he had done, knowing all too well that once I knew, we would be finished. And we were. But after reading this, seeing how you could easily switch out the words sex addiction for alcohol addiction and it would parallel in description, is heartbreaking.

Is that what this is?

Is that how he feels?

Addicted?

Imprisoned?

If this is true, then maybe this explains the times he couldn't get hard.

When I hit the next paragraph, it explains the differences between men and women with sex addiction. I click on the link for men and am directed to another page with the title "Satyriasis" in large bold text. Apparently, that's the medical term used for sexual addiction in men.

I continue to navigate through various pages that discuss all aspects of satyriasis. The more I find, the more I *want* to find. Because everything in me wants to understand everything in Kason. So, I read until I get to an article that explains possible progressions of satyriasis. Words pop out at me, and I become frightened by what couldn't possibly ever be Kason. Words like sexual predator, rapist, child molester, sexual sadist, stalking, exposing . . .

I slam the lid down, my stomach is in knots, and I feel the onslaught of a headache forming behind my teary eyes. Confusion, denial, and the realization that, aside from the last few things I read, most of what I found describes what he was trying to tell me.

But I don't want it to be true. I don't want there to be something wrong with Kason. I care about him more than I care about myself at this point, and it scares me to think that this might be what is going on with him. It scares me because, even though he's telling me the same things as these articles, I don't see him that way. All I've ever seen is an exuberant desire for closeness and affection. If I was around, he wanted to be holding my hand, hugging me, kissing me, any connection he could get. I never felt like he was pushing me for sex, and if I said stop, we stopped—no matter how hot and heavy. When I was ready to take that step with him, it was me who asked for it, not him. I can't even picture him like the type of man these websites are describing. Maybe that's because he only showed me what he wanted me to see.

A sweet, loving, and patient guy who would never intentionally hurt me, or anyone for that matter.

At the same time, if this is what is going on, then I want to help him. No one deserves to suffer in silence the way he's admitting to doing.

Time passes slowly, and with so many thoughts bearing down on me, I do what I can to busy myself. After finishing my homework and then reheating leftovers for dinner, I flip on the television. But mindless reality shows don't remain mindless when I start reflecting on all the times Kason and I would make out on this couch. There isn't a place I can find that doesn't hold at least one memory of our time together.

Eventually, the sun sets, and I grab my keys and phone and head out the door the same time my mother is pulling up the driveway.

She lowers her car window. "Where are you off to?"

"I'm going over to Kason's for a while."

With inquisition in her expression, she hints at a smile when she asks, "Are you two back together?"

There's no ignoring the part of me that wishes I could say yes.

"We're just hanging out, Mom," I tell her when I open my car door. "By the way, he wanted me to thank you for the flowers you sent his mother."

"Tell him hi for me. And don't stay out too late."

The drive up north is all too familiar, and though it was only a month ago that we broke up, it feels much longer with the burden of space that's been wedged between us.

His old Camaro is parked in its usual space, and I pull up beside it. Jitters nag me when I knock on his door, and I start to wonder what I'm even doing here. I come with no purpose other than to simply be near him.

The door opens, and he stands there in a pair of shorts and nothing else. His hair is wet, and I can smell the soap from the shower he must've just gotten out of.

"I was just getting dressed," he says, walking straight back to his room. I follow but stop short of the doorjamb. He pulls open a drawer to his dresser and grabs a T-shirt before shrugging it on.

The air is silent between us, and I wish I knew what to say. Instead, I stand here feeling as if I'm loaded with my own secrets. Secrets of knowledge from my earlier internet search. For some reason, I feel like I've crossed some ambiguous line. As if I've trespassed on information I shouldn't be privy to. It's a strange sense of consciousness of a situation, and I wonder if he's ever looked into it the way I did.

"You want to come in?" he invites, and I take a slow step into his room. "Why does this feel so awkward?"

"I don't like it."

"I don't, either," he says as he walks over and sits of the edge of his mattress. He looks up at me with eyes that seem so innocent, but I know they've seen more than I can comprehend, yet right now, they're adrift. Just like my heart. "Come here."

I go and sit next to him, my leg brushing against his.

"What have you been doing all afternoon?" he asks, and my need to want to help him begins to find its way to the surface.

My eyes lock with his, and I'm met with the reminder of his honesty, never once hiding from the truth no matter the consequences. Armed with knowledge that could possibly shed some light for him, I take a hard swallow and admit, "I did some reading online. And . . . I-I was only trying to make sense out of what we had talked about yesterday."

He fidgets uncomfortably, his hands wringing together.

"Maybe I shouldn't have done that," I recant. "I'm sorry."

He shakes his head, muttering, "It's fine."

"I just . . . I care about you, that's all." He doesn't react, and I decide to pull out my phone. His eyes are downcast as I open up the internet and type "satyriasis" into the search bar.

With nervous fingers, I tap on the first link that pops up, and we can't even look at each other when I hand him the phone.

He reads in silence, and it spans more than what's comfortable. Apprehensively, I turn to see him running his finger along the screen, scrolling up and down, and finally, his brows pinch together and he snaps, "What the fuck, Adaline?"

My heart plummets, detonating a stream of ice through my veins.

"This is what you think of me? That I'm anything like *this*?" he stresses in disgust, handing back the phone only for me to see that he went straight to the bad, reading about deviant behaviors.

"No," I blurt out. "I know you're not like that. But the other stuff—I thought—I'm sorry. I was just trying to help." The revulsion on his face slaps me with the pain of instant regret, and I backpedal as fast as I can. "I thought . . . maybe if you could understand, you wouldn't have to—"

He pushes off the mattress and paces across the room, raging in fervent denial, "That isn't me, Adaline. I'm not fucked up like that. I'm not fucked up like that." He continues to repeat himself over and over, as if he could erase it from existence if he says it enough. I rush to my feet, and he walks straight into my arms. I hold him tightly, but his arms are even stronger. So strong I can feel the fear in the tension of his muscles as he crushes me against him until he finally cracks. "I'm not fucked up . . . am I?"

"No," I insist. "No, Kase. You're not. I'm so sorry. I never should've shown you that. I never should've even thought that could be you."

His arms constrict around me, and I hate myself for two very blatant reasons.

One, I never should've attempted to diagnose him. All I did right now was plant the seed of fear that he could possibly be someone who could harbor such horrific compulsions.

And two, I lied to him when he's never lied to me. I told him no, when my gut is telling me yes, that what he's dealing with could very well be an addiction to sex.

His denial is vehement, and I would do anything to soothe the chaos I set off inside him. But all I can do in this moment is hold him and do my best to reassure him that there's nothing wrong. If he isn't ready to face it, I won't push him. I will never push if pushing means hurting him. Never in my life have I ever wanted to protect anyone the way I want to protect Kason, so that's what I'll do. I'll wrap him in whatever strength I can offer and hope that it'll be enough.

CHAPTER
twenty-five

Adaline

"So, are you coming with us on the senior trip, Guppy?"

Doing what the three of us do best in sixth period—hiding out in the dark room—I respond with a sarcastic, "You mean going to Cancun to get drunk, roofied, and robbed? No thank you."

"Dude, what the hell have you been watching?" Trent laughs. "The trip is in the Bahamas, by the way. Not Mexico."

"Still."

Micah shakes his head at me and smiles. "You got something better going on for spring break?"

Even though it's a little over two months away, my first thought shoots right to spending time with Kason. Maybe that's because it's all I've wanted to do this past week. Since everything happened with his mom, things have been weird between us. Life forced our paths to cross that day, and the two of us have been wading through the murky waters of whatever we are to each other ever since.

After taking the past several days off school to be with his mom, Kason finally returned today. It's been unnerving to say the least. The first class I share with him is the same class Micah is in, too. I wanted to go over and sit next to Kason, but I didn't. Micah's still pissed at him for cheating on me, and I don't know how he would've reacted if I had sat in my old desk. Heck, I haven't even told Micah that I've been talking with Kason this past week. He has no idea what happened with Kason's mother, either. If Molly's reaction to the news is any indication, then I don't want to tell Micah at all.

"You're coming with us," Micah states. "Have you told your mom?"

"Yeah, I told her."

"And she's cool with you going?"

"I don't know. I don't know how she would feel about having me in a room all by myself. And I don't know what she would say if I wanted to room with you two."

"No way, man," Trent pipes in. "That's bunny slamming time."

"You are so gross! I can't believe you just said that."

Trent laughs with nonchalance as Micah tells him, "Dude, don't be bringing a bunch of strays in our room."

"Like I said, I seriously doubt my mom is going to be cool with all this."

"What if you got Molly to come?"

Trent instantly perks up at the mention of her name.

"Molly . . . yes! I miss that chick."

"We'll see," I sluff off, not wanting to clue Micah in on the fact that I'm not Molly's favorite person right now.

The final bell of the day rings, and the three of us walk back into the classroom, grab our bags, and start making our way through the halls. Micah drapes his arm around me, insisting once more, "Seriously, Guppy. You gotta be there."

"I'll do my best to convince her. I promise."

As we walk past the large windows of the main office, I see Kason inside, talking to one of the secretaries. Among the sounds of metal lockers slamming shut and the excitement of the weekend finally being here, I slow my step alongside Micah, saying, "I forgot something in my locker."

"I'll come with you."

"No, it's fine. You go on."

Gripping his hands on to the straps of his backpack, he asks, "You still coming over later?"

"Yeah."

"Come on, man," Trent says, and when they rush off, I turn to see Kason still standing at the front desk.

A few kids bump into me in their dash to get beyond these walls and outside to the freedom of the weekend. But I stand still, staring at the guy who stole my heart and has kept it with him ever since. I never felt I even truly had it back in my possession after we broke up. So, why do I feel like I can't go up to him with ease when we're still so connected?

The secretary hands him a sheet of paper, which he shoves into his bag as he walks out the door to where I am.

"Everything okay?"

Hoisting his backpack onto his shoulder, he says, "Yeah, I was getting all my absences excused from this week."

The last time we spoke, there was so much devastation and an onslaught of emotions boiling over everywhere. Now, I want nothing more than to disentangle ourselves from all of it and just be okay. I have to wonder if I'm alone in these thoughts, though. Yes, he's made it clear that he still loves me, but ever since he confided in me about this struggle he's dealing with, he's been acting a bit *off*. Not that I blame him, but it's made me very unsure of where I stand.

"How's everything at home?"

"It's okay," he says as we start walking out to the parking lot. "Mom seems back to her usual self and will be returning to work on Monday."

"Kason?" I quicken my pace and step in front of him. With so much uncertainty hanging between us, I give up on waiting around for him to give me any sign as to where we stand. "You want to do something?"

He tugs nervously on the straps of his backpack.

"Everything's gotten so messed up," I tell him. "And I hate feeling like I don't know how to talk to you anymore. I was thinking . . . maybe if we got away from all this stress and did something fun that maybe . . ."

The corner of his mouth lifts slightly, and with a nod, he says, "I have the day off work tomorrow."

Relieved that he's on board with my idea, I let go of a shred of worry when I exhale and smile.

"And I agree," he adds. "I don't like feeling this way with you."

"So . . . tomorrow?"

"I'll pick you up."

And with that, my hesitance settles a little bit, and I'm able to walk away from him with a tiny piece of hope that maybe, just maybe, we don't have to feel as if we're strangers anymore.

The doorbell rings and when I get to the top of the stairs, my mother already has the door open and is talking to Kason with a gushing smile on her face. She has always liked Kason, and I could tell it bothered her when we broke up, even more so when I refused to tell her why.

Kason looks at me without a hint of strain in his eyes and smiles. "Get your suit on. We're going to the beach."

"Give me a minute."

I rush back into my room with a lightness in my step. I can't remember the last time I saw him look as relaxed as he appears right now. There's been an ever-constant cloud of gloom hovering over him—over *us*—for too long.

Quickly, I throw on my bikini and cover-up, toss a towel and some sunblock in my beach bag, and grab my sunglasses. I swear there's a bounce in my step as I walk down the stairs, and I welcome the return of the butterflies that long ago abandoned me.

"You ready?"

I give him a nod and then catch my mother wearing a not-so-subtle grin on her face. "You two have fun."

I love her, but, god she can be embarrassing at times.

"What's this?" I ask when Kason and I walk out to a Jeep with two jet skis strapped to the trailer that's hooked onto the back.

"Brogan owed me a favor."

"Nice!"

I jump into the Jeep, which already has all the windows unzipped and is open to the elements. Kason gets in, and with music blasting through the speakers, we leave our emotional baggage behind as we cruise over to the beach.

My hair whips wildly in the air as we drive, and when I tie it back, I look over to find Kason peering my way. Wings flap fiercely around my stomach for the duration of the drive, and for the first time in a long time, I don't feel plagued by heartbreak.

Once we have the jet skis launched and we're zipping across the glassy water, he shouts my way, "Follow me."

With sunshine on my face and salt water on my skin, we circle each other, cat and mousing our way over to a random cove. We slow as we edge toward the shoreline and then kill the engines.

"What are we doing?"

Raising his finger to his lips in a request for silence, I settle back into my seat and wait. The only sound is that of the water lapping against the jet skis as he scans the area around us, and after a minute, Kason's arm juts out and points behind me. I turn in time to see a dolphin fin before it dips back under the water. I stare down, trying to catch another glimpse, when out of nowhere, the dolphin pops out of the water with a gush of air right next to my jet ski. I startle with astonishment and start laughing. "Oh my god. I've never seen a dolphin in real life before."

It comes to the surface again, this time, a little farther away.

"This is amazing." I look to Kason, who's beaming a smile my way, and ask, "How did you know there'd be dolphins here?"

"They're all over these coves. Look on the other side of you."

A group of three fins peek out of the water before they roll up and back under.

"They're so pretty."

"I want to take you somewhere."

"Somewhere better than this?" Seeing these dolphins playing all around us is about the coolest thing I've ever seen, so I doubt anything is going to top it.

He fires up his jet ski. "Come on."

I follow behind him and watch in sheer delight as he cuts through the water. His golden skin glows against the crystal blue water, and when he glances back over his shoulder at me, his smile is so wide, you'd have no clue the torment he suffers.

I throttle hard, laughing loudly when I fly past him, happier than what I've been in a long time, and it's because of him. Yes, what he did hurt me, but I would be crazy to deny that he's the one person who's able to give my heart a new rhythm to live and breathe by. There's no denying the natural connection we've always had. It's unexplainable but not so overwhelming that it's beyond my capacity to feel every ounce of its power. We're undefinable in a way that makes perfect sense.

"See that small island over there?" he calls out when he catches up to me.

I point over to my left. "That one?"

"Yeah. We're going to pull onto the shore."

The tiny piece of land is nothing but white sand and sea oats and can't be any bigger than a half a mile in diameter. We ride up onto the sand, hop off the skis, and strip off our life jackets.

"What is this place?"

"Don't know, but it's been here forever. If you walk around here," he says as we step over to the side that faces out toward the gulf, "you can usually find a ton of good shells."

My feet sink into the powder, and as we stroll the perimeter, I see he wasn't lying. Amazing shells wash up with each wave that comes ashore. I walk out into the water and find sand dollars beneath me.

"Can I take these?" Bending down, I pick one up.

He steps into the water next to me. "You're not supposed to when they're velvety like this."

"Why?"

"Because they're still alive."

I run my thumb over the prickly hairs of the sand dollar before tossing it back into the water. "How do you know about this place?"

"You see that big island over there?"

Using my hand to shield my eyes against the sun, I look out and nod.

"That's Caladesi Island. Micah and I used to kayak over there a lot. This one time, the current was so strong my arms were on fire from fighting it, so I gave up and it drifted me over here."

He takes a few steps away from me onto dry sand and sits. I pause as his eyes lock to mine, and I hesitate briefly before I join him.

Grains of sand stick to his bare chest and arms, and I miss being able to freely reach out and touch him. I can hear his breathing pick up as we stare at each other. I swear, it feels as if my heart is thundering inside my chest. The pressure builds and builds, so much so that it radiates through my skin, and I can't stand that he's no longer mine. The moment I open my mouth to say something, *anything*, is the same moment he opens his, saying, "I hate this unease between us. And I hate how much I miss you."

"I hate it, too."

He then pivots his body toward me and takes my hands in his, sparking a current of electricity through my veins with his touch alone. As much as he's hurt me, and as much as I hear Molly's voice telling me how stupid I'm being, I know he's who I'm meant to be with.

"Talk to me, Adaline." His voice cracks in desperation. "Tell me I can fix this. That I didn't completely break us."

My head drops under the weight of emotion, and when I finally look at him, my need to have him back in my life overpowers me. "You really hurt me." My words strain as they force their way past my lips.

"I will never forgive myself for what I did to you," he stresses as his hand comes to cradle my cheek.

There's no resisting when I lean into his tender touch.

"I want this," he begs on an insistent breath. "And I know I have no right to ask this of you, but I want you. You're all I've ever wanted. My heart doesn't know how to beat without you."

His words wrap around me in a comforting embrace, and I put all my faith into him when I tell him, "I don't want to be without you anymore." His other hand comes to my face, and his thumbs drag beneath my teary eyes. "But I have to trust you, which means you have to trust me enough to come to me if you feel like you aren't getting enough of anything from me."

"You're enough, babe. I swear."

"You know what I mean."

He nods with me in a silent recognition of the craving we

know he's battling.

"I'm serious, Kason. I love you, there's no question about it, but I'm so scared of getting hurt again."

His lips take mine, and I melt on impact. My arms slip around him, soaking in the heat from his skin, and even through the pangs of fear, I feel the safest when I'm tucked in his hold.

"Don't be scared of me," he breathes against me. "I swear, I'll spend forever making this up to you."

I lick the salt from his lips as I kiss him back, and I'm so overwhelmed that I have to fight the urge to cry. Never do I want to be without him again, because it's with him that I'm whole.

He lays me back in the sand, and I'd spend forever baking under the sweltering sun if it meant never losing him again. With his sweat-slicked chest pressed against mine, the broken pieces of our hearts slowly mend one merciful kiss at a time. And between our profound *I love yous*, our hearts are able to sync together, the way they were always meant to be.

CHAPTER
twenty-six

Adaline

'm filled with jitters as I get into my car and head to school. After Kason and I left the beach on Saturday, we went back to his place so he could check on his mom. She was already asleep, so we spent the rest of the evening in his bed, unwilling to leave the comfort of being back in each other's arms.

When he drove me home, I had to swallow back my sadness. A neediness I'm not used to occupied my entire being, and I just wanted to stay with him. We spent the entire night on the phone with each other, the same way we used to when we first started dating nearly a year ago.

As soon as the sun peeked out from the horizon the following morning, Kason was knocking on my door. Dead tired from having no sleep, we went from the couch, to the pool, to the hammock, kissing and napping and cuddling all throughout the day.

If only I could put into words how it feels to be loved by Kason. I've tried, but I have failed every time. I swear the boy breathes and galaxies appear. We soar past gravity's heavy blanket, up so high to places unexplored, and it's there that we become untouchable, unapproachable, and in a way, unnatural. It's there that we have our love, which isn't anyone else's to try to dissect or understand.

But they will.

At least they'll try to.

I felt a sense of obligation to at least call Micah and tell him that Kason and I are back together, but I chickened out. He's been there for me ever since my world came crashing down, offering his shoulder for me to cry on too many times to count. Their friendship took a hard blow in the wake of devastation. Micah hasn't been too kind with his words when it comes to Kason, and now that we've found our way back together, I regret ever telling Micah what Kason did.

I pull into the school's parking lot and find Kason leaning against his car waiting for me. Even something as simple as parking back in my old spot weighs on my conscience.

But worry dissolves when he slips his fingers between mine and holds my hand. He kisses me for all to see before walking into the building. It's a relief to have all my missing pieces back together and no longer having to wander aimlessly through the depths of despair. But relief is short lived when I hear his voice calling from down the hall.

"Adaline!"

In a split second, it becomes harder to breathe as Micah weaves through the students enough to see my hand holding

Kason's. His face drops, and my heartbeat slows.

"What's going on?" he questions accusingly. "You're not back with him, are you?"

I nervously bite the inside of my cheek, and his brows furrow in the judgment I expected would come when he found out.

"You're kidding me, Ady. After what this asshole did . . . you couldn't possibly be that stupid to give him another chance."

"What the fuck, man?" Kason snaps, not liking the fact that Micah is raising his voice at me.

"Do you even have a clue how fucked up she was?"

"Micah, stop," I warn.

"I get that you're pissed at me," Kason tells him. "And you have every right to be. So does Adaline. But you don't need to come down on her like that."

I turn to Kason. "Give me one second, okay?"

He nods, and Micah follows me when I step over against the lockers out of Kason's earshot.

"What the hell did he say to you?" Micah bites under his breath.

"He just explained things. He feels terrible about what he did."

"So, it was that easy? You just forgave him?"

"No, it wasn't just *that easy*. But people make mistakes, Micah."

He glares over to Kason before turning back to me. "That guy's a dick."

"What he did was horrendous. We all know that, even him. But I made the choice to forgive him. I'm not saying you need to do the same thing, but you guys used to be good friends.

You should at least try to put this behind you. For me?"

He shakes his head and sighs in frustration.

"I mean, if I can forgive him—"

"Yeah, okay," he clips. "But only for your sake."

I try to ease the tension when I shoot him a smile, but he doesn't seem amused.

"I'll catch you in third period," he balks before walking away, but he at least acknowledges Kason's presence with a nod when he passes by.

By the time third period comes and goes, I realize that things may never go back to what used to be between our little group. Micah puts forth the effort to appease me as the both of us return to our old seats next to Kason, but the two of them don't speak. When sixth period hits, I'm over being the center of the senior class's headline news of the day. And now I have to deal with Katy's snide remarks. Aside from Micah, nobody—not even Trent—knows what happened between me and Kason, which is a blessing because the last thing Katy needs is that ammo of information to rub in my face. All anyone knows is that we were a couple, then we weren't, and now we are again.

The bell couldn't come fast enough, but by the time I make it to my car, Kason has already left. My stomach sinks a little now that I know the reason why he's always running out of school so fast at the end of the day. We haven't spoken about any of that stuff since the night I showed him that website, but that doesn't mean I haven't thought about it. That fact that he's speeding off because of his compulsive need to get off bothers me. In a weird way, it feels like a rejection of sorts. The fact that he chose to run off instead of coming to me, knowing my mom is at work and we'd have the house to ourselves.

I try not to let it get to me as I head home. I busy myself with homework while Kason's at work, but surprise lifts the burden of waiting when my mom comes home early.

"Well, that's over with," she exhausts when she sets her briefcase on the kitchen counter.

"What are you talking about?"

"Today was sentencing for the Mckenna case. Of course, he's exercising his right to an appeal, so technically it's not officially over, but no judge in his right mind is going to reconsider this case."

"So, what's the going rate for a convicted killer? How many years did he get?"

"Life without the possibility of parole." She pulls out her pearl earrings and kicks off her heels, still frustrated that she lost the case. "What do you say we go out to dinner tonight?"

"Kason's coming over."

"Then we'll drag him along with us." She smiles and leans against the center island. "So . . ." she starts, dragging out the word, and I'm already rolling my eyes at her incessant need to dig for information. "You two seemed happy this weekend."

"Your point?"

"I take it you guys worked things out . . . whatever those things were that you refuse to tell your one and only mother."

I hop off the barstool and open the fridge. "You don't need to know everything, Mom." I pull out a soda and pop the tab.

"Is this how it's going to be? You're getting older and no longer need me?"

"Pity party much," I tease. "And I never said I didn't need you, but I'm almost eighteen. I'm not a little kid anymore."

"I hate that, you know? I swear it feels like yesterday that I was still packing your lunch and putting your hair in pigtails."

The doorbell sounds, and I glance at the clock and smile. I'm saved by Kason.

"Thank god you're here," I exaggerate when I open the door. "My mother's not coping well with my excessive aging."

"Forgive me for wanting to keep you mine for a little bit longer." Her voice billows from the kitchen, which causes Kason to chuckle under his breath.

"What did I miss?" he questions as he looks to her from over my shoulder.

"My baby is about to turn eighteen."

"Don't get her started," I tell him before kissing his beautiful smile.

With her heels back on, she grabs her purse and walks over to us. "You hungry, Kason?"

"Starved."

The three of us head out to the garage, and Kason and my mom slip right back into the comfortable bond they've always shared, as if no time has passed at all. I hop into the back seat of the SUV so that Kason can sit in the front with her.

"What are you in the mood for?"

"Well, this goes against your usual fancy choices, but I could go for a burger after working in the sun all afternoon."

"You're speaking my language today, Kason. After the day I had, that sounds perfect."

We head over to BurgerFi where we sit outside and eat burgers and a big basket of cry fries. The sun begins to set, taking the temperature down with it, and I sit back to enjoy the heat's remission.

"Kason, I never heard if you've made your decision of which college you're going to," my mother says.

The day I found out that Kason was choosing USF was the

same night we started to fall apart, so I never got around to mentioning it. And I've been giving her the runaround every time she asks if I've made my choice yet. There was never any question that I would follow Kason, but when we broke up, everything went right back into undecided territory.

"USF," he tells her. "But I wanted to talk to you about that."

She sets her iced tea on the table and gives him her full attention.

"I've been going over different degree paths and find myself gravitating toward pre-law and wanted your opinion."

"Well, if you're interested in going to law school, I wouldn't suggest a pre-law path. When it comes time to apply to law schools, as surprising as it sounds, they tend to look down on pre-law majors because it isn't a rigorous undergrad degree," she tells him before explaining, "What they're looking for are students with a serious degree that requires a lot of discipline, coupled with a high GPA to prove you have what it takes to apply yourself in law school. So, certainly, stay away from anything arts and humanities."

I sip my iced tea as they continue to talk about different degree options and the areas of law he's interested in. It impresses me that Kason already has ideas and goals for what he wants out of life, especially since I'm clueless as to what I want to do. It's clear my mother is impressed as well when she offers, "If you want, I can make a few calls and see what I can do about getting you into a position that will allow you some firsthand experience with the legal system and how it all works behind the scenes."

"You mean a job?"

"Wouldn't pay much in the beginning, but it might help you decide if this is a career path you want to go down."

His brows lift in gratitude. "You'd do that for me?"

"Under one condition."

"Anything."

"You convince my daughter that college is more than sororities and football games."

"Mom!"

Kason reaches over, squeezes my knee, and gives me an endearing smile. "I'll work on her."

After we're home from dinner, my mom calls it an early night while Kason and I crawl into the hammock underneath the stars. I tangle my legs with his and use his shoulder as a pillow. Comfort never felt as good as what it does with him.

"I've missed this," I murmur as I drape my arm across his middle, relaxing fully against him.

His fingers comb through my hair, and my eyes fall shut. As we sway back and forth under the glow of the full moon, my mind drifts back to earlier today. It's hard knowing that the reason behind Kason cheating on me is something that will forever stay between the two of us. What's even harder is that Micah won't ever understand the reasons behind why his friend behaved so badly. It's the invisible wedge that will always be lodged between us and them.

But a part of that wedge separates Kason and I, too.

One thing I need to help rebuild my trust in him is to have complete transparency. It wouldn't be honest to say that it didn't bother me when he rushed out of school today. The situation is delicate, and I know I run the risk of upsetting him or embarrassing him, but I need us to be different from what we were before so we don't wind up in the same situation.

With a deep breath in, willing courage to speak, I open my eyes and scoot up to rest my head next to his. His breath sweeps across my face so sweetly as we lie face to face, and when he tucks a lock of my hair behind my ear, I force myself to open up to him so that hopefully he will open up to me.

"There's something I want to talk to you about."

He slowly runs his fingers along the tender skin behind my ear and down my neck. "What is it?"

"I wouldn't bring it up, but . . . I want us to be honest with each other."

His lips brush against mine before he plants a soft kiss on them. "You can tell me anything, babe."

I take a moment before I speak. "Today when you left school in a hurry . . . you told me why, but . . ." I pause in the awkwardness, not used to talking about something as sensitive as this.

"But what?"

Tucking my chin down slightly to avoid eye contact, I admit, "It made me feel like you didn't want me."

He releases a pained breath at the same time he pulls me into his arms.

"I don't want to make a big deal about it. I just don't understand why you couldn't come to me."

He leans back with burdened eyes when he confesses, "Because I never want to use you like that."

"You're not using me, Kason. I love you. And if it's something you need, I want to be the one you come to."

I run my hand along his jaw to find it's clenched down, and when it eventually relaxes under my touch, his voice breaks. "It's not that easy for me. I've always been alone in this."

I press my lips to his in a gentle kiss. "But you're not alone anymore."

His expression bears an unspoken need for security, and I

give it to him willingly, asserting, "I love you. Every piece of you. Even the ones you hate." I kiss him again. "I don't ever want you to feel alone. But I don't want to feel alone, either. I want you to want me."

"God, babe, I do. And I'm sorry I didn't come to you when I should have today, but that doesn't mean I didn't want you." He takes in an uneven breath. "It's hard not to want to hide this from you because it's embarrassing. It makes me feel really weak."

"If you're worried about that, don't be. That isn't how I see you at all."

Taking my face in his hands, emotion ridden and fervent, he kisses me. It's open and deep as he spills his love into my mouth, allowing me to taste his vulnerability. We continue to move, hands exploring intimately as we silently plead for closeness. But it's far beyond my skin that I need him to touch. It's what lies beneath. It's the part of me that only he can reach. And when our hands find their way down each other's pants, my breath catches, and I swear it's my soul he's touching.

CHAPTER
twenty-seven

Kason

It's the middle of March. Adaline called me as soon as she woke this morning to tell me that this day a year ago was the day we first bumped into each other at school. I can still remember it clearly, how quickly the new girl crept under my skin. In many ways, I used to be scared of Adaline, but more than anything, it was my own insecurities that I was afraid of. She's so far from the girl I initially perceived her to be, though. She's accepting beyond limits, never once looking down on me or treating me as a charity case. And above all, she accepts me at my worst.

It's been hard to give her the openness she demands from me, but I understand why she needs it so badly. I destroyed her trust. Never did I expect her to forgive me, but she has,

and in return, I hand over whatever it is she needs to help her heal.

Slowly, brick by brick, I've been tearing down the walls I spent years building around myself. Walls I had gotten so used to hiding behind. Walls that kept me safe from judgment and persecution. Confessing to Adaline how badly my body aches killed me, but she took my words into her hands and has been nurturing them ever since, never once using them against me even when they inflict bruises on her insecurities.

She threw me the biggest lifeline when she opened her heart back up to me, and I swore to her that I would be the man that she needed me to be before. The man I was too scared to be. But it hasn't been easy because it forces me to show her sides of me I don't want her to see. She told me a while ago how much it upset her that I wouldn't turn to her to fulfill my sexual cravings. It trampled on her self-confidence and made her believe I didn't desire her. So now, as weak as it makes me, I turn to her, all the while, feeling like shit for using her. She swears it isn't like that, but I taste the bile of truth every time I turn to her for a hand job or a blow job.

There's no denying it—I'm using her—no matter how much she tries to convince me otherwise.

And then there are the times when she can't help me. The days my mind plays tricks on me, and I can't get hard. Those are the days I'm forced to leave her and go home so I can get myself off. She does her best to assure me everything's okay and that she isn't upset. She fights herself to hide it—to hide the fact that loving a guy like me isn't easy. But I hear the pain in her breath. I see it in the red in her eyes. And for that, I vow to love her even harder.

"What are you thinking about?"

I look over to where she lies on her stomach, not realizing how lost I was in my thoughts. Since her head is down at the other end of the mattress and her small feet are resting on the pillow next to me, she's in the perfect position for me to reach over and playfully squeeze her butt. She giggles, biting the pen that's tucked between her fingers.

"What did your mom say when you told her?"

"Knowing I'd still be under your good influence, she was thrilled."

I've been nervous about her mother's reaction when she found out that Adaline had decided to stay here and go to college. I didn't want her to think her daughter was holding herself back for me, even though I know that's exactly what she's doing. But Adaline is strong-willed about her choice and there's no convincing her otherwise.

"I don't even understand what half these courses are all about," she mumbles as she flips through the USF course catalog. "I mean, Human Geography?" She looks over her shoulder at me. "Do you have any clue what that is? And what about this?" she adds, stabbing her pen against the page. "There's a class called The Enlightenment. No joke! It's seriously called that."

I laugh at her annoyed frustration. "You need to put that catalog away."

Slinging it to the floor, she flings her pen too before turning around on the bed and curling up next to me.

"I seriously feel like I'm going to be wasting my time going to college."

"You're not wasting your time," I try to assure her. "Not everyone goes in their freshman year knowing what they want to do."

"You are."

"I'm one person, Adaline. I'm sure there are thousands that are as unsure as you are. Just look at Trent."

She cranes her head back and glares at me. "I can't believe you just compared me to Trent of all people."

"You're so testy today."

I flip her onto her back, and her lips curve into temptation when she teases, "So, what are you going to do about it?"

Her fingers drag along my neck and into my hair, and when I resist her tug to pull me closer, she lifts up to me. Her lips are soft against mine, tasting sweet like candy from the gloss she wears. She drops her head back to the pillow as I lean into her, and when I pull her bottom lip between my teeth and take a soft nibble, she's nothing but breathless giggles.

I drop kisses from behind her ear and down her neck until I find the spot where her heart beats against my lips. While I linger there for a moment and relish her life source as it pulses into my kiss, she gathers the hem of my shirt in her hands. I reach over my head and pull it off, and when I come back down to her, she blushes.

"What's wrong?"

Bashful, she pauses before lifting her eyes that are so damn innocent when she asks, "Do you think we can try again?"

Apprehension surfaces, and I want to tell her no for fear that I'll fuck this up all over again. But she has her fears, too, and rejection is a big one, especially after I broke her trust. She has a hard time understanding that she's the one I've been the most intimate with, and that those other girls, even though I had sex with them, were nothing meaningful to me.

When I see her sinking into herself, I gently push her cheek so she looks up at me. Swallowing my pride, I give her my truth and confess my uncertainty. "What if I can't?"

It's like a switchblade to my heart when I see her eyes fall. "Will you try?"

Before I give her another reason to doubt herself, I tug the strap of her top down and spill my lips along her collarbone. As we move, the voices in my head become louder, telling me I won't be able to get hard and that I'll only disappoint again.

She sits up, and I peel off her top and unhook her bra. When I lower myself back on top of her, I take her in my mouth, sucking gently as my unbounding nerves cause me to break out in a cold sweat. Her hands grip my shoulders as I move to her other breast, but my body is already failing me.

My mind should be on her, on us, but instead, it's only on myself as I try to temper the irritation that's starting to brew.

Adaline turns to her side, and when she crawls on top of me, I close my eyes and will myself to relax. She unfastens my shorts and tugs them down, and I want to die of embarrassment because I'm not the least bit hard. I can't even fucking look at her, and mortification takes an ax to my ego when she puts my limp dick into her mouth.

I'm such a fucking loser, completely worthless to this girl who deserves so much more than this shit.

"Adaline, stop." I push her shoulders away, and I hate the pitiful look in her eyes when she sits up between my legs. "Just fucking stop."

The moment I see her chin tremble, I want to run out on her because I'm so damn pissed off at myself. But I did that once, and I swore I'd never do it again. I don't know how to deal with feeling this useless to someone else.

She grabs the comforter, pulling it over us, and when she lies down next to me, I can't even face her. I turn away, giving her my back. It's not as bad as running out the door, but still a dick move, and I feel like an ass when she selflessly lays her hand on my back with a whispered, "It's fine."

But it isn't fine. None of this is.

"I don't know what the fuck is wrong with me."

"Nothing is wrong with you, Kason."

We both know that's a lie. If there were nothing wrong with me, we'd be having sex right now.

With both of us unsure of what to say, we abandon words. Adaline wraps her arms around me from behind and presses her cheek against my back, dropping kisses on my shoulder blades every now and then. I can't look at her, so I remain quiet as anger festers.

Tension doesn't lift easily, and before I know it, the room darkens as the sun sets and Adaline's breathing deepens and steadies. I finally turn around to find she's asleep, which gives me the strength to gather her in my arms and give her my cowardly, "I'm sorry."

Emotions begin swarming, and without thought, my arms fasten around her more tightly until the pressure becomes too much and wakes her. She stares into my eyes and silently begs to understand, and I can't deny her when I've already let her down in so many other ways. I give her the best I can offer in my own confused state of mind when I say, "Maybe it's because I'm afraid I'll disappoint you."

"That isn't possible."

"I don't even know what's possible anymore."

She nestles herself deeper into my hold, pressing the side of her face against my chest and over my solemn heart. "We'll keep trying," she says, and fuck if that doesn't make me fall even harder for her. Her understanding is far beyond what I ever could have imagined.

"There's something I've been wanting to ask you. I just don't know how to bring it up."

Fully aware of her need for peace and honesty, I grow wary but encourage her regardless. "You know you can ask me anything."

"It feels invasive, but . . ."

Her words drift as she second-guesses herself, and now my curiosity is piqued. "Don't leave me hanging, babe."

"I was wondering how old you were when you first . . . you know . . . the first time you had sex."

She's asked me this once before when she found out about Katy, but the question was easier to dodge back then. Half-truths and misdirections are no longer an option.

"I was young." I stall because I'm worried about her reaction as I think back to the girl who used to sneak off with me after school. She lived in the same complex as me, and we'd hide behind a bunch of tall bamboo that lined against one of the apartment buildings. It started out with innocent kisses, but she eventually started letting me touch her boobs. I can still remember the excitement I felt when she asked to see my dick. Soon those kisses turned into touching, until one day she asked me to put it inside her.

"How young?"

"Twelve," I tell her and then flinch, realizing my lie when my mind flashes back farther than what I intended it to.

She catches my knee-jerk reaction. "What?"

My gut knots as a wave of nausea crashes over me, and I shake my head.

"What is it?"

"Nothing."

Suddenly, a handful of memories fire off inside me, memories I long ago buried. Ribs constrict around my lungs when I push against the questioning look she wears so boldly. Needing space to breathe, I drop my arms from around her and sit up, resting my back against the wall. She pushes herself so she's next to me, and the blanket falls from her naked breasts, but she doesn't move to cover herself.

There's caution in her pause before she asks, "Did something happen before then?"

"I don't want to talk about it."

Her eyes widen in worry at the sternness in my tone, and she knows. Somehow, she just knows. There's a hint of horror that reveals itself against the tense lines of her face.

I can't look at her like this.

Throwing the sheet over my lap, I pull my knees up and drop my head.

"Kason?"

I tense under her touch when it lands softly on my shoulder and shake my head, wishing for the strength my walls used to provide me, the walls I tore down for her. And when she says my name again, my chest heaves as I fight against the visions that play behind my closed lids. Adaline sees right through me. She knows when I shut down. I also know that she isn't going to let me hide from her.

"Will you tell me what happened."

How do I say what I've never said before?

"There's so much about me that's messed up." My voice is weakened in misery.

There's monumental fear within the silence between us, but it's when she finally asks the burdening question, "Did someone hurt you?" that I crack.

With no more fight in me, I give her the darkest and ugliest parts of me when I nod. Her arms lock around me as fast as mine grab ahold of her. Shame and disgust stain me from the inside out, and it takes every ounce of energy I have to keep myself from breaking down. I know I'm holding her too tightly, but I'm on the verge of slipping off the edge. I have no other choice but to cling on as hard as I can, especially when she asks, "How old were you?"

"Eight."

She shudders in my arms as a tear falls onto my shoulder and drips down my back. I pull her into my lap, and my own eyes well up when the memories become too unbearable.

"Who was it?"

I drop my head, unable to look at her when I respond. "A babysitter."

I remember the woman. She was an older lady my mom hired after Shannon went off to college. She used to watch me when I took showers. She'd wash me and touch me . . . put her mouth around me. A heavy breath cracks loudly out of my lungs when I think about the times she'd grab my wrist and force me to touch her between her legs. As time passed, the abuse only got worse. She babysat me for years until she moved away. By then, there wasn't a part of me that woman hadn't violated.

But these are my demons to bear, and I refuse to unleash them on Adaline. She doesn't need to know the sick details of my depravity. I can't stand the thought of her knowing how bad things were for me. She's already crying in my arms right now from what little she's piecing together. My pain shouldn't be her pain.

"Don't cry for me."

"You can't tell me that," she weeps. "You can't tell me not to love you this much, that I shouldn't hurt when you hurt."

She runs her fingers across my damp cheeks and then touches her lips to mine, drinking all of my secrets until I'm empty, until there's nothing left between us. In a single kiss, she strips me bare.

How is it this tiny person can render me naked down to my soul?

I don't know, but she does.

I doubt I'll ever be strong enough to carry the weight of the both of us, but there's no doubt she can. So, with my vile everythings out there, she has me wholly as we kiss through the aching pain of my reality, coming up for air only when absolutely necessary.

CHAPTER
twenty-eight

Adaline

"Promise me you two will be safe."

"We'll be safe," I assure my mom from the back seat as she drives Kason and me to the Tampa airport.

"And make sure you call me every day."

"I will."

"And night."

"Oh my god."

"Don't worry," Kason tells her. "We'll check in twice a day."

I lean forward between the front seats and ask, "If you're so worried, why did you buy us this trip?"

"You're my only child. I'm always going to worry."

"I'm eighteen now, remember?"

Kason tilts his head toward me. "I don't think that's helping, babe."

"Seriously, Mom. Everything will be fine."

For my birthday last month, my mother surprised me with two tickets to go on the senior trip—one for me and one for Kason. It wasn't an easy gesture for Kason to accept, but she insisted, knowing I wouldn't have gone without him anyway. I was shocked that she was okay sending the two of us away together for spring break, but with graduation only a month away and the two of us being eighteen, she figured she'd let us go. Plus, she trusts Kason more than anyone else alive with my safety. There is no way she'd be okay sending me off to stay with someone she barely knows, or even by myself. And she isn't living under a rock. With the amount of alone time we have here at home, there isn't much we could do in the Bahamas that we aren't already doing now.

Which still isn't much.

After Kason told me about what happened to him as a kid, I haven't pushed the sex issue. We've tried only a couple more times, but he's quick to shut down and push me away. Yes, it upsets me, but I try my best to hide it from him. I know he loves me, and I know this hurts him as much as it does me.

Kason has opened himself up to me more these past few weeks, and I now have a deeper understanding as to why he has a difficult time with intimacy. The other girls had nothing to do with closeness or emotions. They were merely objects he used to feed his craving. With the sexual abuse he suffered through as a child and the absence of his mother, he never learned what it was to love and be loved. Not that he doesn't love his mom, he does, but it seems to be a love conceived out of obligation and respect instead of a true emotional bond of

security, trust, and affection. He told me he never had anyone to turn to and that he was forced to deal with everything
alone, which is what made it so hard for him to share his burden with me. I still don't think he realizes how much I want
to be that person for him. A person he never has to fear will
turn their back on him or judge him. A person who can be his
safety net so he doesn't have to always be so strong, that he
can have his moments to unload his pain and know that, with
me by his side, it doesn't mean he has to fall.

We pull along the curb in the departures lane and unload
our suitcases. My mother's nerves crease her forehead, and I
give her a reassuring hug.

"Nothing bad is going to happen. Promise."

"You be safe and have fun, okay?" she says before turning
to Kason and giving him a hug. "Please take care of her. She's
my favorite."

"Always."

He thanks her for the hundredth time for giving him this
trip, and she shrugs it off as if it's no big deal before we say
goodbye and wheel our luggage in. With excitement in the air,
I'm nothing but giggles and smiles on the plane, which is filled
with other seniors from our school, except for Micah and
Trent, who are on another flight. Seeing how happy Kason is,
knowing this is the first trip he's ever taken, makes this whole
experience that much better.

When we land, the charter bus is already waiting to take
all of us to the hotel. We sit in the back with a bunch of our
friends that are more Kason's than mine. I look across the aisle
to see Katy finally has a distraction as she cozies up to Garrett,
who's on the lacrosse team with Rhett, one of Kason's good
friends. It doesn't matter though, because I only have to deal

with looking at her for a few more weeks and then we're officially done with high school.

Once at the hotel, we check in, thankful for the co-ed room my mother signed off on and even more thankful that the room has a king size bed instead of two doubles.

As soon as the door closes behind us, Kason lifts me off my feet, and I'm quick to kiss him as he walks me across the room to the double doors leading to a small balcony.

The moment our lips part and I open my eyes, I'm amazed by the view. "Kason, look."

He sets me down, and we step outside to take in the full oceanfront view. The turquoise water glistens brilliantly against the white sand as waves roll in.

"It's incredible," he remarks, and I turn my attention to him, saying, "*You're* incredible."

"Dudes!" a couple guys shout at us from below, intruding in on our moment. "Get your asses down here!" they holler as they raise their beers in the air, already taking advantage of the eighteen-year-old drinking age.

I shake my head at them as Kason pulls me back inside and closes the drapes so we can change into our swimsuits. But not a few minutes later, we are interrupted by a loud banging on our door.

"Open up, fuckers," Trent's loud voice booms, and when Kason opens the door, Micah and Trent come walking in with high fives for Kason and hugs for me.

It's still a little tense between Micah and Kason, but nothing really ever affects Trent, so he's been able to serve as the glue that still holds us all together.

Trent walks over to the window and rips the curtains open. "Killer view. They stuck us over on the opposite side of the building." He then steps out onto the balcony with a laughable, "What's up, peasants?" shouted to everyone below at the pool.

"Eat dick," some guy hollers in response.

I bust out laughing as he walks back in with a cocky, "Already making friends."

"You're insane."

"Let's go have some fun and loosen you up," he says as he drapes his arm around my shoulders.

The four of us head to the pool bar. The guys all grab a beer while I get something fruity and alcohol free before we find our spots on the beach. We hang out, and when Kason and Trent finish their drinks, they head out on a couple of jet skis while Micah and I stay behind.

"So, when do you leave?"

"The end of July. My parents signed a lease for a condo yesterday," he tells me.

"So, it'll be you and Trent?"

He leans back on his elbows and nods.

I look over at Micah, who's become a really good friend of mine this past year, and wish I could ignore the sadness that creeps in when I think about not having him around anymore. It's weird to think that in a few months, we will all be going in different directions: me in Tampa with Kason, and Micah and Trent over in Miami.

"I can't believe you're leaving," I tell him somberly.

"I can't believe you're staying."

"You know why I'm staying."

He sits up and rests his elbows on bent knees. "What is it about him that makes you willing to stay behind?"

"I love him, Micah. I know it sounds trite, but I really do

love him."

"I worry about you, you know?"

"You don't need to," I tell him. "But it means a lot that you do."

He looks out over the water, and I don't doubt his sincerity when he says he worries. He's made it known many times since Kason and I got back together how much it bothers him that I would forgive so easily. But Micah doesn't know Kason the way I do. He doesn't know the inner battles Kason fights every single day. The shame that plagues him because of the addiction he denies so fervently out of fear and confusion. Kason didn't cheat on me to hurt me or betray me, he did it because he was powerless and starved. I don't excuse what he did, but when I look at it as if he were an alcoholic who fell off the wagon, I can make sense out of it. And essentially, that's what happened with Kason.

But we've been back together for two months now, and in those two months, he's assured me he hasn't gone outside of our relationship for sex, and there's no part of me that doesn't believe him. Even though I've never asked, I know he turns to porn a lot, but I don't consider that the same thing. I've seen the websites on his phone and in the history on his computer. The last thing I want to do is make him feel bad for not being able to control himself, so I don't say anything. I only want to support him and love him until he can get to a point where he can see this for what I see it as—a legitimate addiction.

"You deserve more, Ady."

"He is that more. You can't see it, but I promise you . . . he's more."

Micah drops the subject, and when Kason and Trent return, the four of us catch up with a group of friends and take out a catamaran for the rest of the day. The guys continue to drink and enjoy themselves, becoming a bit too loud and obnoxious, so I join a couple girls who are lying out on the trampoline tethers at the bow of the boat.

With my sunglasses dropped over my eyes, I eavesdrop in on their mindless chatter as I bask in the sun, and occasionally, sea spray cools my heated skin. It's only when I hear a commotion toward the back of the boat that I sit up to find Trent . . . naked and completely wasted.

"Suck on this, bitches," he shouts to the guys before taking a running leap off the boat and into the water as everyone laughs and cheers him on.

"Don't look at that shit, babe," Kason hollers my way through his own laughter from the middle of the craziness, and all I can do is giggle and then lean over the edge.

"You better hope nothing nips at your little thingy," I tease as Trent wades in the water.

"Who're you calling little? Woman, I'm a beast!" he proclaims before someone throws him his board shorts. He's too drunk to catch them, and they end up slapping him across the face. "Dude! Respect."

When the ruckus dies down, Kason breaks out of the crowd and comes in my direction. He's only wearing a pair of board shorts and a backward facing baseball hat, and the sight makes my heart flutter as I gawk at him from behind the privacy of my shades. I'm forced to bite my cheek to hide the giddy smile that tugs on my lips. Inside and out, there's nothing about Kason that's unattractive.

I catch glances from the two girls when Kason joins me on the tether. He lies on his back, twisting his hat forward, and I sidle myself next to him, draping my leg over his. With beer on his breath, he kisses my hair before whispering honestly into my ear, "I need to get out of here."

My heart sinks because I know the reason behind his words and there's nothing I can do. We're out here with a large group, and I don't see us heading back any time soon.

"Is that why you're drinking?"

Pulling the bill of his hat over his eyes, he nods as he tugs me in closer.

It's near sundown by the time we return the boat. Hand in hand, Kason and I head to our room after making plans to meet everyone in the lobby in an hour to go to dinner. I can feel Kason's anxiousness in his hand that's clenched around mine. Today is the first time I've been hyperaware of the fact that Kason isn't able to simply go out for the day without his cravings gnawing at him.

There's a neediness inside me that pangs to take care of him, so I don't even think twice when the door closes behind us and I pull his lips to mine. He's electric against me, moving with purpose as we stumble across the room and fall onto the plush bed. I crawl on top of him and drop kisses down his neck and along his chest, tasting the salt from the sea as I trail lower.

Peeking up, he watches me intently as I unlace the tie to his board shorts and tug them off. He's already hard, and the moment my lips are around him, his eyes close, and he drops his head back onto the pillow as he lets out a loud exhale. It's times like this, where we can be together without complications, that I savor the most, wishing it could always be this easy. It isn't until he knows sex is on the table that he shuts down. He can be hard one second, and in the next, he's not.

But right now, he is. He's content and free as I take my

time with him. His hands lose themselves in my beach-tangled hair. With his touch on me, I relax and sink onto the bed between his legs. I love being able to give him this, even more so now that I know how badly he needs it, as if his survival depended on it. Maybe to him, that's exactly how it feels, and that thought alone makes me want to give him more.

I debate saying anything for fear I'll ruin this moment when he needs it so badly after abstaining all day. We've tried so many times in the past, only to exhume the bitter emotions of disappointment and sadness we both feel every time we fall short of what we both want so much. I want to feel his love. I wish for it—dream about it. We try so hard to have that level of intimacy in our relationship, only to be denied it time and time again. But I love him, so when I slip my lips off him and he looks at me, it's all I can do to murmur my request in desperate timidity.

"Please?" A single word, barely even a breath.

He pulls me to him and peers into me with eyes that hold a slight buzz from the alcohol he slowly consumed throughout the day. Our hearts beat against each other, both yearning for the same thing, except mine falters off tempo when his hand grazes the side of my hip as he slowly pulls the string to my bikini bottoms.

The bow falls open along with every rib guarding my heart. He kicks off his trunks and rolls me onto my back, still hard between my thighs. The part of me that's scared he will lose it if we wait too long wants to force him to hurry. But there's a look in his eyes, a look I haven't ever seen before, that stops me from rushing him. It's a look of conviction. His usual hesitation seems to have dissolved within the chemicals of intoxication. He isn't drunk by any means; he's only fueled with enough to relax him.

Soft lips fall onto mine.

He kisses me slowly, but so very deeply that I no longer know whose breath I'm breathing. Our tongues caress, tasting love in its purest form, and I sway into him as we move in this new way together.

His fingers undo the ties to my top, and he drops it to the floor before tossing my bottoms there, too. With the two of us bared to each other, and for the first time, knowing this is about to finally happen, it's *my* apprehension that breaks through the surface.

"Are you okay?"

My heart kicks a hard beat out into the open, no longer protected in its cage, and I shake my head ever so slightly but enough for him to see.

"You're trembling."

"I'm scared," I quietly admit.

His breath catches, and his forehead drops to mine. "I am, too."

"But you've done this before."

"No," he confesses thickly. "I've never done what we're about to do."

I run my hand along his jaw, and when his eyes open, I see the sincerity in them.

"I love you, Adaline."

The space separating his words matches the rest and rhythm of my heartbeats. He says it again as his lips spill over my breasts, and each silence between his *I love yous* is a breath he breathes inside my veins.

I open my legs, feeling every bit of him pressed against every bit of me, and I become overwhelmed by my unyielding adoration for this man I've completely and wholeheartedly fallen for.

My thighs begin to shake nervously against his hips when he reaches between our bodies and grabs himself in his hand. He runs the heated tip of himself along my softest everything, and I swear I feel my bones melting from inside my skin.

With my hands wrapped firmly around his shoulders, he hesitates. "Shit." His eyes dart to mine. "I don't have a condom."

"I don't care." My response comes instantly because we've worked so hard and for so long to get to this point, and we're finally here. There's nothing I'm going to let stand in the way of us making love.

"Adaline—"

"I don't care. I'm not waiting any longer," I insist. "Just don't come inside me."

There's worry etched in the lines between his brows, but he wants this as much as I do. He begins to move again, closer and closer, putting an uncomfortable pressure against me, and I coil back slightly.

"What's wrong?"

"I want this . . . I'm just . . . I'm scared it's going to hurt."

He runs his one hand down my cheek and between my breasts, holding my heart as best as he can. "Do you trust me?"

"With everything."

He bends down, and we kiss as he slowly pushes his way inside me. I gasp loudly against a silent cry and dig my fingers into the roped muscles of his arms. My legs quiver, and my belly tightens against the burn of him opening me in this foreign way. The intense pressure has me rendered still, fearing that any movement will only bring more pain.

I feel myself tensing even more, and he stops.

"Am I hurting you?"

I give him my complete honesty when I nod.

"Just try to relax," he breathes, his eyes swimming in his own pleasure.

He doesn't push any deeper as he drops his lips back to mine and lavishes me in slow, deep kisses. His mouth moving gently over mine as he palms my breast in his hand. My fingers get lost in his unruly hair, and eventually my body softens and my legs fall open. When this happens, my entire body, my every nerve, stops what it's doing for a split second as he sinks all the way inside me.

And this is the moment.

This right here.

Feeling, for the first time, love touching my body from the inside.

I hold him tighter than ever before as my body adjusts to having him inside me, and he holds me just as tightly. The both of us are entirely consumed by the weight of this moment that it becomes hard to breathe.

Kason draws back, and as I look up at him, tears flood my eyes. When they begin to bead down my temples and into my hair, he leans in and lays a kiss along my brow as he cautiously begins to move his hips.

Unsure of what to do, I let him take the lead, biting back the ache that comes with each new movement. Soon, my body responds to him, growing more aroused and making it easier for him as he slowly makes love to me.

"God, baby," he whispers hard against my skin, "you're everything."

Flesh on flesh, with nothing in this world separating us anymore, I wrap my legs around his waist and pull his chest to mine. And all the butterflies he's ever given me return, migrating from my stomach up to my heart. They find their way down my arms and into my hands, which tremble as I touch him. The sensation moves into my hips as they sway gracefully and then it reaches my thighs and wobbly knees that hug against him.

My body radiates in anxious energy.

Every flutter speaks of him.

He gazes at me, and lips that have touched nearly every part of my body lift into a tender smile as they proclaim, "I love you so much."

"I love you, too." And I do. Kason's the most beautiful human I've ever known, and our love is one that doesn't need convincing.

It never has.

It's a truth felt deeper than our bones.

CHAPTER
twenty-nine

Kason

I often see myself in colors. It's a conscious choice I make. Looking at myself in this simplistic way makes it easier to get through the days. Cuts down on the questions. Narrows the dimensions. I don't have to dissect what I feel or the reasons why. I don't have to delve into my past to pinpoint an instance that has ingrained triggers inside me. For the most part, I'm merely blue or gray or purple—a stained bruise in its various stage of life.

I'm simply a color, no longer an equation for which there is no answer.

It wasn't until a year ago when I met Adaline that I started to identify with different shades. I still see the markings of dankness, but they're now intermingled with rays of brightness.

And today . . .

Today, I see hope in the color of amber.

Adaline and I never made it to dinner last night. We never made it out of this room—this bed.

There's a slit between the drapes where a blade of morning sunlight slices through the room, highlighting a sliver of her soft face as she sleeps in my arms. I think about the only other time we shared a bed and the misery of having to lock myself away from her in the bathroom for hours. But last night was different. Finally, after us having to deal with all my bullshit, I was able to give her what she's been patiently waiting for.

It's hope . . .

Because *she's* hope.

She understands me when I don't even understand myself. She's forgiving when I refuse to forgive the things I've done. And she gives me hope in the eye of hopelessness.

Being able to give myself to her and have her give herself to me is more than what I could imagine. Never in my life have I felt the way she made me feel last night. It was soul-consuming to be inside her as tears slipped down her face while she clung to me. Seeing her need me as much as I need her gives me even more certainty in us.

And I need that certainty, because there's been so much unease inside me since we got back together, knowing how badly I broke her trust. On top of that, opening up to her about all the shit in my life, I often feel like our relationship is walking the thin line of a tightrope and any minute we're going to slip. I wouldn't blame her for faltering with all the baggage I come with when all I strive to be is the strong man she deserves. But it's hard to feel strong when I've exposed so many of my weaknesses to her.

She's taken everything with love and acceptance, and while I would never give her up, a part of me still feels undeserving.

As I push my fingers through her mussed up hair, her body stirs and she tangles her legs with mine. I shift in the bed when I feel the initial constricting of my dick as it begins to harden.

Bless the effects of alcohol, because I had absolutely no issues keeping myself hard last night. I was finally able to relax, and once we finished and I had more confidence on my side, we were able to go for a second time in the middle of the night. And now, I'm ready again even though there's a morsel of hesitation when I think about how she's going to react with my need for more.

She knows how much I get myself off every day, but now that we've crossed over into new territory with sex, it's all I could do last night not to wake her up more than just that one time. And even after that, I hated that I had to sneak out of bed after she had fallen asleep to rub one out in the bathroom.

With her arm draped across my stomach, she runs her foot along my leg and giggles lightly under her breath when her knee grazes my hard-on.

"I thought you were sleeping."

With the most beautiful smile I've ever seen, she nuzzles into me.

"What's so funny?"

She lowers her arm and runs her hand over my dick with a playful, "*This.*"

I grab her wrist with one hand and her hip with another as I pull her on top of me. "You shouldn't laugh at that," I tease, feigning seriousness.

Her smile fades into captivation, and when I reach up to

hold her face in my hands, she asks so sweetly, "Can we lock ourselves away in here all day?"

Her request hits me like a drug blazing through my veins. Still naked, I lift off my back and gently suck her nipple into my mouth, feeling it harden against my tongue. Her arms circle tightly around my neck as she holds me against her chest.

Needy to be with her, I reach down to guide myself inside her at the same time I feel her body shift, wanting me to be on top. I wrap my free arm around her waist to keep her in place, saying, "I want you like this."

She blushes innocently with uncertainty in her eyes before dipping her head down.

"What is it?"

With reluctance, she admits shyly, "I don't know what I'm doing."

I kiss her, which is a feeble attempt to soothe her insecurities, considering my body is straining for hers. "I'll show you." I breathe the words against her lips.

She parts her mouth from mine and stares into my eyes, speaking to me with words unsaid but felt within a mutual understanding of her self-consciousness. She has nothing to be unsure about because there's nothing this girl could do that wouldn't be perfection.

Scooting up, I lean my back against the headboard. When she timidly lifts on her knees, I slip myself between her lips, find her opening, and slowly lower her onto me. Breathless, her head falls into the crook of my neck, and she hugs me close. I have to take a second to keep myself from getting too worked up with how insanely good she feels, but when I can't take her stillness for another second, I slide my hands around her hips and begin to guide her up and down. She's tight around me, tugging me as I move her, and I force myself to make this slow so I don't come too soon.

Her breathing picks up, heating my neck, and eventually turning into tiny ragged whimpers of pleasure. As times fades between us, she loosens her grip around me when she becomes more comfortable. She starts to move on her own, and it's the most beautiful thing I've ever seen as I sit back and watch her. Everything about Adaline . . . each little piece from the inside out, has taken me wholly. I've never felt as much peace in my life as I do when I'm with her.

It's a quietude that never leaves us as our week in paradise goes on. Our connection grows deeper and more powerful with each passing day as we savor this time together. But too soon, we're forced to step onto the plane that will take us back to Tampa.

Amid the chaos of the seniors who are on our flight, we're able to tune everyone out. With her tucked under my arm, she sneaks kisses whenever she can, giggling and cuddling against me. Everything feels different when we get off the plane, this week forever changing our trajectory as a couple, bonding us in a way I never could've predicted.

When we walk out of the airport, Cheryl is already there, waiting for us with a big smile. When Adaline exchanges my arms for her mother's, I load our luggage into the back of the car.

We kept up on our promise to call her twice every day to remind her we were still alive and well. Adaline even called my mom a couple of times to tell her about all the fun things we were doing, which I thought was incredibly sweet.

Cheryl catches me a little off guard when I walk around the side of the car and she pulls me into the same motherly hug she gave Adaline. I hug her back, grateful that I have someone like her in my life that accepts me as unconditionally as her daughter does, to help fill in the gaps that are left behind by my own mother. My mom is a caring woman, but there's always been distance between us.

"Did you have a good time?"

"The best," I tell her before we all climb into the SUV. "I can't tell you how much I appreciate you giving me that trip."

She smiles as she pulls away from the curb. "I'm glad you had fun, but I have one more thing I think you'll be excited about."

I glance over in curiosity.

"I found out a few days ago, but I wanted to tell you in person."

"You're killing me here."

She laughs and then tells me, "I got you an assistant job at the firm I work for."

"Are you serious?"

"You'll be assisting my senior legal analyst full-time this summer, and then I'll drop you to part-time when fall semester begins. It doesn't pay much, but I'm sure it's more than you earn cleaning pools. At least this will give you a good idea if law is something you want to move forward with."

I sit, speechless that she would arrange this job for me. Adaline leans forward and gives my arm an excited squeeze as I stare at her mother. "I don't even know what to say."

"If you're good with me being your boss, all you have to say is yes, and the job is yours."

"Yes," I practically exclaim, blown away by the opportunity she's giving me, which isn't something I would've had if it weren't for Cheryl. I always thought, even though I've worked my ass off to get into college, that most of my aspirations would wind up being nothing more than pipe dreams. But with everything lining up the way it has been, I'm starting to see even more glimmers of hope in the familiar color of amber that only Adaline can make me see when I turn my head and kiss her.

CHAPTER
thirty

Adaline

My mother's eyes overflow with somberness when she walks into my bedroom and hands Kason a few more folded down boxes. I watch her from over my shoulder as I grab an armful of clothes from inside my closet. She takes a slow scan of the room, which is already halfway packed, and turns her head to me. A tear wells up and spills down her face.

"Mom . . ."

"This is too hard to watch," she murmurs before walking out of the room.

I take my clothes and lay them on the bed next to where Kason is unfolding the boxes and taping the bottoms shut.

"She's acting like I'm moving to the other side of the world."

"I think this is a lot of change for her all at once," he says, and when I eye him suspiciously, he reveals, "It might have come up during lunch the other day."

"I don't know how I feel about you two working together." I snicker as I drop a stack of clothes into one of the boxes. "What else is she saying about me?"

"It isn't like we sit around and talk about you. It was lunch. She was asking questions about the semester starting and happened to mention how she felt."

"Did you tell her to relax a bit? That I'm only going to be a thirty-minute drive away?"

"She's my boss." He chuckles while putting together another box. "I'm not about to tell her shit like that."

I go back into my closet to grab more clothes, amazed by how quickly time has passed. After our senior trip, graduation came and went all too fast. Before I knew it, we were getting our diplomas and heading into our last summer before college starts. With Kason now working full-time for my mother, I wound up spending most of the days with Micah and Trent.

In between, I made sure to stop by and visit with Sharon. The doctors say that her liver is failing her, but she seems to be doing better. I admire Kason for taking care of her and making sure she's getting to all of her doctor appointments. I know it takes a toll on him.

Molly never came out this summer, but that didn't come as a surprise. We've sort of grown apart. Maybe that's what distance does to a relationship, or maybe it's the fact that I've changed. I'm not the same girl I was when I was living back in Texas. It always used to be the two of us and boys were in the background. That isn't the case anymore. I'm happily lost in love with Kason while Molly is doing her thing, having fun with all of her girlfriends. Last I heard, she got accepted to Baylor University.

And now here I am, packing my room and getting ready to move into the dorms that my mother insisted I stay in. She wanted me to get the "full college experience," which she even said using obnoxious air quotes. I would think that since moving out was all her idea, she wouldn't be quite so upset about my no longer living here, but that clearly isn't the case. Truthfully, it makes me sad, too. I don't like the thought of her coming home to an empty house every night. A big chunk of my heart worries that she's going to get lonely.

I asked her a couple months ago if she was ever going to start dating, but she laughed it off.

"*I don't have time to date*," she told me.

I hate that she's been alone for the last five years when my father has already moved on, remarried, and had a new baby. She deserves happiness and someone to love her. She deserves it more than my father.

I stop what I'm doing when I come across a stack of pictures that are tucked in the back of one of my dresser drawers. I stare at the photos that I never reframed after they were shattered in the burglary last year.

At the top of the stack is me with that purple bow in my hair, sitting on my dad's knee, and it makes my heart twinge to look at it. It's been almost a year and a half since we last spoke. He never bothered to call or send a card when I graduated. He's made no attempt to reach out at all. I think he's officially given up on me and has moved on with his life with his new family.

Kason's warm hands cover my shoulders when he steps behind me and looks at the picture I hold. My heart hangs heavily in my chest, the way it always does when I think about my dad, which is why I hid these photos in the first place.

Abandonment is a hurt that doesn't go away easily.

"Do you think he still loves me?"

I set the pictures aside and turn to face Kason as I lean back against the dresser.

"It's hard for me to believe that a person could find you unlovable."

"It's weird, you know? That so much time has passed. That I have a sister who I don't even know." I grip my hands on the edge of the dresser and hang my head.

"I know it's not easy." He runs his hands up the length of my arms to the sides of my neck where he cradles me. "One thing I've learned the hard way is that we only have so much say over our lives, and the rest is out of our control."

"It's hard to deal with. The fact that my whole world is changing so fast and he has no idea. He doesn't know that I'm moving out, where I'm going to college, that I fell in love."

"What if you reached out to him?"

I press my head to his chest, and he gathers me in his arms, my place of safety and comfort. "I can't handle being rejected again."

He plants a kiss to the top of my head and continues to hold me, and after a moment passes, I ask, "What about you? Have you ever thought about finding your dad?"

"No."

"Does it bother you that you don't know who he is?"

"In a way, yeah. I sometimes wonder how my life would've been different if he had been in the picture, but I try not to let my mind go there. It stirs up too much shit for me."

I lift up on my toes and give him a kiss, and with all the

changes taking place in our lives, I hang on to the anchor he provides me. He's the constant I can depend on, and I don't know what I would do without him.

"I don't ever want to lose you." The words spill out before I even think about speaking them aloud. "I'm sorry. That sounded really needy."

"It's okay to be needy. I need you, too," he says, taking my face in his hands. "I don't want to imagine a life without you."

After a few more hours, most of my room is packed in boxes and loaded in the back of my mother's SUV. She sheds tears, and Kason gives us the evening to ourselves. She calls in dinner, and we sit out by the pool. We eat and talk about school, Kason, *life*. When the moon meets its peak and I'm alone in bed in my half empty room, it finally hits me.

Nothing will ever be the same when I move out tomorrow.

I pick up my cell phone and call Kason.

"I'm not good with change."

"You're a pro at it," he tells me.

"I still don't like it."

"You have nothing to worry about, babe. I'll be right there with you."

I spend the last night in my bed the way I've spent nearly every night—talking with my love until I fall asleep.

When morning comes, my mom follows me in her car as I drive over to the university. There's an energy in the air when I step out of the car. Students scurry about after picking up their room assignments and keys. Once I've checked in at the resident advisor's table, my mom and I begin unloading boxes.

"You girls need help?" a guy wearing a fraternity shirt asks when he approaches the SUV with a large dolly.

"Saved by the frat boy," my mother says with a tinge of salaciousness.

There's no controlling my eyes when they roll back. "Forgive her. *Please.*"

The guy laughs and holds out his hand. "I'm Liam."

"Ady," I introduce.

"Freshman?"

"Was my parental chaperone too much of a giveaway?"

"Pretty much," he says lightly before reaching into the back of the SUV and grabbing a box. "Well, let's get you moved in, Ady."

He loads more boxes onto the dolly, and when I tell him my dorm number, he leads the way, asking, "You from around here?"

"Hyde Park."

"South Tampa girl," he exclaims. "Where did you graduate from?"

"South Shore High."

"I was a Tampa Prep brat, myself. Don't hold it against me," he jokes before we round the corner. "Here we are. Home sweet home."

I unlock the door to find that half the room has already been moved in to.

My mother drops her purse onto the empty twin bed, and a part of me already misses home.

Liam unloads the boxes and stacks them along the wall near the window as I take in the small room.

"Why the long face, dear?"

I give my mother a shrug. "You know . . . change."

"That about does it," Liam announces as he stacks the last box.

"Thank you. You saved us a lot of time and sweat," my mom says.

"Not a problem." He then turns to me. "So, Ady. You plan on rushing?"

"Rushing?"

"Greek life."

"Oh," I stammer with a shake of my head. "I wasn't planning on it."

"You're missing out. It's legacy night tonight for all the chapters. You should stop by."

"I'm not a legacy."

He shoots a wink with a sly, "Lucky for you, I'm good at keeping secrets."

He grabs the dolly and heads out. "I'm a Kappa Sig, by the way," he adds, and when I shut the door behind him, I turn to my mom with my jaw nearly on the floor. "Oh my god! Was he flirting with me?"

"What I wouldn't give to go back in time to my freshman year."

"Seriously, Mom?"

"I'm just saying." She walks over and opens the first box. "These years are going to be some of the best years of your life."

We start unpacking and putting my side of the room together. Once the bed is made, pictures of Kason and I are hung above the built-in desk, and my clothes are put away in the closet, the door opens.

"Aaaah!" a perky redhead squeals as she bounces on her feet with her arms outstretched. "I was wondering when my roomie would get here." She gives me an equally bouncy hug, making me laugh out at her enthusiasm. When she pulls away, she says with a big smile, "I'm Lana."

"Ady. And this my mom, Cheryl."

"Nice to meet you, Lana."

From over Lana's shoulder, I see Kason step into the doorway. "You're here!" I run and leap into his arms.

"Took me forever to find a parking spot. This place is crazy."

"Well, now that I'm outnumbered, I'll take that as my cue to leave."

"Mom, you don't have to go."

She picks up her purse and, with a forced smile I see right through, she walks over to me and gives me a hug. "It's okay. I'll get out of your hair and let you settle in."

Her eyes begin to water, and she quickly slips her sunglasses on.

"Mom."

"Remember, you're my favorite," she says tenderly before feigning a shred of sass when she adds, "Don't you dare forget about me."

"You're insane, you know that?"

She gives my forehead a peck and, with fake composure, turns to Kason, saying, "I'll see you in the office tomorrow."

"Yes, boss," he says teasingly, which cracks a tiny smile on her lips before she ducks her head and walks out.

"So," Lana says, dragging out the word. "Who's this?"

"Oh, sorry. This is my boyfriend, Kason. Kason, this is Lana, my roommate."

The two of them shake hands. "Have you moved in yet?"

"I live off campus," he tells her.

"Nice!" she says as she walks over to her bed, which is covered in bright, colorful pillows that are about as vibrant as she is. "Are you coming out with us tonight?"

Kason raises his brows at me, and I shrug.

"It's legacy night, and I so happen to be a Chi-O legacy! Since you're my roommate, it's practically a requirement that we go to our first party together."

"I'm out on this one," Kason tells her before turning to me. "You heard your mom. I have to be in the office early in the morning to sit in on a strategy meeting."

"Maybe next time," I tell Lana.

"Uh-uh. No way. You're totally going."

"She's right. You should go out and have fun."

"See! Even your boyfriend agrees."

"Are you sure?" I ask Kason, and he nods.

"Perfect!" Lana announces. "Now that we've settled that, what do you say we grab some lunch? I'm starved."

The three of us head over to the Student Center and grab a few sandwiches. As we eat, Lana tells us all about Sarasota, which is where she was born and raised, and that she's the oldest of four sisters. She talks about her family, and the more I get to know her, the more I like her. It's been too long since I've had another girl to hang out with that didn't have some sort of jealousy and dislike for me. But we're not in high school anymore. Right now, it's just Kason, Lana, and me—no labels.

I turn to Kason and give his leg a squeeze from under the table. He's being his usual quiet self whenever he's around someone new. The same way he used to be with me in the beginning. Not quick to open himself up to anyone, he sits back and lets Lana and I talk and get to know each other.

After lunch, we walk through campus back toward the dorms, and I can tell by the death grip Kason has around my hand that he's in need of some alone time. With no more privacy with my new living situation, I tell Lana that I'll catch up with her later.

"Eight o'clock," she says. "You'll have to help me pick out the perfect outfit."

"Eight o'clock," I confirm before Kason and I head to his car to go back to his apartment, knowing his mom will be at work for the next few hours.

For the most part, sex with Kason has come effortlessly, although there are still times when he is so stuck in his own head that he can't get an erection. I don't take it personally anymore, understanding now that it has nothing to do with me. On the flip side, I know it still really affects him, and for that, I do my best to be supportive.

I try to always make myself available to him, but there have been times when it's become too painful for me to have sex because of how often we're intimate. After we came back from the Bahamas, I was riding the high of finally being able to be that close with him that we'd find ourselves having sex multiple times a day, but it started to become too much. Knowing he craves it that often, I was scared to turn him away, so I stayed silent. That is, until we made love one time and he found streaks of blood on the sheets afterward.

I finally had to tell him about the amount of pain I was experiencing during sex and how sore I had become. He felt so much guilt and really beat himself up about it. I did everything I could to ease his worries.

From that moment on, he made me promise to communicate with him about how I'm feeling both physically and emotionally. So, when he slides the condom on and asks, "Do I need to use lube?" I tell him, "Yes."

We make love, and he takes it slow to make it last as long as possible, but I know it isn't enough, and I wind up giving him a blow job later before he drives me back to the dorms.

"Call me if you need me, okay?"

"I will," I assure.

"I'm serious. If you're ready to leave and she doesn't want to, call me and I'll drive you back to the dorms. I don't want you walking around by yourself."

With one last kiss, I tell him, "I promise," before hopping out of his car.

CHAPTER
thirty-one

Adaline

"What about this one?"

I shake my head at the slinky black dress Lana is holding up. "It seems a little . . ."

"Slutty?" she answers for me. "It's okay. You can say it."

Her bluntness makes me laugh. "Well, I didn't want to offend you."

"Are you kidding? I'd be more offended if you let me walk out of here looking like an easy piece of ass." She hangs the dress back in the closet and starts rummaging through the hangers. "Speaking of ass, you scored in the boyfriend department. How long have you two been together?"

"A little over a year."

"Is he always so quiet?"

"At first," I tell her as I sit on my bed and brush on a touch of mascara.

"Well, he seems nice." She then pulls out a pair of black shorts and a silky green top. "Better?"

I give her an approving nod. "Much."

My cell vibrates when I toss the mascara back into my makeup bag.

Micah: Miami misses you.

Me: How can it miss something it never had?

I walk over to the closet and pull out a similar outfit to Lana's, and after I change, I pick up the phone to find another text waiting for me.

Micah: Exactly. You should be here!

I hated saying goodbye to Micah a few weeks back when he moved. It's weird not having him around after spending so much time together. Without him, and the fact that Kason has been working so many hours, I've had to fend for myself in the barracks of boredom. And even though Micah and I text and talk on the phone, it isn't the same as having him here. I look over to Lana, who's rifling through the obscene number of shoes she has, trying to pick out the perfect pair, and I smile. It's the thought that maybe my mother was right when she said these could be the best years of my life that thrums excitement inside of me. Yes, change is tough, but I met Lana, who, with her perkiness, could ease this whole transition for me.

Me: You'd be proud. I'm going out to a party tonight.

Micah: With who?

Me: A feisty redhead Trent would lose his mind over!

Micah: Is this your new roommate?

Me: Yeah.

Micah: Have fun, Guppy. Miss you.

Me: Miss you, too.

"By the way, you never told me if you were rushing or not."

"Honestly, I never really thought about it until today when some guy mentioned it."

Lana straps on a pair of wedges. "You mean one of those hottie frat boys that were helping everyone with their boxes?"

"Yeah. One of those guys."

"Did you catch his name?"

"I think it was Liam. Said he was a Kappa Sig."

She stands and smooths her hands over the fabric of her top. "How do I look?"

"Perfect," I tell her before slipping my feet into a pair of strappy sandals. After pulling my long blonde hair into a ponytail, I slip my cell phone into my back pocket. "You ready?"

"No purse?"

"Never been a purse girl."

"We're going to have to change that," she snickers as we head out.

Leaving Beta Hall, we decide to walk over to the Greek Village instead of trying to fight for parking. When we arrive, the whole village is packed with people.

Lana grabs my hand, and her face lights up. "This is going to be so much fun. Come on! Let's find the Chi-O house."

I keep up with her as we weave through people crowding the busy sidewalks that lead to the house. Standing out front are a couple of girls wearing T-shirts that proudly display their Greek letters, and they smile and wave us inside. Lana goes off to do her thing while I roam aimlessly around the first floor. I take in the small clumps of girls that are scattered about, wearing their bright sorority shirts, dark tans, and social standing with pride. I'm approached by an uppity blonde.

"Welcome." She's much too chipper. "Are you a Chi-O legacy?"

"No. I'm here with a friend who is, though."

She continues to chat, asking me if I'm rushing, if I've declared a major, and blah, blah, blah. Her questions come at rapid-fire pace, and I quickly excuse myself. Stepping back outside, I take a seat on a small bench and people watch as I wait for Lana. I start questioning what it is I'm doing here, feeling as if I'm in a completely different world rather than a place that's only thirty minutes away from my house. The thought reminds me to text my mom.

Me: Lana dragged me out to a Greek thing tonight. I doubt I'll be out very long. Love you.

"Ady?"

I look up to see the familiar face of the guy who helped me with all my boxes from earlier.

"What are you doing sitting out here by yourself?"

I tuck my cell back into my pocket. "I'm waiting for my friend."

"In there?" he asks, motioning to the sorority house.

"Yeah."

"You're going to be waiting all night. Those chicks run their mouths like talking is going out of style."

I smile and nod to the large piece of luggage he's holding on to. "You doing your own moving?"

"Nah. Just a few party snacks, that's all."

"In a suitcase?"

He chuckles. "You know how it goes."

I shake my head, clueless as to what he means, and he smiles. "Come on. You don't want to spend your night sitting out here, do you?"

"I should really wait for my friend."

"You mean the one who's apparently ditched you?"

I look over my shoulder at the Chi-O house to find its door is still wide open but Lana isn't anywhere in sight, and then I relent, "Okay. Only for a little bit."

I fall into step beside him as he wheels the suitcase between us. The noise grows louder as we get closer to the Kappa Sig house. Music blasts through the wide-open door, and when we step inside, Liam is greeted with a rumbling of loud cheers.

"Is this the typical reaction when you walk into a room?" I shout in jest over the chaos, which is far louder than the last house I was just in.

"Like I said, I have the party snacks."

I follow him into the kitchen, where he picks up the suitcase and drops it onto the counter.

"It's about time," a random guy says when he walks over.

Liam unzips the bag to reveal a slew of glass bottles.

"Fuck yeah, man," another one says as he high fives Liam.

They all start grabbing at the various bottles of booze, and when Liam unscrews the cap off a vodka bottle and pours a little in a red plastic cup, I decline.

"You sure?" he asks, and when I tell him I'm sure, he downs it himself.

A hand slips over my shoulder, and when I turn around, I come face to face with Kason's friend, Rhett.

"What are you doing here?"

"I was going to ask you the same thing," he says.

"I didn't know this was where you were going to school."

"Where's Kason?"

"At home. He has to work in the morning."

"I can barely hear you." He tips his head toward the living room.

"I'll be right back," I tell Liam, and he gives me a nod before I follow Rhett over to a small sofa sitting in the corner of the room.

"Who are you here with?"

"My dormmate dragged me out."

"Beta Hall?" he asks.

"Yeah."

"Me, too."

"Mady!" Liam announces as he walks across the room with a cup in each hand.

"It's Ady."

He holds out one of the cups. "You can't turn down a drink when you're in someone's house. I've heard it's bad manners."

"Is that so?"

He smirks, and when I take the cup from his hand, I politely take a sip, and I'm surprised by the decent taste. "What is this?"

"Some stupid punch one of the brothers threw together. It tasted like juice, so I figured you'd like it."

I give my approval when I raise the cup in the air and take another drink.

"Yeah!" he encourages before turning his attention to a group of guys sitting on the couch adjacent to Rhett and me.

"Who is that guy?" Rhett asks.

"I don't know. I met him today during move-in." I take another swallow of the punch. "So, I take it you're going to be rushing?"

"My father was a Kappa Sig, so he's pushing me to follow suit."

310

He then asks about Micah and Trent and if they're liking Miami. I tell him how they're doing and continue to drink as we go back and forth. I don't even know how much time has passed, but my cup is now empty, and I've started yawning.

With each yawn comes a small wave of lightheadedness as Rhett and I continue to chat. When I feel my eyes fading, he takes notice.

"Are you feeling okay?"

"I don't think I drank enough water today or something."

"Stay right here. I'll go get you some."

I lean back into the couch as a strange feeling begins to wash through me.

"You already drunk? Damn, you're a lightweight," Liam jokes when he shifts to face me.

I look across the room and see Rhett walking toward me, but he streams out of focus.

"Here you go."

I take the bottle of water from his hand but have to exert extra effort to twist off the cap. Once open, I down a few big gulps.

"Better?"

I nod even though I don't feel any different.

"I'm going to head out. You want to walk with me back to the dorms?"

"You're leaving so soon?" Liam says. "What about your friend? Shouldn't you wait on her?"

I look at Rhett and agree. "I should probably go find her."

"You sure?"

"Yeah. I'll finish this water and be fine."

My vision begins to go spotty, and he says something else, but his voice muffles out and then he leaves.

My phone buzzes from my pocket, and I struggle as I pull it out before opening up my texts.

Kason: Just wanted to tell you that I love you. I'm hitting the sack. Call if you need me.

Hyperfocusing on my fingers, I type my response.

Me: I love you, too.

"Boyfriend?"

Liam is looking over my shoulder, and I shove my phone back into my pocket. "Yeah."

"Damn. Sucks for me," he says. "Or maybe him. After all, he's the one that isn't here."

"Does that stuff actually work on girls?" I joke, but my words feel too slow coming out.

"No," he admits through a chuckle. "Never, which is probably why I'm still single."

I lift the water bottle back to my lips, but my arm is too heavy and then the bottle slips through my fingers, spilling all over my lap.

"Damn." Liam takes the bottle and sets it of the table in front of us, and everything continues to move in slow motion, fading in and out of clarity.

"I should probably get going," I tell him as I push myself off the couch, but I stumble, and he quickly grabs on to my arm. The room spins around me, and when I fall back to the couch, I ask, "How much alcohol was in that drink?"

"Are you okay?"

His voice filters in from far away, but he's right next to me behind waves of color and splotchy light.

"I feel dizzy."

"Let's try calling your friend so she can come and get you," he says, and I nod even though I'm unable to fully attach to his words.

I close my eyes, but everything continues to spiral from behind my lids. Sounds mix and mingle, eventually drowning out into a hollowness. Movement comes, and when I open my eyes, I can't focus in on anything. It's all a fuzzy haze, blended into nothingness.

Pressure wraps around me and prevents me from falling, but the sensation only makes me foggier as my head hangs lifelessly. I try to move my feet beneath me, but either they weigh too much or my muscles are too weak—I can't tell.

I blink, and I don't know how long it takes me to open them again, but when I do, everything is quiet and I'm lying on my back, stuttering, "I n-need to call-I need-I—" Thoughts fail me, and I lose my words, eventually giving up when the dense fog turns black.

CHAPTER
thirty-two

Adaline

I stir and roll from my back to my stomach before blinking my eyes lazily as I begin to wake. When they finally open, it takes me a minute to realize that I'm not at home in my room. With another blink, I remember that I'm in my dorm room. Turning my head to the side, I don't recognize anything around me.

In a complete haze, I try to take in the unfamiliar room. It's nothing like the one I just moved into. When I shift my head to the other side, my heart stops. Like a jackknife, I sit up and look at a guy who's naked and lying face down next to me.

For what feels like a solid minute, I have no heartbeat as my body breaks out in a prickling cold sweat. Paralyzed where I sit, my stomach buckles in a knot of nausea as my mind swims in utter blank space. Frozen still, I can't for the life of me figure out where I am or how I got here or what the hell happened.

The moment I'm able to move, I look to find that I'm naked from the waist down.

I suck in a painful breath when my heart slams into my ribs. A bullet shoots straight through my chest, collapsing my lungs, and I can't breathe. Everything goes blurry as my eyes fill with scalding hot tears that splash like acid as they rip down my face. The pieces of the puzzle are beginning to fit together.

The ax of terror dangles above me, threatening to break me in two as my eyes dart around frantically.

The used condom lying on the floor.

My underwear and shorts tossed across the room.

The phantom intrusion I feel inside my soul.

And then the guillotine drops.

No.

No, no, no!

FROM THE
author

Did you enjoy CRAVE, Part One?

Don't miss the conclusion in CRAVE, Part Two when it
releases on October 16, 2017.

Pre-Order HERE
www.ekblair.com/books

acknowledgements

It took many people who love and support me to help me see this story come to fruition. I wouldn't be able to do what I do if it weren't for the following people.

To my fans, I cannot thank you enough for continuing to love my characters and support my stories. Your loyalty means the world to me. The greatest joy is being able to open my heart and share what's inside with you.

To my husband, none of this would be possible without you. You're the best Mr. Mom I know. Thank you for taking care of our children, our house, the laundry, the dinners, and so much more to allow me the time and privacy I need to write. I love you!

Sally Gillespie, you are one of my biggest blessings! The time you sacrifice for me is simply incredible. Thank you for helping me in the creation of this story. It wasn't always easy, but you never let me give up.

Ashley Williams, wow! Just WOW! How do I even thank you properly? The hours upon hours you have devoted to this book are downright incredible! You make my words strong, even though you bust my balls to do so. From the early mornings to the late nights, and everything in between, you are always there for me. You are an amazing editor and friend!

Jennifer Juers, thank you for your honesty and time. I love that you don't sugarcoat anything! You never try to appease me; you only want to help me. The time you put in to making this book the best it can be is invaluable!

My sister, thank you for, once again, advising me on all the medical situations that arise in this story. We laugh way too much, but you always take the time to clarify and explain everything I need to know to create an accurate storyline.

Bloggers, there are too many of you to name, but each and every one of you are equally important. Thank you for your undying support.

OTHER TITLES BY
e.k. blair

THE FADING SERIES
New Adult/Contemporary Romance

Fading (book 1)
Freeing (book 2)
Falling (book 3)

AUTHOR ANONYMOUS
Contemporary Romance

SECRET LUCIDITY
New Adult/Contemporary Romance

THE BLACK LOTUS SERIES
Dark Romance/Erotic Thriller

Bang (book 1)
Echo (book 2)
Hush (book 3)

www.ingramcontent.com/pod-product-compliance
Lightning Source LLC
Chambersburg PA
CBHW030605180626
46816CB00005B/1684